SUCH A LOT OF WORLD

A Novel

Roshan Paul

To my parents,

Lily and Mathew,

for beating a different drum.

Cover photographs by Gautam Shah

Cover design by Kainaz Unvalla (Kai Design Sense)

4

Table of Contents

Prologue

I wanted to resist the cigarette offered to me by an anonymous policeman, the red spark glinting in the darkness, a rare flash of light on the deserted highway towards Amritsar. Not a smoker, I didn't intend to become one. Just then, the cold air of the northern highway rushed at me; I shivered, and almost of its own volition, my hand reached out and plucked the cigarette from the officer's outstretched hand. It was so dark I could barely make out the khaki uniform behind the arm, let alone read the name on the badge, so I just took a long drag and passed it back with a nod and quiet word of thanks.

We were on an empty stretch of highway about an hour outside Delhi, twenty meters after a set of speed breakers designed to slow traffic down just for spot checks like this one. The police had erected their usual checkpoint - three yellow steel fences placed at angles to the road so that cars had to very slowly maneuver between them and stop for inspection if needed. Two policemen with large torches and intimidating semi-automatic rifles slung over their shoulders armed the gates, shining their lights in the eyes of drivers before sending them off with a cursory inspection. The interstate buses and occasional car weren't the target - this was just for show, to make sure word got out that the watch for terrorists and drunk drivers was still being taken seriously by the Delhi police. With you, for you, always.

By the side of the highway, two police jeeps and a van lay waiting with their lights off. A third car, the one I'd arrived in, was the only vehicle with a light on. Under the inside light, I could see Mira Chopra and the Chief Inspector taking turns scribbling on a large notepad, with her assistant director in the back seat looking on as they went over the plan for at least the fifth time. The Chief Inspector looked patient and bored. But Mira seemed on edge. After sitting through the first three times they went over the plan, agonizing over any possible hitches, I had stepped out to stretch my legs and breathe in the night air. Not for the first time, I wondered why Mira had offered to let me tag along on the mission.

As I watched, the Chief Inspector received a phone call, then turned to Mira and all three of them stepped out of the car. As the door closed, the inside light went off and the darkness closed in on the little group even more. Under the faint moonlight, Mira beckoned to me.

"The *chaiwallah* called", she said. "A large dark colored van just passed him, heading this way. Very fast." It was an ingenious scout. Every time the police needed to check someone out, they paid a tea stall owner at a *dhaba* fifteen kilometers away from the speed breakers to be on the lookout and then alert them. Checkpoint ChaiWallah, the Chief Inspector liked to call him. This gave the police just about ten minutes to get into position. "We're going to stay behind the car", she continued, "just in case it gets out of hand".

It was just the two of us behind the car. Mira's assistant director, retired from both the police force and the security business, walked away with the chief inspector. Although unarmed, he wore a bulletproof vest and wanted to be in on the action. It was his contacts with the police that even allowed Mira access at this level - he knew the right buttons to push, the right people to influence, and how to charm the Chief Inspector and his boys whilst on the job. Without him, we wouldn't be here. The police, after all, hated this mission.

The policemen began to move into position. A handful, heavily armed, crouched behind bushes flanking the highway. Another small group remained in the jeeps, where drivers were on the alert in case a chase was necessary. The Chief Inspector and Mira's assistant director stepped up to the two officers by the barricade to pass on final instructions and a quiet word of encouragement. Headlights suddenly appeared in the distance, and they scuttled back into the darkness beyond the road's edge. The sound of a fast-moving car got louder and louder, and suddenly slowed. "They're at the speed breakers", Mira whispered. After that the sound reduced to a quiet purr – the driver of the van had seen the barricade ahead. But he wouldn't think this unusual. He would likely have been stopped here before, and allowed to pass unobstructed since the policemen's quarry was a terrorist suspect or inebriated businessman worth a few thousand rupees in bribes. Or, if busted, he carried more than enough cash to convince the police to step aside. Another reason why Mira's assistant director needed to be in the thick of the action.

The van appeared at the barricades. It was a nondescript vehicle with a white paint job, utterly commonplace on streets across India. One of the policemen approached the driver, torch flashing in his eyes. His partner casually moved to the other side of the van to have a clear shot at the passenger-side window. The driver's window rolled down and a conversation began. Standing behind the car on the side of the highway, I sensed more saw Mira's whole body go tense. I felt more than glimpsed a few tendrils of gray hair escaping her bun and hanging down beside her eyes. I imagined more than noticed the delicate lines emanating from her eyes become more pronounced as she squinted into the darkness. And then I saw the policeman by the car flash his lights skywards. Once, twice. It was over before it had even begun.

The cops behind the bushes swarmed out, guns leveled, and surrounded the car. The driver frantically re-started the engine. The van lurched forward but then, seeing the numbers against him, the driver's sense of self-preservation took over and he braked, the van shuddering to a stop. The door was wrenched open and the driver pulled out and flung to the ground. The trap had been sprung so efficiently that he had had no chance, no choice. The policeman on the other side pointed his weapon at the man in the passenger seat, keeping him covered. The Chief Inspector strode up, pulled the driver to his feet and led him to the back door of the van. Shaking with fear, the driver opened the door and two accompanying policemen threw it wide open as the inspector shone his torch into the van.

All at once, a yelling filled the night. It was part wail, part cry for help, all fear. Whoever was inside clearly didn't see the police as friends. But this was all the signal Mira needed. She raced around the car and ran towards the road. I was right on her heels. As we stepped onto the road, I saw the two men from the van being led towards the police cars, each escorted by three policemen. When we reached the van, the Chief Inspector wordlessly shone his torch inside. The beam of light struck a young girl in the eyes; she shrank from it, covering her eyes and turning away. He moved the torch and it hit another girl, who did the same. As the light swung back and forth across the hollowed-out interior of the van, I saw it was filled with bodies, mostly very young girls. There were too many of them to count right away, but beyond the ones closest to the light were silhouettes of many others, piled like dirty laundry into the back.

Mira spoke then, quietly but firmly, telling the girls not to be afraid, that the danger was over, that they were safe now. The girls fell silent – too silent. It wouldn't be till morning they would realize that Mira was telling the truth.

Chapter 1
Band-Aids for Loneliness

I paid my bill and left. The live band from Nagaland was chasing a tuneless rendition of *Bad Moon Rising* with an awful cover of *Long and Winding Road*. They were a mournful crew: uniformly lanky, wispy-goateed, shaggy-haired, with black t-shirts featuring album covers by Hendrix, Metallica, and Dire straits. Your typical wannabe rock-stars. I'd had enough.

When I entered an hour ago, there had been a gorgeous female lead with a husky Tracy Chapman-esque manner. She wore a low-cut tank top under a slightly oval face the color of melted butter. She didn't wear a bra but she was one of those girls who didn't need one. Not that I cared; I'm an out-and-out ass man. The tank top stopped short of low-slung blue jeans that fell perfectly into black leather boots. Perfect. Give me jeans and a tank top over a sari anytime.

When I walked past the band on my arrival, she flashed a stunning smile and then stole glances in my direction as she crooned what's most generously described as an innovative interpretation of John Lennon's *Imagine*. Noticing I had put my menu down, she pointed a waiter in my direction without missing a note. I wondered idly if this was a come-on but there was something too efficient, too professional, about it. She disappeared after *Imagine* and her cadre of merry goatees launched into the staple repertoire of most Indian live bands – rock music from the '60s to the '80s.

Now, as I walked past the band on my way out, I put my hands together in a noiseless clap. The band smiled in acknowledgement. I'm not sure why I clapped; they had been pretty ordinary. But I appreciated the honest effort and had enjoyed the opportunity to sink into something familiar, notes and lines I knew well, in this unfamiliar capital city I was living in.

My molten-buttered beauty was sitting at the bar and, as I walked past, she smiled that dazzling smile again and mouthed

"Thank you." I'd have kissed her feet for another smile like that. But I also saw that she was the consummate professional, dependent on this bar where she sang for her supper. She needed to make the customers feel welcome. And she was way out of my league.

Out in the street again, I took in the rarity of a pleasant evening's weather, and decided to walk the beer out of my head. It was a half hour walk home but that didn't matter. I had nothing else to do. Another Saturday night on my own.

**

The beer is disarmingly foamy and satisfyingly cold as I swallow, my whole body unwinding, relaxing on the barstool. But then it becomes fiery, sparking all the way down my throat until it falls, expired, into the crucible of my stomach. I lean my forearms forward on the polished mahogany bar, stretching my neck sideways each way to ease the tautness that always forms when I'm on stage and aware of eyes on me, greedy, yearning male eyes. That's why I smiled at the boy with the open face when he walked past. He checked me out all right but not in the way that pictures me naked. For a change I felt complimented not leered at, and a grateful smile danced out automatically. V has that same way about him, that ability to flirt with a simple glance that lets you know the ball's in your court and whatever you choose is fine by him. Yet that sort of detachment is maddening when you're in love with its owner; when, like five hours ago, I lay in V's arms, my lips against his chest and my leg draped around his waist, but still sensed his mind was even more removed than the faraway thud-thudding of his heart, faint like a distant drumbeat carried over hills by a gentle wind. I lay coiled around him but felt like a branch of driftwood bumping against a forbidding cliff-face. Then the alarm went off and he went home, leaving me to pick myself up, alone, and come to work. Yet, I missed him even as I pulled on my jeans and I'm missing him more with every song I sing. You may say I'm a dreamer, but I'm not the only one. *The boy who passed me on his way out looked so much like a younger care-free V that my smile – unbidden – bursts through again and I'm thanking him for making me remember what the possibilities are, why I'm still V's. If only he'll allow me in.*

**

Back home, almost out of habit, I settled into the beanbag with a book. My two flat mates were out of town for extended periods – Laks had gone home to Chicago to assure his parents that he was still in one piece after several months in India, and Ilona was accompanying one of the bands her company managed on a nation-wide tour. I had the flat to myself for almost a month, and it often felt like the beginning again. Like when I first moved to Delhi.

I can still remember those first months vividly. My work was challenging but enjoyable; I was on a steep learning curve so the days sped past. It was the evenings that were tough, and the weekends intolerable. After all the expectations of working life we unconsciously imbibe growing up, perhaps the most insidious is that the weekend is your time of leisure and relaxation. What we don't learn is that this depends on whether you have someone to spend your weekends with. If you're in a new and unfriendly city, famous for its extremes of weather, without many friends or the money to make new ones, the weekends can be interminable. You go to bed on Sunday nights with a smile on your face because you get to go to work when you wake up.

In those first few months in Delhi, my books became my best friends and security blanket. My degree in Economics and then an MBA meant I'd spent little time reading anything that wasn't academic. So I read everything I felt I should have already done by this point in my life. I began new relationships with new writers. The 'Indian Writing in English' bazaar was stocking more and more produce by the day, it seemed. The sheer volume of literary fruits and vegetables made up for the fact that much of it quickly went rotten. So I stuck to the biggies, devouring everything by Salman Rushdie and V.S. Naipaul and Amitav Ghosh and Anita Desai. As Western tabloid journalism infected mainstream Indian press with epidemic speed, I burrowed deeper into my books, understanding what Graham Greene meant when he said that novelists are writing the truth and journalists are writing fiction.

But underneath it all, I read because I had little choice. Reading helped me forget about dinner some nights, in those early days when my salary only covered the rent. Reading helped fold the grimy room I was renting into the pages of another world. It allowed me to ignore the gigantic cobwebs on the corners of the ceiling that resisted all attempts at destruction, the layer of dust that caked the floor and all furniture surfaces, the algae growing in the bathroom that I shared with four Bengali call-center employees, the ants and cockroaches and rats in the cubby-hole that passed as a kitchen but was never used as one, and the fact that my soap had to sit on my stack of books and my plastic bottle of snack food jostled my shaving cream and shampoo for space on the window ledge. Most of all, reading helped me get through the endless weekends.

I started to carry a book with me everywhere. To work, in buses, to meals (I usually ate alone), and always to the toilet. I became addicted to turning pages. So now, separated from my flat mates, I looked forward to feeding the habit. So I was smiling as I snuggled into my beanbag that Saturday night with the latest Amitav Ghosh for company.

Things had gotten better since those early days. After several months as an 'intern', my salary now afforded me a modest amount of financial security – I could eat at a decent restaurant a couple of times a month and have a couple of drinks every other weekend. I'd made new friends in Delhi, and moved into a neat little *barsati* with my friends as flat mates instead of call-center ghosts who only moved at night and chattered in Bengali despite (or perhaps because of) being fully aware that I couldn't join the conversation.

Yet, not enough time had passed to help me forget the loneliness of the big city. There are few forms of loneliness worse than feeling lonely in a city of over ten million people. You wonder how other people in your position – the young, single professional – are spending their weekends, where they are eating and drinking away their disposable income, where they are fighting and where they are fucking. When you think about it realistically, you know they're probably stressing out over how to hide their lovers from their parents or how to stretch their salaries to pay the cell phone bill. But this likelihood of shared anxieties doesn't usually feel right in your head when you're lonely and at a loose end. You feel certain that everyone else has a great party to go to on this Saturday night, and you're the only one not having fun.

Sitting down with the book, I embarked upon my starting-a-new-book ritual: gaze at the cover until I soak in every detail of the picture or cover-art, turn the book over to slowly read the synopsis, the fragments of reviews by well-known publications, and endorsements by famous writers. Then, open the front cover and read the writer's bio and list of previous publications, paying attention to the years in which each book was sent out into the world, writing my own little biography of the writer's life. Then read the dedication, wondering how dear Johnny or Amy or mom and dad had done to deserve a whole book in their honor. And finally, I read the acknowledgements, which also tells me about who this writer hangs out with and, I imagine, what they went through as they put their words to paper. I am procrastinating starting the actual book, putting off reading that first sentence until I can taste the anticipation and something inside me is screaming, "Get on with it, already!"

Friends have laughed at my visible excitement when I pick up a new book by a beloved writer. They say I talk about the book for days on end until it's clear to everyone that it's not the book I'm enjoying so much as the fact of reading a favorite novelist again. And that I have little else going on in my life.

Ritual over, I opened the book. After a couple of pages, I got up from the beanbag to fetch myself a glass of water, and then went to the bathroom to pee. Returning to my seat, I wriggled and squirmed until the bag settled just right around my body. Time slows down when you're on your own. I become very conscious of these routines, my little habits and movements and activities. I tend to think through tiny things that wouldn't occupy mind space if I were busier. So, last weekend on a walk back home from a nearby market, I found myself trying to figure out just why I am incapable of reading more than one book at a time, unlike most people I know who can effortlessly juggle two or three books simultaneously.

Paradoxically, when time moves so slowly, rather than just following whatever whim occurs to me, I find myself becoming excruciatingly organized. I decide to get up and re-fill my glass of water after reading precisely 'x' number of pages, and then read another 'x' number of pages before, say, bringing dry clothes in off the line, and then make lunch while skimming the paper, and then nap for exactly 'y' minutes, then make tea and sit outside for 'z' minutes before...and so on and so forth. Every tiny action becomes carefully ordained.

I don't mind it though. Putting simple movements in some kind of arbitrary order is as good a way of occupying your mind as any other. A number of people have told me how much they hate walking into a restaurant and eating alone, or even living alone. I barely notice these things since my first months in Delhi made me very accustomed to doing most things alone; only once in a while did I meet the few friends and acquaintances I did have. It often seemed that everyone but me had a busy social life. When a friend would call at the last minute to change the plan to another day, forcing me to abandon my evening, I had no choice but to politely say "Ok, next week's fine too." So I'd spend another evening alone but since I usually had nothing happening on the day they suggested postponing our coffee meeting to, I had no real reason to refuse the suggestion. I discovered that while I hardly ever got bored, I did get lonely. And, with my aloneness sitting heavily within me, I suddenly couldn't wait for the weekend to be over.

**

Another thing about spending so much time alone on a meager salary is that you will endure hours of boredom for a free meal or round of drinks and some random conversation with strangers. Like that time my office received an invitation from the British High Commission to the launch of a new initiative on Counter-Terrorism. (What on earth does counter-terrorism mean anyway? An eye for an eye? Wouldn't Anti-Terrorism work better?) We had no clue why we'd been invited and none of my colleagues were interested but the High Commission was an important donor so I offered to go.

The launch largely comprised the predictable yawn-inducing speeches. I began to doze off in my seat, waking up when I dropped half my drink on the person sitting next to me. He was a good sport about it though, and we ended up chatting outside the marquee tent over a few more drinks and some fish 'n' chips.

After five minutes in his company, I realized he was a cinch for James Bond. About 6'5", blond, tanned, shirt opened halfway down his chest in the chilly Delhi night, an effortless charmer. He claimed to be a communications analyst who had now been deputed to Delhi to work on the new initiative. He even called himself Pierce Cunningham, a spy's name if I ever heard one.

Mr. Cunningham had that ability – which I imagine to be an integral part of spy training – to talk a lot without actually saying anything. The more I quizzed him on what his new job was about, the more he deflected me with fulsome praise about the wonders of Delhi:

"So, does your job require a lot travel?"

"Oh, bits and pieces, but you know Delhi has so much to offer that I wouldn't want to spend much time anywhere else."

Long pause.

"Are you going to be working with the government or with grassroots organizations?"

"Well, you see...Oh waiter...waiter! Yes, may I trouble you for another of those fish fingers? Ah, lovely. And a crab nugget? Great. Thanks, mate.... So, where were we? Ah yes, Delhi really does have such a fascinating history, all these old cities built on top of each other. Bloody marvelous, innit?"

A few more unsuccessful forays into the world of Cunning-ham, and I grew a little tired of his Delhiphilia. "How long have you been here?"

"Oh, I got off the plane 3 hours ago", came the smiling reply.

Ha! So Delhi hadn't even sunk in yet. Sure, he's done his reading but he had much to learn, I thought. This James Bond needed some more training. But he didn't let out a single clue about his job in over thirty minutes of gentle probing.

**

It was in these times of loneliness that I would wish that I was the kind of guy who could easily meet new people, or smoothly pick up new women – in a bar, coffee shop, party, wherever. But I can't. It doesn't help to be an introvert. It also doesn't help to have an oddly puritanical mental leash that yanks me back whenever I want to approach a girl for the sole purpose of seduction. I try to unwind this leash pressing deep into my neck by rationalizing that I only want to talk, and get to know her better. But the leash is smarter than I, and can't be fooled. It yanks me away from the girl every time. Most of all, it doesn't help to be shy or diffident. Confidence works. An older and wiser female friend once told me that a man wins half the battle when he is conscious of his own attractiveness.

But just knowing this doesn't do anything. This kind of confidence is either something you are born with or you slowly gain; it's not something that can be donned with the aid of clichés like 'What's the worst that can happen? She'll only say no' or even that glassy pearl from T. S. Eliot "Only those who risk going too far can possibly find out how far one can go". Nope, if it's a mask you put on for the night, your quarry will see through it even before the first tequila shot.

I did get lucky once though. A few months after moving to Delhi, I was in a bar with Ilona and some of her college friends. It was a large group in a crowded nightclub and so we inevitably broke off into smaller groups of twos and threes. I found myself talking to Nadia, a petite primary school teacher from Hyderabad who was visiting friends in the city. She told me she had a Muslim mother and Hindu father. She was dressed in loose jeans and a shirt but something in her eyes and carefree demeanor indicated that the conservative attire was more out of habit than active choice. She wasn't dowdy under the surface. We were soon engrossed in a discussion about the perils for women travelling alone in India, and we moved to a corner away from the speakers in order to chat better. She said she had a fascination for Japan and was trying to find a reason to go live there for a while. Not ever being inclined towards Japan, I confessed my ignorance but added that I'd recently become a fan of the Japanese writer Haruki Murakami, especially the way he often brings pop culture into…

I didn't ever finish that sentence. "You like Murakami!", she squealed. "I lov-v-v-e him. And so few people have even heard of him, let alone read any of his books. Not even the well-read types."

It was like a switch had been turned on. Though probably it was just that the alcohol had dripped into our blood and began heating it up. Soon she was leaning into me as she talked about other Japanese writers and how she was single and how nice it was to meet a guy working in education for marginalized children and how sad it was that most guys didn't like girls who read a lot. Soon, hands and thighs and knees and shoulders began touching and bumping, and I began wondering "What's going on here?" More drinks came, as the club got more crowded. We couldn't see any of the rest of our group, most of who were on the dance floor. We were laughing too heartily at each other's jokes, and after one exaggerated guffaw she buried her face into my shoulder, and, did I imagine it, bit me softly.

What to do? I chose the conservative option – that I had imagined it. But now she was staring at me like I was an idiot. So I kissed her.

As lips and tongues met, and arms went around shoulders, my first thought was "God, it's been a while." She began to pull away and look around between kisses. I suggested we go for a walk. We tried to make it seem casual as we strolled downstairs into the now-closed mall in which the nightclub was located, and found a semi-private corner before launching at each other like trapeze artists high above the ground in a circus tent. We pushed aside restraint and top layers of clothing as we became less heedful of our surroundings. I pulled her shirt up to cup and kiss her breasts as she bit, much harder now, into my exposed neck. My arms cupped her ass and pulled her hard against me as I straightened and found her lips again. She moaned and began to suck on my tongue.

A few moments later, I was starting to wonder what next, when she took matters into her own hands. She unzipped my pants, put her hand inside, caressed, and asked, "Do you have a...you know?"

I was taken aback. This kind of fooling around was surprising enough for a girl who you've just met, but this...this was a whole new world. Maybe all those *India Today* surveys about the new, sexually liberated Indian woman had some merit after all. I thought I'd like this new India very much indeed.

"Yes", I breathed, fumbling in my wallet for the condom I always carried, more out of hope than expectation. I had never before needed it. This one was several months old but seemed intact.

"Great", she whispered, not asking the obvious.

Above us the din from the techno beat had the walls quivering. I was vaguely aware that we had been leaning against the window of a trendy ladies brand of semi-casual blouses and shirts. The mannequins seemed to be looking down at us with knowing smiles. It was eerie, but also reassuring; their half-smiles saying that they'd seen it all before; we weren't the first and we wouldn't be the last.

"Shit, I should have worn a skirt", she cursed as she struggled out of her jeans. We laid our pants on the floor for cushioning, left our shirts on, and as I entered her I prayed that the security guards were sleeping and other randy couples would choose other corners.

Several months later, when a newly arrived Laks asked me how easy it was to get action in this seemingly ultra-conservative city, I recounted the gist of the story over an after-work drink at Defence Colony's Gola's pub.

"Cool", he grinned.

I assured him that it had been the only such instance in almost a year and had been book-ended by lengthy dry spells. "So don't get your hopes up."

He didn't reply for a moment, seemingly lost in the contemplation of a 1960s movie poster on the wall. "Murakami, eh?" he muttered reflectively, and then looked back at me. "Well, that's the best reason to read random Japanese literature I've ever heard."

Chapter 2
Landlords and Other Rodents

_____

Let's start at the very beginning, Julie Andrews tells us. *It's a very good place to start.* I met Ilona in the way many lonely people of a literary bent imagine making a new friend: on a sultry Saturday afternoon in a favorite bookshop. I was browsing the bookshops of Khan Market, searching in particular for Italo Calvino's poetry-prose novel *Invisible Cities*. But none of these much-touted bookshops had it in stock, and I was running out of hope when I glimpsed one copy on a shelf in the bookshop called *The Book Shop*. Just as I reached out and picked it up, I heard an annoyed grunt beside me.

"Shit, I wanted that too." A woman in her mid-twenties was scowling at me. "Of all the damn books in the place...", she muttered.

She was of average height, neither too thin nor overweight, with light-brown streaks in her pony-tailed long black hair, and dressed in standard modern casualness: thin-framed spectacles, dangling silver ear-rings, look of annoyance, tight white T-shirt, and loose cotton pants.

"Maybe they have another copy", I suggested. We looked. We asked. They didn't.

"Oh well, ladies first", I said. "Why don't you take it? I'm sure I'll find it somewhere else."

My attempt at gallantry only deepened her scowl. "No way, none of this 'ladies first' nonsense. You picked it up first, you take it."

I was intrigued, as I usually am by outspoken feminists. "Hmmm....ok, tell you what. You take the book and, in return, you can buy me coffee. Are you busy?"

She hesitated. I wondered if I had been too suggestive. It wasn't like me to say something so forward. But then she looked up, narrowing her eyes, "No, I don't think so. You take the book, and *you* can buy *me* coffee."

I laughed, happy to go along for the ride. "Ok. Let's go."

I paid for the book and, leaving the store, we moved down the row of shops to a nearby café. Ilona, it turned out, was from Kolkata but now working in Delhi with a well-known celebrity and event management company. Before her current job, she had been a political news reporter for *The Indian Express* and, before that, an administrator with the United Nations Development Program. She had first come to Delhi chasing a master's degree in International Relations from the Jawaharlal Nehru University.

Everywhere in the world, and Delhi is no different, announcing which college you attended always produces stereotypes in other people's heads. It places you in a neat little box of mental constructs, and informs how everyone else relates to you. As soon as Ilona told me where she did her Master's degree, I guessed she was smart, opinionated, and probably left-wing.

"But why come all the way to Delhi to study? Doesn't Kolkata have the best colleges in the country?"

"It used to", she replied. "But Delhi is better these days. Actually, too many people still believe that Kolkata is the intellectual and cultural capital of India. But that hasn't been true for a while. I can guarantee you that the quality of education and caliber of students is much higher in Delhi. Plus, I wanted to live on my own for a while. Home had become just too...I don't know...stifling."

"Are you glad you came? How are you handling Delhi after Kolkata?"

People from all over India, but especially the South and the East, find it very hard to ever feel settled in Delhi, whose inhabitants we often perceive as being rude, aggressive and permanently on edge. This, in addition to the abominable weather three-quarters of the year.

Ilona sipped her coffee, and carefully wiped away the white froth that stayed behind on her upper lip. "Oh, it's not been too bad. I had a few problems when I first came but I've been here, what, three or four years now, and I'm used to it. Delhi has a lot of problems but Kolkata is pretty unbearable these days, given its identity crisis."

"What do you mean?"

"Well, today Communism in Kolkata is mostly lip-service. In college, I used to support the Communist leanings of my fellow Bengalis but then, in the days when I was trying to decide where to go for my master's, I opened the paper one morning and, believe it or not, there was an advertisement taken out by the Communist Party asking its cadres to 'loosen some of their ideological stances' and help the government invite the multinational companies in. *An ad. In the paper.* Although this was against their beliefs, it was now" – Ilona raised curled fingers exaggeratedly, in the international gesture for quoting something – "necessary for the good of the State" that foreign companies be allowed to set up shop in Kolkata. The moment I read that, my mind was made up. I thought I was in a Vaclav Havel play and I'd rather read them than live through them."

She sat back in her chair and opened her arms wide. "They're openly welcoming capitalism into their tender embrace while bashing it for votes every time an election comes up. I needed to get out, and I figured that since Delhi is proudly capitalistic and doesn't pretend to be otherwise, I may as well go there. So here I am."

"Wait...I don't get it. Are you for or against capitalism?"

"I'm not debating it. One of the things I learnt in my master's was that arguments about things like capitalism or communism are just mostly hot air. Time-pass. A good way to practice debating. But that's it. I'm undecided about capitalism...and I find I don't care too much one way or another. What about you?"

"Me? Well, there's this Winston Churchill line about democracy. How democracy is the worst form of government..."

"Except for all the other forms of government", she finished the line for me. "Yeah, I know. But what does that have to do with capitalism?"

"I think it's the same thing with capitalism. It's the worst economic system except for all the other systems. Churchill also said that the best argument *against* democracy is five minutes with the average voter. I think that applies to capitalism too. You know all these super malls that are opening up? In Gurgaon and Noida here, but also in every other big city...well, the best argument against capitalism is five minutes with the average mall goer."

She laughed and raised her eyebrows. "How very snobbish of you and Sir Winston", she said, smiling so I wouldn't take offence. "But you know Churchill was also a racist asshole, right? He was against Indian independence because he didn't think we would be able to govern ourselves. Or something like that."

"Yeah, but he's always good for a quote or two."

**

Look at them chatting and laughing. You'd never think they had just met. After a year in this job I can usually tell straightaway whether the people at a table are strangers or old friends: just by their body language, the way they sit, the formality of the words they speak to each other, the amount of attention they pay to the item-girls dancing in the music videos on the ceiling-mounted TV. But these two are so at ease with each other that if he hadn't asked her where she was from, as they waited for me to filter their coffee, I would have bet they were old friends, maybe even related. First impressions tell you everything, Mr. Manager likes to say. Dress neatly, shave, keep your hair tidy, avoid pimples – he parrots on as predictably as the BJP invoking the Foreign Hand. I think it's all a load of bullshit. It's not what you wear but how you wear it that counts. I could be freshly shaved and suited-and-booted but put me next to either one of those two with their casual clothes and uncombed hair, and anybody would tell you that I'm from a lower class. Mr. Manager is full of bullshit. And such a dickhead the way he orders me to ask oh-so-innocently if the customer would like ice-cream with his coffee, or hazelnut flavor or chocolate sauce as if that extra stuff is free, and then add another twenty rupees to the bill. Mostly, customers just sigh and pay up. Some argue a little but then give in since they don't want to seem cheap in front of their friends or colleagues. But every now and then a maverick – like that Italian chap yesterday – will blow up, call his server a thief and a rat, and threaten not to pay at all; just in order to make a scene and embarrass the café. The look on Mr. Manager's face when that happens is priceless. It's worth putting up with all his nonsense just for those once-in-a-while moments when he looks like he's been caught with his pants down in front of a crowd.

**

Ilona and I quickly became friends. We had so much in common that we could have been related. We sat on the same side of the political and social spectra, although since my views were not forged in the left-wing crucibles of Kolkata and Jawaharlal Nehru University, I was usually comfortable slightly closer to the center. At some point in our lives, we'd both worked in a social service organization, doing "development work". We were fiercely territorial over our books and, with our young stomachs, adored the rich Punjabi cuisine that dominates north India. She even liked cricket, and could speak knowledgeably about the game: it's not every day you meet a girl who can name all four members of India's spin quartet of the 1970s. Yet, somehow, there was no physical chemistry between us. So even potentially loaded evenings such as the one when we met for dinner in Vasant Vihar and she drove me home while we exchanged stories about past lovers and bemoaned the lack of present ones, ended platonically with a hug and a "see you around". We joked that we had been married for decades in a previous life, which is why we no longer had any romantic mystery to uncover and also how we shared so many of the same tastes.

On returning home from that particular dinner with Ilona, I found my landlady waiting in the tiny garden outside the front door. She was a Disney caricature of the wicked witch from the east, with her wispy greying hair, buck teeth and crooked mouth curling over an anorexic frame. She was also tight-fisted and foul-tempered.

Not long after I moved in, her husband came over to tell me they were raising the rent from Rs. 3,500 to Rs. 5,000. Since it was barely a couple months after I'd moved in, I objected and refused to pay so much more so soon. After this to-and-fro went on for a while, he finally relented and said, "Listen, you have to pay some more. My wife was furious with the rent we had initially agreed on. She said we can get more for this room than that. But I know you come from a good family. Also money is not everything and I know you really needed this place. But my hands are tied, so I tell you what. You give me Rs. 4,500 and I will tell her that you are paying Rs. 5,000."

I stared at him. He went on hurriedly, "She doesn't handle the money or the bank account or anything like that so all I have to do is tell her you agreed to Rs. 5,000, and that'll be enough. What do you say?"

I said that I couldn't afford to pay much more than what I was currently paying as this was the bulk of my salary in any case. So how about Rs. 4,000?

After some more hemming and hawing, he agreed, and I breathed a little easier.

But now, seeing my landlady lurking in the shadows of the garden, I knew that the game was up. She had come to do her own dirty work. I wondered how the scene had played out in their home. I could easily see her reducing her timid husband to a cowering wreck before storming out to tackle things herself.

Our severance scene started out normally enough. If this were a tennis match, it began with neither player going for the lines. She asked me for more money, and I politely refused. She served me a line about my having had girls spending the night in the house, in violation of the rules of my contract, and moved in to the net, eager to volley away the winner. I sent the return back down at her feet by replying that my friends had come over on occasion but none had ever spent the night, and whoever told her that was lying. (I knew exactly who had fed her this story. One of my housemates had been openly coveting my room, which was much bigger than his. He'd often talk about it with some of the other residents of our four-bedroom house, assuming I couldn't follow their Bengali. But Bengali isn't so dissimilar from Hindi that I couldn't catch the gist of what he'd been saying. The bastard! What else had he been telling her?).

She then threw up a lob, asking, or rather commanding, me to share my room with another tenant. Although this is a fairly common practice in these types of paying-guest accommodation arrangements, I valued my space too much to share it with someone I didn't know and had made that fact clear from the beginning. So I refused again, reminding her of the deal, emphatically smashing the lob away.

The early rallies dispensed with, it was now time to pull out the big shots and I steeled myself to hold my ground against a string of demands and accusations.

She began to weep. I was now totally at a loss for what to do. She said that her daughter was getting married and they needed more money for the wedding, and her husband was useless, a total 'duffer'. She was very worried because the boy's family was so much richer than theirs and they needed to put on a good wedding. It wasn't her fault, but they had to have more money, so they were raising the rent. It was a good move; I'd been expecting a pounding from the baseline but she'd moved in to the net with heavy topspin. I called her bluff, knowing that this tug on my heartstrings was her final weapon. But, after that easy pass down the backhand side, things got ugly.

Still half-weeping, she began to scream, questioning my manhood and parentage. But in her incoherent rage she had lapsed into Bengali, and I barely understood. Seeing this too had no effect, she stormed out but not before saying that she was going to move into the spare room for a few months because the house was in a mess and she intended to clean it up and make sure we boys knew who was boss. I may have won the set, but the match was far from over.

Soon after I closed the door behind her and went back into my room, I heard a knock. I opened the door to Debu, standing there in a vest and trousers, and asking if he could have a word. Of the group of four Bengalis I lived with, Debu had always been my favorite. He was the quietest and shyest one, and often spoke in

English if I was in the room. Although none of the others followed suit, obliviously carrying on in Bengali, I'd always appreciated his effort. But Debu now appeared different. He seemed a little shaken and even more hesitant than normal.

"Sorry", he began, "I was in my room and I overheard most of that. But there's more to the story than what she told you. You should know what happened before you came in."

I cleared room for him on my bed, the sole piece of furniture I possessed. But he remained standing at the threshold, with his usual diffidence and anxiety to intrude.

"She actually came in earlier", Debu started, "looking for anyone she could talk with. It's my night off, so I was at home. She told me she was planning to move in here and take care of the place. I was horrified because, as you know, she is quite angry all the time. So I tried to politely tell her that we didn't need that. She then said the neighbors had complained that we were drinking and being loud every night but I told her that that was a lie because usually you are the only person here at night and we would have known if you were having parties. She was lying from the beginning. She then began to ask me all kinds of questions about you. Stupid questions…they didn't make sense. Anyway, I didn't know much so I didn't have anything to tell her, but she seemed to be looking for bad things about you. Then she got a phone call from someone and walked into the kitchen. But from where I was sitting, I could hear her side of the call, and from that much itself I knew that her husband was leaving with another woman. The poor guy, I don't know how he lasted even this long. After the call, she came back and started crying. I tried to console her but I didn't really know what to say or do. She began crying that she would commit suicide and how that would make her husband and children sorry and remove all her problems. She said it two or three times. Then she began to look at me in a funny way. I was wearing this *banyan* then also and at one point she reached out and touched me on my biceps. It was disgusting. I told her I needed to go to sleep and we could talk about the changes when everyone was here. I went back to my room, and soon she left. About fifteen minutes later, you came in and she was with you. I heard what she said to you. I don't think what happened with you was personal. She would have fought with whomever came home next."

I was partly appalled and partly amused at the thought of my crone of a landlady making a pass at my 28-year-old shy housemate. "This is ridiculous", I said at last. "What are we going to do?"

"I am moving out", he said. "And I recommend the same for you. This woman is a lunatic. What if she moves in here, and one day she really does commit suicide? What if one day one of us walks into his room and finds her hanging from the fan? Do you know how that would look? We could get into so much trouble from the police. I've been thinking about this sitting in my room after she left, and I have decided to leave. She is very unstable and capable of anything. And so rude and bad-tempered she is that even if she wasn't crazy, living here will be a nightmare if she is sharing with us."

Debu had a point. He said he would leave as soon as possible. I agreed and said I would move at the end of the month, no matter what. It was time. I had become fed up of this glorified hovel and needed a change. Evidence of my landlady having turned the bend was just what I needed to overcome my inertia.

I began looking for a new place, adamant that it would be in South Delhi since I didn't want to commute too far to work. But this decision made it tough to find something in my price range. I combed the newspapers and visited loads of potential paying-guest options but had no luck. Any place I could afford was either too communal or too filthy or too bare bones or had too many rules and regulations. I was done roughing it out; I wanted at least a modicum of comfort and freedom.

In the end, however, my search was in vain and I began to resign myself to sticking it out with my batty landlady for a few more months. Just as I sadly made that decision, Providence at last looked my way

**

My cell phone rang one evening as I finished up in the office. "Yo, whassup, dude…Whaaassssuppp!" The trying-hard-to-be-Harlem accent at the other end of the line belonged to my friend Lakshmanraja Chawla. Or Laks, as he introduced himself to Americans who hadn't a prayer of rolling their tongues around Lakshmanraja.

"Check it out, dude, I'm moving to Delhi", he continued. "Coming to hang out with my homies in India, by which I mean only you, my brother from another mother. It's going to be sick! Get ready to hang with the Laks-man."

"What the hell are you talking about, Laks?" The nickname had stuck, it seemed, from his Chicago childhood.

"Yeah, I'm coming to live in India for a while." He dropped the hearty mano-a-mano bonhomie that he irritatingly puts on when he gets hyper, and began to speak normally. Or as normal as Laks gets. "Yeah bro, I got fed up with this Wall Street crap and we've been reading and hearing so much here about how India is 'where the action is', the 'next big Asian tiger' and yada yada yada, that people keep asking me questions about India. And I look at them blankly, you know, like I have any freakin' clue about all things India. So I decided to come over to the mother ship for a while and get to know my roots a little better. Plus, I miss you my man. It's been too long, and I thought to myself, 'Avraan is in Delhi so how much fun would it be to go chill with the sexiest playa Mangalorean I know and get my fill of the fatherland while I'm at it'."

"Motherland", I said.

"What?"

"This isn't Nazi Germany, Laks. India is feminine. The *Bharat-mata,* 'India as mother' concept is quite a big deal over here."

"Yeah, whatever, dude. Don't sound like you got a stick up your ass. So I got lots to learn. Anyway, I was thinking we could find a place together and hang out, you know. Check out the waddering holes at night. It'd be like old times. Whaddya say?"

Like all good speakers of American, Laks often pronounced 't' with a 'd' sound. Water morphed into wadder, daughter was daughdder, fatter became fadder. This clash of dictions was in fact how we had first become friends. My college in Bangalore participated in an international exchange program with an American university, in which the American university would bring students from around the world to its campus in Iowa for one semester, in which these students would take a full load of classes at the university whilst interacting with students from America and around the world. The program also recruited students from the home university to participate and, in turn, get to experience and understand the lives of fellow college students from several different countries. I was selected to go from Bangalore. On my first day there, as I was leaving one of our orientation sessions to head back to the room I shared with a genius Bulgarian tech geek, I heard a voice from behind calling my name.

36

One of my fellow classmates was jogging up to me. I had noticed him during orientation as he was the only other Indian in the room. In India he would be considered a little over average-height but in America, he was a little shorter and stockier than average. He had an Arab-like swarthiness with a fast-growing stubble under a luxuriant mop of wavy hair. It turned out he wasn't Indian but Indian-American, and was one of the local students from the host university.

"So, what do you think so far?" he asked.

"Oh, it seems pretty good. Early days yet, though", I responded.

"Yeah. By the way, I heard you speak during the introduction session...thought I'd mention a couple of things about speaking American English, if you don't mind."

Not giving me a choice but to accept his unsolicited advice, he continued, "We say schedule like this, see, *skedjule* not *shedyule*. *Shedyule* is British English, and I saw a lotta blank faces when you said it back there. You don't mind me saying this, right? I'm just looking out for my fellow *desi*."

"No, I don't mind", I said, a little amused. "Any other tips?"

"No...well, ok, yeah, just one more. When you say 'conservative' – and you'll say that word a lot because most debate in this country is framed in terms of the conservative position vs. the liberal position like there is nothing in between – you say it like this: The first part is not 'con' as in convict but 'con' as in cunning or...um...cunt. And the 'va' part is not like in 'vain' but like in 'visit'. So, it's more like cun-ser-vit-ive than con-ser-vait-ive. You getting me?"

Yes", I replied. "Thanks."

"Ah...but it's tricky. It doesn't always work that way. For example, with the word 'vitamin', we say 'viitamin' and you say 'vitamin'. We make it a long 'i' where you cut the 'i' sound in half. It's the opposite of what happens in conservative. Weird, no? It's all so arbitrary; you'd never think it's the same language. Anyway, you'll pick it up as you go along. Actually, you speak English pretty good for an Indian", he ended with what he must have thought was a generous compliment, and looked for acknowledgement.

But he had just stepped over the line. I knew there was a good chance that my English was better than his, regardless of pronunciation technicalities, and since I prided myself on my English language ability so I couldn't just let this example of American provincialism go unheeded.

"Thanks", I said, "So do you...for an American."

He blushed a little, even through his brown skin, and then recovered with a laugh. "Hey, that's cool, dude. Good one. I may use that myself sometime. So where are you heading now? You wanna grab some lunch? My name's Lakshmanraja but just call me Laks."

And so Laks became the best friend I made in my five months in America. He had an easy charm and a generosity of spirit, which meant that despite his average looks, he often had a bevy of willing beauties to pick from, attracted – as they would confess to me when they plumped for information about my friend – by the 'soulful beige' of his deep-set eyes but which I could see was just the enviable way in which he could turn on and off the charisma as if flicking a light switch.

We spent most of our time together during those few months and did all the things new male friends do. We played sport (tennis), drank alcohol (rum) and talked about girls, struggled through Microeconomics problem sets, ate long lunches (Mexican and Italian) and watched lots of movies (drama). There were differences: I liked to read while he played a lot of video games, he was crazy about basketball while I stayed in touch with all the cricket news on the internet, and perhaps most importantly, we had totally different tastes in women. He liked the petite, ultra-feminine kind that looks up to her man as protector and decision-maker, and I was attracted to the casual, feminist, self-assured kind. We were a perfect blend.

But it had now been over four years since we last met, and we'd both changed a lot, so I wondered if our relationship would still remain the same. Laks had graduated with a degree in Sociology but then went to work for a major investment bank on Wall Street. He was acclaimed in our Iowan campus as a poster boy for the American liberal arts education, which likes to believe that college is to help you learn *how* to think and not *what* to think, and therefore you can go anywhere and do anything with a liberal arts degree. Most of the international student community tended to view this reasoning as a sad attempt to justify offering 'useless' subjects like Art History or Gender Studies. But at the time Laks graduated, the world of American financial services seemed to concur with the liberal arts position, and Art History students were just as sought after as those who had focused on Advanced Statistical Analysis.

I had never believed that Laks would enjoy the Wall Street ethos of work-hard-play-hard cutthroat competition. Yet he had seemed to dive in with zest and, for a few years, he lived that life and raked in the money. All, it seemed, was going very well. So, after telling him about my recent house-hunting woes and how this was perfect timing since it meant I could start looking for a proper flat to rent instead of continuing my journey through the paying-guest circuit, I asked him what had prompted this move.

"A rat", he said.

"You're going to have to explain that".

"A few weeks ago, I took my lunch break alone. Went to get a burrito at Chipotle. You remember Chipotle?"

"How can I forget? There's no good Mexican food in India. I miss those gigantic burritos."

"It had been a rough morning. I worked my ass off for two months to clinch this huge deal with a biotech firm and then my boss took, like, total credit for it at the monthly senior staff meeting. I've never been so mad in my life but that's how the fucking system works. There was nothing I could do about it except take a long lunch to cool off. Ever had whiskey on the rocks for lunch? Don't do it – just makes you more depressed. Anyway, I was walking back to the office when I saw a small circle of guys standing and looking down. Now, this is New York City, right? Nobody stops to look at anything – if you've lived here for any amount of time, you've seen everything in the world. I was curious so I went over and there it was, lying beside a manhole: a huge mangy grey rat. Dead. Its tongue was hanging out, like it had suffocated. The manhole cover was broken, and the rat seemed to have washed up onto the street. Picture the sight, dude. A circle of Wall Street folks, in their dark blue suits and black shoes with carefully chosen red or yellow or pink ties to add that splash of color, and they're standing around a dead rat. These guys who are the fiercest on the trading floor and the loudest in the bar, and here they are stunned into speechlessness by the sight of a dead rat. You know where I'm going with this, right?"

I hadn't a clue.

"Well, come on, you can't escape it, can you? A dead rat washing up on Wall Street. I immediately remembered that old line – once you're in the rat race, no matter how far you go or how fast you get there, at the end of the day, you're still a rat. And suddenly, looking at the rat and the guys standing in silence like mourners at a funeral, I had, like, this epiphany. Like my blinkers had been removed. I realized that we were all mourners at the funeral for one of our own. Trippy, huh? Then I was thinking some more and I had to admit that the reasons I was in the rat race were the money and the pace and intensity of this lifestyle. It wasn't the work itself that I liked; in fact, I hated it. And so I was walking slowly back to my office and thinking about all this talk about India being where its at these days, and how here all I have to look forward to is my asshole boss stealing my work until I can get promoted and then steal some other kid's work... That rat was a goddamn sign, Avi. I know, I know, all very clichéd and all, but there it was. So I went back to the office and handed in my two weeks notice and came home to decide what to do. And the more I think about it, the more I became sure that I wanted to come and live in India for a while."

The flash flood of words finally ebbed. I could hear him taking a breath, through his mouth, which is how Laks has always breathed.

"How did your mom and dad take it?"

"Oh, they were cool, in the end. A bit shocked when I left New York and showed up back here in Chicago, but they accepted it well. Deep down, I think they're actually psyched that I want to come to India. It makes 'em feel like they kept me in touch with my heritage and I haven't become totally Americanized like most of their friends' kids. These days, it reflects well on parents here if their kids are still interested in India."

"Any idea what you want to do here?"

"Oh I have a job already. One of Dad's partners is related to one of the big shots at NDTV, so he was able to swing me a job

41

there. I'm starting as a trainee in production but I'm hoping to eventually do some live reporting myself."

"That's awesome, Laks. It would be great to see you again and hang out. But are you sure I should look for a place for the two of us? You're not afraid I'll cramp your style?"

"Are you shitting me, dude? I've never lived in India before, let alone Delhi, which everyone keeps saying is going to be a handful. Uh-huh, I'm going to need you to hold my hand while I find my feet. And I'll help you pick up girls in return. Find us a pad, *hermano*. We're on!"

**

After all those afternoons of hopeless trudging from one sorry paying-guest flat to another, things suddenly started to fall into place. I found a flat not through using a broker or the classifieds but through that timeless way of asking every one I knew to ask everyone they knew. The grapevine.

The very next day after my conversation with Laks, I received a call from a friend who said that the yoga instructor of the sister of his friend had a *barsati* she was looking to rent and would I be interested to go take a look.

The yoga instructor's house was in a lovely part of South Delhi, close yet equidistant to both my office and the NDTV offices. A wiry Nepali housekeeper with a pencil moustache opened the door and ushered me in to a spacious living room, where a woman in a pearl-white *salwar kameez* was talking softly into a cell phone. She looked exactly like how I'd imagine a rich housewife-turned-yoga-instructor would look. Tall, lithe, flowing black hair, light-colored skin, and enough about her to suggest that a couple of decades ago she was one of the hottest girls in town. She had married a telecommunications tycoon and had a son who was now, unsurprisingly, studying Economics at Oxford. She spoke English with the slightly drawn-out diction common to the old-moneyed of Delhi. It always sounded put-on but I liked it nevertheless. Her name was Priyanka and she was, to a T, the quintessence of Delhi's elegant Punjabi elite.

When she got off the phone, she turned out to be very brisk and business-like, which I warmed to from the beginning. She was looking for young professionals to rent the *barsati* upstairs. Although some students had expressed interest, they had wanted her to provide meals and 'countless other accessories' and she was 'just not into running a PG-type situation'. No, she wanted tenants who would be happy to take care of the place themselves and manage their own cooking and cleaning.

We walked up three steep flights of stairs to the roof, and she opened the door to let me see the place. For a *barsati*, it was massive. It had two bathrooms, a decent-sized kitchen and, of course the terrace, which we would have to ourselves. I loved it, except for one catch. It had three bedrooms, not two.

We stood in the empty front room, and discussed what to do about the third room. I couldn't think of anyone who might be interested, so I asked if she would give it to us at a lower rent, which she refused. In the end, we decided to wait a couple of weeks to see if anyone else came along to take the third room.

As we walked back down the stairs and stood chatting at the front gate, I could see she was keen to let us have the place. In my now rather extensive field experience as a house hunter, I'd learnt that landlords in Delhi were happy renting to South Indians because they perceived us to be quiet, well mannered, and generally unproblematic. Moreover, Laks was a foreigner, and an American at that. From a landlord's perspective, it doesn't get much better than this. I began to feel that if she didn't find better tenants in the next few weeks, she would let us have it at a lower rent. Unlike my previous landlords, money mattered less to Priyanka than us staying out of her hair. Although she and her husband would like the extra money, they didn't want to manage unpredictable tenants for it – for them, the opportunity cost of the marginal loss of revenue was potentially huge. I was tired of house hunting and eager to close the deal but knew we just needed to wait a bit longer.

But there was still one thing to check. Most landlords have a long list of rules and regulations for their tenants, particularly in a paying-guest arrangement, but also often for rented apartments or *barsatis*. These rules can often be quite rigid, especially the ones relating to curfew and which visitors were persona non grata. I knew one instance where two women renting a flat were forbidden to have any visitors, male or female; on one occasion, one of the girls' brothers had been rudely denied entry by the landlord. But I valued my freedom and I knew that Laks would never accept any restrictions on his movements.

"If we took this place, what rules would there be?"

To my delight and surprise, she dismissed the idea. "Rules? Oh no! You guys are adults, responsible for your own lives and decisions. The staircase to the *barsati* is outside the house, as you can see, so you can come and go without disturbing us. We don't believe in curfews or anything like that. You can bring your girlfriends or boyfriends home whenever you want. All I ask is that you take care of the place properly and don't expect us to provide you with food and a maid - like those students wanted. And the quieter you can be the better."

I was zapped. Zonkered. And other meaningless words at the edge of the known universe because that's where Priyanka seemed to have come from. Had she just said we could bring *boyfriends* home? Right then I knew we would take this place. Although neither Laks nor I had a girlfriend at the time, we lived in hope like everyone else. Sneaking lovers in and out of your apartment is always a problem no matter which city in India you live in. This was simply too good to pass up. I told my prospective landlady that I would soon be in touch and left with a spring in my step.

Later that evening, I met Ilona for a drink in Defence Colony. Still full of excitement at this new possibility, I told her in detail about Priyanka the yoga instructor. When I got to the line about bringing girlfriends or boyfriends home, Ilona reacted just like I had. Her eyes grew wide and her mouth fell open. "Are you serious? She really said that?"

"Yes", I nodded.

Ilona tried to whistle but didn't quite make it. "That's incredible. Hey, if you guys don't end up taking this place, let me know. I'll take it. I'm looking to move out anyway."

Ilona had been having problems with her landlord too. She was dating a photojournalist but it was always a problem to spend quality time together since they both worked full-time, he stayed with his parents, and she wasn't allowed to have him spend the night. And now her landlord had been trying to impose a curfew on her, much to her horror.

"You know...", I began, uncertain, with the glimmer of an idea that seemed a little far-fetched. "If this woman has no problem with us having girls over, then maybe she'll have no problem if the third roommate *is* a girl. Would you be interested?"

"That would be great! But I doubt it. She sounds cool, but she can't be *that* cool."

"Well, it's worth asking, isn't it? Let me call her right now", I said, pulling out my cell phone. Again, to our astonishment,

Priyanka said she had no problems with a woman living there with two men, as long as the woman's parents had no problem with it. I relayed the message to Ilona, who nodded at once.

"Priyanka, we'll take it... Yes, I'm sure... Of course you can meet the girl first; her name is Ilona... Yes, her parents can call you to confirm they are comfortable with it... Great! We'll move in by the end of the month."

And just like that, I got two wonderful housemates, a great little rooftop apartment, and a new faith in the humanity of landlords. Things were looking up. When Ilona and I toasted our good fortune, the bar was playing the reggae hit *Get Busy* by Sean Paul. For the rest of our time in Delhi, *Get Busy* became our anointed theme song. Whenever we heard it played, Ilona, Laks and I would get up to dance together.

Julie Andrews knew a thing or two. *When you know the notes to sing, you can sing almost anything.*

Chapter 3
Angel Safari

Monsoon season in Delhi has the flavor of a one-night stand: sandwiched between the summer's hot and humid slices, sensual yet slimy, and all too quick: bringing showers of affection but very soon coming and going.

When the monsoon hits, one of the most noticeable changes is the perking up of the city's bird life. After the long, tortuous summer of 45-degree days and 40-degree nights, the first rains always brought a buzz to my little colony. For a tiny concrete rectangle in the midst of South Delhi, I'm always surprised by the bird life it supports. In the last monsoon, there was the falcon couple whose nest was almost as large as their wingspans, an army of pigeons, hundreds of sparrows, and a pack of parrots. As the rains continued, mynas arrived, singing merrily, and one morning I communed with a hoopoe as I ate a breakfast of papaya, toast and honey. But the highlight surely was the graceful appearance of the prince of them all: a large peacock who flew right past me and perched on a neighbor's roof. As I hopped around in excitement, trying to get a picture, Uday, the housekeeper, gave me an avian-weary smile. "This is pretty normal", he said. I begged to differ.

But monsoons, as the birds well know, have a dark side too. The wind shrieked like a banshee one Friday morning, waking me up at 5 a.m. and keeping me awake as I listened to windows, doors, and shutters fly around and slam into walls in all the buildings in the colony. I finally gave up on sleep at 7 a.m. and walked out to my *barsati's* front door with its glass panes that provide a view of the terrace and, beyond, the colony's tiny park. The wind was now bringing rain, driving it along at a geometrically elegant forty-five degree acute angle to the ground. Suddenly a flock of pigeons rocketed overhead at an astounding speed. The electricity flickered, and then died. Only then did I notice that the tree at the other end of the park was being battered by the gale, swaying back and forth like a punch-drunk boxer listing against an implacable opponent, branches flailing like arms as if the tree was making futile attempts to land a few punches of its own. The falcon's nest in its upper branches was bearing the brunt of the storm's fury, whipped about so mercilessly that Mama and Papa Falcon were circling it in despair, screeching in impotence. Or screaming out a prayer.

**

Wildlife also featured on my first working day in Delhi. I was heading to the office but after taking a set of wrong turns discovered myself in the middle of an African safari. Except that, on African safaris, wild buffaloes are part of the so-called "Big 5", one of those animals without seeing which your safari isn't complete. Here, wild buffaloes can stampede down a main road. I had stopped my auto rickshaw to ask for directions in the Jamia Milia area when we spied a herd of about seventy-five buffaloes heading straight towards us. They were big, almost as large as their savannah cousins, and had the long curling horns and other assorted weaponry to match their African brethren. They seemed skittish, marching through the Delhi traffic like protestors walking past a police cordon, eyes rolling around in their sockets to spot the angle from which a stick or club might descend upon their heads. They bore down on my autorickshaw, the driver frozen in shock, but then galloped around us, terrifying a biker who skidded to a stop when he realized that these bulls weren't playing Chicken. In that moment, watching tons of bovine muscle descending upon a brittle human being, I feared for his life. But at the last moment, the herd dodged the biker and ploughed into the path of a Ford Ikon. The Ford man, who was talking on his cell phone, had to stop as well, and wait like the rest of us whilst the buffaloes did what they wanted to do.

I couldn't help chuckling at the scene. On a crowded Delhi street, dozens of huge black buffaloes were streaming past a man on his cell phone in his air-conditioned luxury car. In other parts of the world, people paid hundreds of dollars per day to take photographs of these animals. Here, they were part of traffic and there was not a camera in sight.

Feeling good about being in Delhi, relishing the new narrative that was beginning in my life, I found the way to my new office and rang the doorbell, eager to begin.

**

Three days later, I sat in an autorickshaw, struggling to fight back tears. My first day as a teacher had been a complete disaster, and the thought of returning home to my miserable paying-guest accommodation with its surly roommates and conniving landlords was almost more than I could stand. When I decided to move in there, I had hoped my job would make up for the squalor I lived in but now, after such a calamitous beginning, I wondered whether that kitchenware sales and marketing position I had turned down – with its healthy salary and generous signing bonus – hadn't been such a terrible option after all. Was I really sure that I wouldn't be able to bury professional ennui under an avalanche of money? So many people do it all the time; was I really that different? One day of teaching in a slum had drummed into me emotionally what I had till then only understood intellectually: that I was from a different world. I didn't belong there.

The kids – my wards – seemed to sense my alienation from the minute I walked into the asbestos-covered shed that served as a makeshift classroom and tried to quiet them so we could start. And once they sensed this uncertainty in their midst, they honed in on my weakness like piranhas sensing a feast, exploiting it with the utter ruthlessness found only in children and great leaders. They drowned my voice out in their bickering, bullied and taunted each other, threw things around the room, refused to take seriously any of the exercises I had painstakingly devised, and generally ran me ragged.

The lowest blow came from the least likely source: a girl of about ten who looked and moved like an angel but in whose beautiful brown eyes shone a gleam of truly demonic mercilessness. Towards the end of our session, which was coinciding neatly with the end of my tether, she stood up and addressed me in a tone of total boredom that would have been convincing if not for the deliberately cruel yawn that accompanied it. "Avraan *bhaiyya-ji*, why don't you learn Hindi properly first and then be our teacher?"

Jeering laughter engulfed the classroom as rage and shame enveloped me. How could I explain to a slum girl from Delhi that most parts of her country don't speak Hindi very well, if at all? It was hard enough trying to explain that to richer and better-educated *Dilliwallahs*. This was crunch time. I knew that if I didn't have a good comeback to this angel-coated insolence, I'd have to work for weeks to regain any semblance of credibility. But I have no quick-thinking smooth-talking skills. And being conscious of the importance of the moment just made me tenser. My skin felt hot and flushed, as it sautéed under the gaze of thirty pairs of bright young eyes. I became aware of sweat streaming down my sides and soaking my shirt.

And then, horror of horrors, I could taste the Dust. My old childhood bogey, filling up my mouth in a swirl of powdered sand and grime, coming back to haunt me as always in my moment of fear. As soon as I felt my tongue sag under the coarse weight of the dust, I realized that no clever answer would be forthcoming.

I opened my mouth to attempt a stern, disciplinarian approach but even that failed to materialize. I opted to stall for time. "What's your name, again?"

"Bips", said Lucifer's handmaiden, holding my barely-disguised glare steadily.

"Bips", I repeated.

It wasn't meant to be a question, but it came out sounding like one. *"Yaar, she thinks she's Bipasha Basu"*, drawled a boy called Anuj sitting at the other end of the room from Bips. A few kids snickered, the laughter rippling gently but unmistakably through the room. Clearly, Bips wasn't the most popular girl in class. But, bless his heart, Anuj had drawn her attention away from me.

"Just shut up", Bips turned on him. "I don't want to be Bipasha Basu. You know very well that my Dad named me Bipasha because he is in love with her. I hate my name."

What separates the ruthlessness of children from that of great leaders is that children are far more easily distracted. In the end, I didn't have to answer Bips as the session took off neatly from the sparring exchange initiated by Anuj. But I had no illusions that I'd get off this easily next time.

So, now, in the autorickshaw, I turned to my colleague Reena and said, "I don't think I'm cut out for this. There's no way I can even control those children, let alone teach them anything."

"Relax", she said. "You did fine. Everyone finds it hard in the beginning. It's not easy, with the backgrounds we come from, to be able to gel at once with these kids."

I was about to snap back at Reena that she didn't have to state the bleeding obvious when she put her hand on my arm and squeezed it empathetically.

"You must remember that these children have hardly any formal education. They aren't used to sitting in a classroom. Especially when it is so much more fun to be playing on the streets. When they can play and earn their living by wandering freely on the streets, what incentive is there to sit in a classroom? When you were in school, how much did you like sitting quietly in class listening to the teacher? Didn't you find yourself counting the minutes till break-time when you could go out to the field and play? I definitely did. And I remember the boys in my class would play book-cricket all through the History period since the teacher was practically blind. These kids are no different, Avraan; it's just that, unlike us, they are not brought up with the conditioning that going to school is not a choice they get to make. Many of them have parents who aren't keen on the work we are doing, because it means that their kids spend less time earning money on the streets."

She broke off to tell the auto-driver to turn right once we got off the Trans-Yamuna Bridge and then leaned back. "That is the biggest challenge of our work – getting the parents to buy-in. And until parents start to care, in a big way, across the whole city, we're always going to be fighting an uphill battle getting the kids to even attend class, let alone concentrate. So chill out. You will become better at handling them in time. Like jujitsu, you will learn how to use their energy to your advantage."

I was skeptical. "We'll see. But you know, you could have told me this beforehand. It may have helped. During the training, perhaps."

Reena nodded. "Yes, I know. Our training is a bit of a joke, isn't it? What to do, we are under-staffed and over-worked as it is. We'd like to spend more time and resources on training. We budget for it each year, actually, and spend so much time planning better training methods since it's the only way to take this work to a larger scale, being able to train lots of people to do this, I mean. But in the end, in the immediacy of deadlines and meeting donor schedules, training our own staff and putting proper systems in place never seems as immediate, or urgent. We are paddling so hard to stay above water all the time – always this session to plan for or that official to meet – we end up throwing the newbies into the deep end with us."

**

The training *had* been a joke. That first morning, after my encounter with the buffaloes, I walked in to an office that was a riot of colorful *salwar kameez* and estrogen energy, fluttering back and forth in energetically organized chaos. I perched myself on the incongruous barstool by the front door and waited for Reena, whom I'd been told to meet on my arrival. As office life bustled around me, I counted seven women and one man, most of whom gave me curious looks when they breezed past, seeming to want to stop and talk but eventually choosing to press on with their work. I didn't mind being left alone, glad for the opportunity to sightsee this workplace busyness on my first day.

A shorthaired woman wearing chunky earrings and a pink *salwar kameez* approached me, carrying a handful of files and folders. "Are you Avraan?"

"Yes."

"Ok. Hi. I'm Reena. I'm your team leader, and your timing is perfect because someone has just quit and we need new teachers desperately. You know what we do and all that?"

"Just the basics. Teaching non-curricular skills to slum and street children. Stuff like peace, tolerance, conflict resolution."

"Exactly. Except that we don't actually call it 'peace, tolerance, conflict resolution'. Those are very loaded words these days, along with social justice, human rights, secularism, gender sensitivity, etc. So we lump them together in a basket we call 'life skills'... Well, everybody calls it that, actually... Basically, we're trying to get youth thinking more about the world and the people around them, and even more importantly, reflecting about themselves. In the process, they will hopefully become better citizens."

"Got it", I nodded. In theory, at least.

"Ok... Well, here are some of the training materials. You'll find some documents talking about the methodology, and then some lesson plans and session outlines for the actual modules we cover with the children. Why don't you read these for now, and I'll be back in about half-an-hour and we can talk more if you have any questions."

"Should I just sit here?" I motioned towards the barstool.

"No, of course not. Let's go find a table for you. We may have to clear some space, though. And I can introduce you to everyone along the way."

She turned on her heel and walked through a psychedelic Rajasthani curtain that led to a large living-room of sorts – like many offices in Delhi this too was set up in a space designed to be an apartment. There was hardly any real furniture. Most of the room was covered in a thick carpet upon which cushions and bolsters lay strewn haphazardly. Seating was on the floor; "some of us like to feel grounded as we work", Reena explained. The walls were covered in an array of activist inspirational posters and framed photographs of office celebrations. Along the bottom half of one of the walls stood the only concessions to furnishing: steel chairs facing an assembly line of desks with computers on them. I was finally introduced to my new colleagues, all women except for the accountant. Reena tossed names at me – Yamini (one of the founders), Pinky, Monica, the sisters Nivedita and Anandita (we call them Nivvy and Annie), Ayesha, Imran (who'll be glad to have male company) – and each person looked up and smiled or raised their hand in a slight wave.

Seeing all these people fairly well entrenched in their nooks and crannies of the office made me nervous: the newcomer, the outsider. I clutched my batch of folders and followed Reena as she made space for me at a desk near the bathroom door, and then promptly disappeared into the next room. I began to read about the techniques I would be employing to enable slum children to start thinking about issues like communal harmony, environmental awareness, and gender sensitivity.

Reena's half-hour turned into two hours. I finished reading and engaged Imran in conversation. We were joined by some of the girls, who questioned me curiously about my background and motivations for taking this job. Reena re-appeared and shooed everyone away. "Did you bring lunch?", she asked.

"No."

"You're welcome to share mine, if you don't mind simple home food."

"Of course not. That sounds great." Like I was going to refuse eating my new boss' home-cooked meal.

"Ok, follow me. I know a place where we can talk in peace."

Reena led the way through the corridor and out to the terrace, where we interrupted a couple of colleagues on a smoke-break. More introductions followed, and then more polite chitchat, until Reena grew restless.

"We're going to eat lunch on the water tower", she announced and beckoned me with a toss of her head to follow her. Around the corner, in a niche in the wall, stood a rickety wooden ladder leading to the top of the building and up to the flattop water tank that rose like a squat chimney from the roof. Reena hoisted her cloth bag across her shoulders and climbed, calling out to me over her shoulder to be aware of "the third step, because it's cracking, and of course, the fifth step has already broken off so be careful there."

We emerged on top of the water tank, from where I could see across the roofs of the colony in which my office was located. As always, I was struck by the sight of neatly arranged houses interspersed with trees and roads, fanning outward from where we stood. Townships and colonies in Indian cities always seem so planned and ordered from above, and so completely chaotic from below. This space between the viewer and their object, like the shimmering cloth of a veil, promising exoticism yet in reality only concealing the blemishes.

Reena followed my gaze. "Nice view, isn't it? On clear days, we can sometimes see as far as Nehru Place from here, and even beyond, to GK and Sirifort."

This wasn't a clear day. The air was thick with smog and dark clouds suggesting first a *loo*-storm and then a downpour, and I could barely make out New Friends Colony next door. I gave up looking at the view and plunked myself down beside Reena, who was withdrawing an array of steel tiffin boxes from her bag containing the staple meal of North India: *roti, dal, bhindi,* and *acchar.*

"Did you read through the material?" Reena asked. "Any questions?"

"Well, I get the methodology, getting them to reflect first with personal examples and then apply those reflections to the exercises and games we conduct to show how their thinking has relevance to major social issues. Taking them from the inside out, so to speak. That makes sense. And I guess I'll learn how to best facilitate these exercises with time. But I was just wondering..." I trailed off, not quite sure how to phrase my question.

"What?" Reena tore off a piece of *roti* and scooped up a healthy portion of *dal*, which she carefully placed in her mouth with one hand cupped under her chin to catch any drips.

"I was wondering...um...if these topics, these social issues, are really relevant to slum youth. I mean, in addition to having fun like all kids, surely they are most concerned with making a living and supporting their families. Why would they be at all interested in talking about secularism and the environment and issues like this? Aren't those kind of topics better suited to rich kids? Shouldn't we be focusing more on basic education, like Maths and English?"

"You'd be surprised, actually", Reena replied. "And that's a good question. It goes to the heart of the work we do; in fact, it's related to how this organization started in the first place. Do you know the story?"

I shook my head. "I know it began after the Gujarat riots in 2002, but that's it."

"When news of the riots reached here, there were days when Delhi was tense – the whole country was tense I guess – with the worry that what was happening in Gujarat would spread. It didn't spread, thankfully, but over here people's memories of the anti-Sikh riots in 1984 and then the Ayodhya riots in 1992 are still fresh. In 2002, three of us – Anu, Yamini and myself – were all working as social workers in the East Delhi slums, doing exactly what you just suggested we do. We were teaching English and Maths and a mix of other subjects that weren't being taught well at school or, more often, weren't being taught at all. It was like the after-school 'tuition' classes that rich kids go for. But during the riots, the elders and women in the slums would come to us to ask about the likelihood of the riots spreading. Everyone was thinking about 1984. 'What were we hearing from other parts of the city and country?', they wanted to know. And so we started talking about the local tensions, which characters were likely to start something off and who may be able to help if things got out of hand – that kind of stuff. Naturally, this led to talking about how to prevent such things in the long-term. As we talked more with these community leaders, we saw an opening to introduce issue-based learning into the kids' lives. We suggested that instead of teaching what their kids should be learning in school, we could introduce other ideas, get them thinking about identity, religion, communal relations, and so on."

Reena paused to throw a small piece of *roti* towards a crow that had landed hopefully on the ledge a few feet away from us. The crow cawed and waddled towards it quickly. It scooped up the morsel and hopped away to chow it down.

"Well, these women loved the idea", Reena continued. "They promised that their children would attend the sessions. And so it began. We quit our social work jobs and started this organization focusing on building life skills. We only worked in that one slum for the first year, as we designed, developed, tested, and refined our methodologies. It was pretty successful. And this year we received funding to spread our work to two more slums, also in East Delhi. You'll be working in one of the new slums."

"Wow", I said. "I never realized that slum dwellers would care about social issues. I mean, for most of us, *they* are a social issue."

"Yes, it's a common misconception. Of course, slum and street dwellers are very absorbed in basic needs and worries about livelihood. That will always be their primary concern. But they are also very involved in making their communities better and safer. And if you think about it, that makes sense. Unlike rich people, they don't have the option to ignore their social reality; they live right on top of all the problems, so of course they want to do something about it. Every time calamity strikes, whether it's a natural calamity like floods or a human calamity like riots, it's always the poor who are the most affected, who lose their lives and homes and livelihoods. You may not believe it but I've met more slum youth concerned about the destruction of the environment than upper-class youth. For them it's not a community service project to get into a good college. It's their life. So, yes, absolutely there is a place for what we do, don't worry about that. It may not be as important as ensuring basic education but then, on another level, maybe it is. Maybe it's even more important."

I was suddenly excited. This all sounded new and innovative and cutting-edge. I couldn't wait to begin. The one other area of concern, I told Reena as I put a final handful of *roti* and *dal* into my mouth, was my salary. It seemed too low for comfort.

"Don't worry, it will increase over time", she assured me. "Your first six months are sort of a probation period. Many people don't last much longer than that, so we have to be careful what kind of investment we make in our new recruits. You'll get a raise after six months and then another after a year."

She paused. "If you last that long."

Now packing up her empty lunch boxes, she smiled, "I remember when we started out. We weren't making very much when we were social workers but we had to take a pay cut even from that when we began to do this life skills work. When I told my mother what my new salary was going to be, she whistled and said, 'Really? That's even less than your phone bill'."

"Thanks, Reena", I said. "Very reassuring."

"Hey. Don't mention it."

Reena was right. My second session was easier than my first, and my third easier than my second. Over time, like with any job, I established comfort zones and discomfort zones. I learnt how to persuade the kids to focus on the sessions rather than on the countless other things they would rather be doing. I learnt how to get the girls to assert themselves in class, even towards their male classmates, which Reena said – in a way that made me feel like I was flying – was a considerable accomplishment. I learnt how to see when a fight was brewing during lessons dealing with sensitive topics, and to head those fights off before they began.

Thus it was that one day, as I stepped into the autorickshaw with Reena to return to the office and she made her usual query, "How was the session?", and I replied, "Fantastic", I realized, with a joy made sweeter by the fact that it was laden with relief, that I was thoroughly enjoying my work.

And what's more, I even became friends with Bips, that willful, rebellious, ten-year-old tomboy who had sabotaged my first day on the job but who, although she rarely smiled, could give you a look so beseechingly tender that you had no choice but to fold her into your heart.

**

Freed from my performance anxiety, as I got to know my students and their lives better, I also started to notice where in the world I was. To see through the opaque and easily dismissible fact, or structure, of the slum to the individual pixels that make up this complex form of human habitation.

Pixels that all my life, passing by in a car or bus or autorickshaw, I had obliviously and at times literally overlooked. The brown lumps on the roads that were not those of cows or dogs but of human beings who lacked anywhere else to defecate. The shops selling intoxication – *paan, arrack, bidis* – outnumbering all other kinds of shops, catering to a population trying to avoid the shattered fragments of the rose-tinted glasses they had worn when they left their villages to seek economic refuge in the metropolis. The need for survival that persuaded young men to sell their bodies for activities ranging from sorting garbage to swelling election rallies to creating a mob every time a leader decides it's time for some good old-fashioned rioting. The yearning for a better next-life that leads the older ones to court fines and police violence by casting garlands of marigolds as religious offerings into the River Yamuna, despite every conceivable step taken by environmentalists to prevent the asphyxiation of the majestic river. The eighteen-hour days of backbreaking toil to build homes and lives that could, with a little grease under the table from building contractor to city official, be demolished without so much as a warning.

Day by day, the lifelong opacity of my view towards this world began to dissolve into these little grains of life, of lives, of living. Plato famously said that the unexamined life is not worth living, to which Martin Luther King Jr. retorted "But the examined life is painful". The ancient Greek was dwelling on outcomes; the fiery preacher reminding us of the process. These days, 'process' is in vogue: in sport, in business, in technology, in marriage counseling. But how do you react when the process of surviving every day for those you're with involves greater struggle than you've faced in all your life?

**

"You need a complete renovation", Bips tells me.

"What?" It takes a few minutes to establish that what Bips means by renovation is in fact a makeover. We are sitting outside the hut she lives in, after class one day. I lean against the wall, my legs stretched out in front of me, and Bips sits cross-legged by my side. Her mother brings me a glass of milky tea and I take a long sip to hide my amusement at receiving fashion advice from such an unlikely source. If it's come to this, I must really need renovating.

"What do I need to change?" I ask.

She looks me up and down, from the overgrown hair curling ungracefully to my dust-encased sandaled feet. "Well, to start with, you need a manicure and a pedicure."

I wonder, not for the first time, how she knows about these things.

"You definitely need a better haircut. This one is terrible."

"You think it should be shorter?"

"Not really. You can just comb it once in a while." She puts her hand on different points of my head and pats down tufts that are popping up as if to see the world. Then she sits back with hands on her hips. "Don't you know how to buy proper clothes?"

"I guess not. Why don't you come and help me the next time I go shopping?"

"Yay! Can I really come?" She claps her hands in excitement.

"Definitely. So, I need a manicure, pedicure, haircut and new clothes. Is that all?"

She looks at me searchingly. Then, with her brow wrinkled as if engaged in a deep internal deliberation, she says, "Can you get new ears?"

One morning in my third month at work, towards the end of another riotous session, I heard a knock on the door behind me, and a female voice called out, in the high-pitched drawl that adults use to attract the attention of children, "*Namassssstteeee!*"

I turned to see an elegant grey-haired woman standing at the door. She wore an amber cotton sari, with matching bangles on each forearm. Her glasses were old-fashioned, bifocals with thick brown rims. She looked frail yet somehow wiry; the broad smile on her face softening her weathered features.

Behind me, I heard the sound of bodies rising, feet scraping against matting, and a rush of air as my class mobbed the woman, yelling "Mira *didi*, Mira *didi*".

"Hello, everyone", she laughed and began to talk to the kids, handling their hyper-active energy with a comfort and ease I'd never be able to acquire, no matter how many years of lesson plans I delivered. The kids adored her; every one of them felt as if she was speaking to them alone. Bips was at the front of the crowd, jumping up and down to ensure she received maximum attention. The woman clucked and cooed with the kids for a few moments and then looked up. "I hope I'm not interrupting too much, Reena. I was passing by and I thought I would say hello. I haven't seen the kids in so long."

"Not at all", Reena replied. "And let me introduce you to Avraan, our new teacher. Avraan, this is Mira Chopra. She works with trafficked women, rescuing and rehabilitating them. A lot of those women live in this slum. Many of these kids' mothers owe her their lives."

"Shush, Reena, don't make me blush", Mira said and then looked over at me. "They're quite a handful, aren't they? Don't worry; they're all little darlings really."

Then, switching to Hindi for the kids' benefit, she said "I have to be off. I came here on work after all and I'll be tempted to ignore that if I spend any more time with these angels."

Her host of angels collectively preened. I said nothing; awestruck by the veneration they had for this tiny woman. Reena herded our reluctant angels back to their seats. "We'll be done in about half an hour, Mira. If your meeting gets over by then, why don't you join us for lunch?"

An hour later, I learnt what Mira really did. How she led missions into brothels to rescue women who had been sold into prostitution. How, when she received a tip that a truck was carrying trafficked women, she would contact the police and accompany them as they stopped the truck on the highway and forced the crew to release their miserable cargo. How she brought these women to safer places and slowly began the painful and painstaking process of healing them – psychologically, emotionally and physically. How she provided them some kind of vocational training so they could begin life anew.

To my surprise, Mira had no qualms about using the word 'prostitute', unlike most social activists, who insisted on the term 'sex worker'. She dismissed such politically correct terminology. "When did prostitute become a bad word? Was there a memorandum that I missed? Or maybe they do it via email in this modern age, which I can't be bothered to use!"

We laughed as Mira continued. "It's the situation that's the problem, not the word. All these prim and proper people who say 'sex workers' or 'victims of commercial sexual exploitation' or 'women in the flesh trade'... Oh, it's just getting more and more

65

complicated all the time. We spend so much time arguing over these semantics that we waste energy that would be better spent trying to defeat the traffickers. And sex is not work, for God's sake!"

Fighting human trafficking is another world away from controlling a class of energetic children. Organized trafficking is not only illegal but also a high margins industry, and these two facts bring some very unsavory players into the game. Mira's life is forever under threat; she is careful never to reveal any information about where her family lives or who they are. She gets several death threats a month, and is often physically assaulted. She showed me her arm – a mess of twisted and scarred flesh that bore little resemblance to a human limb. "It's been broken ten times", she said. "At least they're consistent. They keep going to work on the same place. It could be worse."

She spoke of it lightly but I had suddenly lost my appetite. My head spun, and I saw that Reena had gone pale. There was more.

"The worst thing actually is that I have to seek protection against these trafficking mafias, but the only people willing to protect me are the competing mafias. There's a price on my head in West Delhi; no protection covers me in there. I won't come out alive. I'm safe in East and South Delhi, and it's risky to go into North Delhi, but I take my chances there."

"Why West Delhi?", I asked

"The mafia there is at the center of all the trafficking that goes through Delhi. My work has cost them lots of money."

"Can't the police help you?" I wondered.

She snorted. "The police are for sale, sometimes at a discount. Every time I ask them to come with me on a raid, they hem and haw and do everything possible to avoid me until I threaten to go to the media. Only then they cooperate."

"How much does it compromise you to use the East Delhi mafia's protection?" Reena wanted to know.

"That's a painful question. Taking their protection means that I have to look away when certain things happen. It used to bother me a lot at first but it was the only way to continue my work. Fortunately, the East Delhi mafia isn't involved in trafficking...the West Delhi crowd has total control of it. My husband, who is an economist, says that the "barriers to entry are too high" for the East Delhi mafia to enter the trafficking market. No, they are mostly involved in extortion and the drug trade."

"What kind of extortion?" I queried.

"Oh the usual stuff. They go to small businesses and threaten to beat and kill people and destroy shops unless they are paid off. What's called a 'protection racket' in the West and what we call 'double taxation'. It's quite common all over India. Most small shops and street vendors in Delhi have to accept the double taxation system. This is the stuff that I have to turn a blind eye to. The promise I made to myself is that I'll live with this as long as they stay away from trafficking. But if they too start trafficking, then I don't know what I would do. The consequences of not having their protection are too terrible to think about."

Mira looked down, absent-mindedly twirling her fork through the remaining chicken noodles on her plate. She seemed to be struggling to hide an emotion. When she looked back up, she was a different person. The vivacity and humor had drained away. Under her bubbly exterior, she looked like a deeply tired senior citizen.

She managed a smile. "Anyway, what's the point of an old woman laying all her troubles on your young shoulders? It's not good to dwell too much on some things. We should go, no? We all have more work to do."

Chapter 4
Bitten

Although the monsoon has its moments, Delhi really comes to life in late Autumn, when temperate days follow cool breezy nights and the *Raath-ki-Rani* whispers fragrantly through the air. After the many months of irritable heat, a sense of tranquility descends on everyone's mood. Drawn to the good weather like mopeds to the spaces between cars in Delhi traffic, art and culture sweep through the capital this time of year. Festivals abound: of international film, regional theatre, pottery, sculpture, and even leather. Auditoriums host jazz concerts and classical dance recitals. Sufi music celebrations occur in the foreground of historical monuments. Then comes Diwali, with lusty shopping sprees and traffic jams, but also delectable combinations of light and sound. Wedding processions weave through traffic heedless of the commuters stuck in their jam. And the evenings of Ramadan lift Old Delhi into a flurry of buoyant nights without end.

One such Friday evening in November, Ilona and I decided that we should all attend a music festival at the grounds surrounding India Gate, which itself was vibrantly lit up for the occasion. I arrived after work and found Ilona had spread out a blanket on the grass under one of the floodlights. From there we had a good view of the performers but weren't part of the primly seated audience. Kishori Amonkar was on stage, grumbling and cranky as usual before she uses her voice to do what it does best. Jali – my new girlfriend – was late as ever, but I was surprised not to see Ilona's photographer boyfriend Nikhil. Our plan was to go out for drinks and dancing after the concert, where Laks would join us along with his current girlfriend Mitali. It was such a rare occasion that the three of us and our partners were all in town that we were keen to make the most of it. A night like this had been long in the planning, with Nikhil an enthusiastic advocate, so his absence immediately struck me as odd.

"Where's Nikhil?" I asked, sitting down on the blanket beside Ilona

"He couldn't make it", she replied. "Something came up."

But she had paused too long before answering, and looked away from me towards the stage. Something's happened, I was thinking, as Ilona turned back to me and asked, with studied casualness, "So, how was your day?" If I hadn't been alert or if we hadn't been sitting under floodlights, I'd have missed it but, as it happened, her hair swung aside from her neck as she turned towards me and I glimpsed a dark purple bruise on the side of her throat.

"Ilona", I said almost reflexively, "Is that..."

She gasped, clasping her hand to her throat. "Shit... you saw?"

I nodded slowly, as it hit me: if Ilona had come from work, she wouldn't have been able to see Nikhil. Was the hickey from someone else? "Something came up for Nikhil, huh?" I grinned.

Even under her brown skin, I could see Ilona blushing. "Ok, ok. I told him not to come. He hates classical music anyway; says it always sounds like a funeral to him."

"So who's the lucky guy?"

"Mind your own business", she retorted. Then, with a wicked grin, "Doesn't a hickey leave you with this delicious feeling of having been well and truly...done? I'm just sorry for the general public that's not getting bitten."

We laughed at that. Just then Jali arrived, forcing a change of subject.

I met Jali a few months ago when a mutual friend passing through the city on work arranged to have coffee with both of us.

71

It was still early evening when our friend left to catch his train but Jali and I stayed on in the café, talking endlessly over several cups of milky tea and dry pastries until the waiters kicked us out at closing time. She was a dance therapist whose name came from an untranslatable Swahili word meaning a combination of love, respect and honor, a remnant of her parents' East Africa upbringing. They had reverse-immigrated from Uganda to Baroda when she was in her early teens. After high school, Jali left what she felt was a restrictive Baroda for college in Delhi, and had been here ever since. We met again for drinks a few days later. When we parted, she invited me over to dinner the next weekend. After that meal, we stopped spending so much time just talking.

Now, as Jali sat down on the blanket and snuggled against me, drawing my arms around her, a Sufi singer replaced Kishori Amonkar on stage. We grew quiet as the sorrowful melody drifted across the lawns, softly enveloping us in the moment and removing any inclination to chatter. My thoughts drifted to the romantic adventures of my enigmatic flat mate.

Ilona often seemed like one of those girls who had never really grown up. At an age when even the most cosmopolitan women get into relationships with one eye fixed upon permanence, she appeared to actively seek out the men who wouldn't work. When a man moves from girl to girl, he's accused of being afraid of commitment. It must work both ways.

Yet Ilona often claimed that Nikhil was her soul mate. They had met at a university party early in her first year in Delhi and had been on-again off-again ever since. Born to be a photographer, Nikhil took the same fastidious care with Ilona as he did with his photographs; this ability to be careful and considered was a priceless foil for Ilona's bursts of neuroticism and whimsicality. Their romance thrived in the conducive setting of a university campus and they joined the same newspaper after they graduated, full of the thrill of seeing each other every day at work. But as their careers developed and new people entered their professional and personal lives, Ilona and Nikhil settled into a more relaxed arrangement, without the pressure to meet every day or even stay fully updated on each other's lives. Nikhil's photojournalism entailed frequent travel and he was often away for weeks, even months, at a stretch. This didn't seem to bother either of them. Ilona often joked that they were like an old married couple that actively looked for things to do without the other person. However, only when Nikhil was around did she seem truly at ease.

Still, this latest indiscretion wasn't the first time Ilona had cheated on Nikhil. A few years ago, during a nine-month period in which Nikhil was sent to Ahmedabad based on his editor's hunch that Gujarat was about to implode, Ilona had gotten involved with a budding industrialist. The playboy heir to a construction empire, our industrialist prince liked flashy cars and clothes, was ethically ambiguous, annoyingly street smart, unabashedly money-hungry and, when you got down to it, a complete boor. He was, in short, everything Nikhil was not. And, in a way that Nikhil would never be able to match, he wooed Ilona with fancy weekend trips and nights of endless fun until she decided to go along for the ride.

And was torn apart for it. Just as she prepared to call things off with Nikhil, the prince told Ilona that he could never marry a Bengali and would have to agree to the match his parents were arranging for him within their community. When asked why he had been making her promises he couldn't keep, the prince shrugged nonchalantly and said it was because she was great in bed. He then proposed she be his mistress even after he was married. At this point, the shreds of Ilona's dignity gathered for one final stand and allowed her to walk away.

Almost immediately after, she found herself floored by the devotion of a colleague at her new job with The World Health Organization. He was a research-analyst tracking the spread of dengue fever in South Asia. Like the prince, he was persistent, but in the exact opposite way: he went out of his way to do nice things for her, showed her the ropes as she settled in to the politics and bureaucracy of a UN organization, lent her an empathetic shoulder to cry on, and generally let her know that he was hers to do what she wanted with.

In the meantime, Nikhil had become increasingly distant and unreachable as he click-click-clicked his way across a Gujarat destroying itself in the post-Godhra riots of 2002. Devastated in the aftermath of her failed affair, and needing some serious pampering, Ilona sought comfort in the arms of her new admirer. But when the last scabs fell off her healed heart a few months later, she began to feel that her current lover was just a little too similar to her boyfriend. He possessed all of Nikhil's goodness but lacked that vital spark – the indescribable x-factor – that drew Ilona to Nikhil. So when Nikhil finally returned to Delhi, Ilona called off her rebound fling as gracefully as she could manage and went back to her boyfriend. She hadn't strayed since.

Nikhil remained unaware of Ilona's dalliances in his absence just as, it must be said, did she of his. They seemed to tacitly agree not to ask too many questions of each other. "He either doesn't think I could be with anyone else", Ilona said, "Or he has something to hide himself." Regardless, she felt they were both better off not knowing.

But now it seemed Ilona was getting involved with someone else, and this time with Nikhil mostly in town. I wondered if this latest paramour was more like the construction prince or the dengue fever analyst.

Such indecisive, almost dilettante, wandering points to a girl petrified of commitment. But with Ilona (as with most accused of commitment-phobia) such a conclusion is simplistic, incomplete. Like all of us, she was certainly seeking that someone who brings the right blend of excitement and stability, with both physical and intellectual chemistry. But she also needed more. A few nights ago, during a weed-enriched post-dinner conversation on our *barsati's* terrace, she confessed that ever since she was a little girl, she'd had the feeling that she was born for a purpose, that there was something she was meant to do in her lifetime. The feeling grew stronger when she arrived in Delhi, like a mock treasure hunt when the treasure-hider announces you are getting warmer as you get closer. In Delhi, Ilona felt closer to discovering what she truly wanted to do and that the only way to find her purpose was to continue searching; to keep following the intuitive breadcrumbs that led towards the treasure of her enlightenment.

I looked at her sitting beside me, within arms' reach, head bowed, swaying gently with the Sufi melody and lost in her own contemplation. I realized then that Ilona's quest for a lasting love would only be fulfilled once she resolved her other life quest. She looked up and smiled to see me watching her. It was an uneven smile, more melancholic than joyful. And although my arms were tightly wrapped around my girlfriend, at that moment it was my flat mate I wanted to hug.

**

The revelation came, as revelations often do, late one night in the presence of alcohol. We were sitting under the stars on the terrace deck of our hotel in Khajuraho, on a vacation sponsored by Laks' parents as a birthday gift to their roots-burrowing firstborn. The deck possessed a lovely view of some of the more famous temples, which themselves looked ghostly in the benevolent gaze of a full moon. (Of course, in another frame of mind and without the booze, the moon may just as easily have seemed malevolent. But we were mellow and tipsy, and thus the yellow-white orb was telling us it had our back).

It had been a hot and sultry day of poking around the temples, trying to make our guide reveal something – anything –

75

about the historic temples that wasn't out of a porn fantasy. He steadfastly refused to cooperate. And so, the famous vertical series of sculptures on the Kandariya Mahadev temple, of a couple making love where the woman straddled her upright man with the helping hands of simultaneously masturbating handmaidens, was, to our guide's complete certainty, a depiction of the ideal couple's successful sexual progression, 'like high school, college, and post-graduate performances'. When not making things up, he bragged about how he specialized as a guide for Japanese tourists, and would we like to hear his Japanese for it was very, very good. We declined. He looked crestfallen. A few minutes later, Ilona, a gleam in her eye, pointed to a couple about fifty feet away and conjectured, "Hey, are those people Japanese?"

Almost immediately, our guide instructed us to climb a flight of steps and examine a certain statue for the sheer wonder of its intricate detail. When we came back down, he had vanished, along with the Japanese couple. Glad to be rid of him, we sat down beside the Kandariya Mahadev and watched the sun set over it, its final amber rays slow-dancing with the bougainvillea shrub around the temple. Laks started to scribble on the back of his guide map, giggling a little. When he raised his head, he read out a little poem. It was called *Friendliness in Khajuraho*, he said, and began to read:

"Are you married?" "Where are you from?"
"Can I find you a guide?", they chant in a throng
"For the Eastern group temples, can I get you a cab?"
"Or for the waterfalls?", they're so eager to grab
A few hundred rupees from
Another set of tourists
Dazed by the storm
Of a tourist economy where even a deal on a cab
At the end of high season is worth a big grab.

Chuckling as Laks finished, we rose and made our way back to our hotel deck. Given that we were in Khajuraho, it was perhaps inevitable that our post-dinner rum-drenched conversation would flirt with, dance around and then finally settle on the subject of sex. Not that this was unusual for us. Few subjects are taboo in my book (even if I don't often say much), Laks has been obsessed with sex ever since I've known him (with a relish for graphic descriptions of his encounters), and Ilona's public health work during her World Health Organization days made her not only comfortable but also often forthright in discussing sex. Then there was the total ubiquity of sex in modern pop culture; if you have your eyes open in urban India in the early years of the new millennium, you can't get away from sex. Thus, the location and the alcohol were mere catalysts, the gravy that eases your meal down your throat. A typical exchange would go very much like the one that started our whole conversation off:

Laks: Did you see that sculpture of the guy pleasing three women whilst standing on his head? Now there's an experience I'd like to have.

Ilona: Dream on, little horn ball; there's no way you can handle three women at once!

Me: Three? Two women would be too much woman for Laks.

Laks (placing arms behind head and smiling): Really? That's not what your mothers said to me last night.

Me: Typical crass American. Don't you realize that mother jokes are the lowest form of humor?

Laks: True. But they're funny, aren't they? And who says crass isn't effective? Like, sometimes, all you want to do is sit back and get a blow job. Nothing more, nothing less.

Ilona: Does your mind *ever* emerge from the gutter?

Laks (grinning lasciviously): Nope. Why don't the two of you join me down here? It's way more fun than the stiff upper-lip world you grew up in.

And so on, and on. On this particular night, encouraged by our third Cuba Libre (as Laks insists on calling a rum-and-coke), someone brought up the topic of our first sexual experiences. Laks, happy to go first, painted a portrait of how during a community service trip to Mexico during a college vacation, a much older woman seduced him in an office building, to which Ilona commented that if any guy other than Laks had told such a story, she wouldn't believe it. Then it was my turn, and I gave a brief summary of how I had once been asked to dance at a party during my first year in business school, which we did, until my dance partner said, "So, are you going to be happy just dancing all night?" and led me away to a bedroom.

I would later wonder why Ilona hadn't just told us about the time she lost her virginity, or the moment of her first kiss. She could have shared just about anything, but the combination of the night, the alcohol, comfort with her friends, and perhaps just the need to share the burden, conspired to let her to reveal what she did.

She at first declined softly when her turn came, saying it was too personal. We were having none of it, however.

"Don't put up the price like that", I said.

"Yeah, not fair to hold out. Spill the beans, woman", Laks piled on the pressure.

"You don't want to hear it", Ilona shot back. "You couldn't handle it."

As soon as those words were out, Ilona realized she'd made a mistake; we greeted her comment with 'ooohs' and 'aaahs' and then more creative catcalls. Forced on the back-foot, she said, "It was with my uncle."

The smiles left our faces to make a ghostly cameo on Ilona's. "See, I knew you wouldn't be able to handle it."

"Ilona, you don't have to say anything", I said, feeling she should be offered a way out if she didn't want to talk. But, after all those years, the skeleton needed to emerge from its closet.

"I've never said this aloud to anyone before", she said. "It was my mother's eldest brother. He was staying with us at the time, since his wife and children had moved to Delhi...I forget why. I only remember that he stayed with us for a couple of years. I was ten or eleven years old then."

She took another sip of her drink, and then blew her nose loudly. She seemed to be wondering how best to give voice to memories long suppressed. Finally, being matter-of-fact at heart, she opted for the clinical route. She spoke as if she had rehearsed what she would say a thousand times, describing it to others in her head over and over – if only to be able to process it herself, make sense of the senseless, and then store it away somewhere.

"In the summer, it would get very hot inside the house. The nights were worse than the days, if anything. My room didn't have a fan so I would sleep in my parents' bedroom with them. But after a while, their bed got too hot with three bodies in it, so I began to sleep on a mattress in our living room balcony, where the night breeze was cooling. One night, my uncle came into the kitchen to get a drink, and saw me lying there in the balcony. The moon was out, and I had lain down in a little puddle of moonlight that seeped through the balcony grill. In hindsight, I wonder if that's what made him first come up to me. He sat down and we talked a little. Then he began stroking my face and hair, and then my legs...gently...just running his fingertips across them, and up past the hem of the nightdress I wore, up along my thigh. It was ticklish, and I giggled, still blissfully unaware. "Sssh", he said, and put a finger to his lips. "Be quiet, don't wake up anyone". Then he got up and left. I fell asleep. I don't remember how much later it was, but I woke up to him stroking my hair again. Now I was a bit puzzled. He looked loving and tender, and I smiled at him, which maybe was what pushed him to cross the line."

She paused, thinking for a moment or two. We sat silently, listening. "Or maybe it didn't start him off, because he had clearly come back to me with some sort of plan, something pre-determined. But maybe my smile encouraged him. He took my hand then, and rubbed it gently. I wanted to go back to sleep, so I told him I was sleepy but he said, "In a minute, *beti*. You can sleep soon, and you'll sleep so nicely. Just one minute." Then he took my hand and kissed it. And then he placed it on his groin, above the cloth of his pajamas. His penis was hard. Back then I was clueless what this meant. I had only seen men naked a couple of times on the street, and once by accident my father when he was changing clothes. Their penises had seemed small and soft and wrinkly. So this bigger, hard, throbbing thing was totally new to me. He then began guiding my hand to rub him. I opened my eyes wide in shock, but he covered my mouth with his other hand, and said, "Don't worry *beti*, there's nothing wrong here. You're just showing your love for your uncle. You do love your uncle, no? Then this is the right thing to do." I had no idea what he was talking about but I was just very sleepy so I let him stroke himself with my hand. After a little while, he came. Then he said, "That's all. Don't tell anyone, ok, *beti*. This is our little secret. I know you like secrets, don't you? So you must keep this one. Go to sleep now." He bent down and kissed me on the forehead, and then left. The next morning I woke up feeling weird, a little dirty, and something else, a new sensation that today I would call feeling violated. But I shrugged it off, and went to school. Late that night, he came to me again. This time, he had unbuttoned himself, and he placed my hand inside, directly on his penis, and started me rubbing again, all the while repeating that everything was normal. By now, I knew that this was not normal. Or I didn't exactly *know*, but I sensed it. Everything within me was screaming that this was wrong, that I was not supposed to be doing this. But I felt like I had no choice. I did love him dearly then. He was always very kind, and would spoil me no end, since I was his only niece and his own children were far away. So I guess I believed him when he said it was the done thing, or I convinced myself to believe him. It happened a couple more times that month, and then he left our house to join his family in Delhi."

"So now you know why I said you wouldn't want to hear it", Ilona finished with a wry smile. She plastered her best face on, but recounting and reliving this experience hadn't been pleasant for her. "He just kept saying it was ok, it was good, it was normal... It was only later that..."

For all his crude street talk, Laks can also show immense tact. While I sat there shell-shocked and tongue-tied, wondering what to say or do, he leaned forward, took her hand, and said. "Thank you for trusting us enough to share that, Ilona." But he stopped after that. There was not much else to say.

Ilona wiped a tear away, and said, "The wicked uncle. So fucking clichéd, no?"

"Anyway, it never happened again", she continued. We didn't see him for a couple of years, and after that every time they visited Kolkata or we went to Delhi, I made sure not to sleep alone but to always have my mom or my cousins – his children – in the same room. I saw him looking at me in a funny way a few times after that, especially as I grew up and my body started to take shape, but I never gave him the opportunity to be alone with me."

"Why didn't you tell anyone, your parents, for instance?" I asked. "Guys like this shouldn't be allowed to be near children. Maybe he was also abusing his own kids."

"I wondered about that", Ilona admitted. "I guess if I actually saw with my own eyes that he was doing it to someone else... But on my own initiative, I never wanted to speak about it."

"But you should have", I persisted. "I see this in the slums sometimes, and the only way to make some progress in stopping it is for the women to speak out. But too many women stay silent, sweeping it under the rug of family stability." In the back of my mind, I knew I wasn't being sensitive, that this wasn't the time or place for a 'what's to be done about this?' conversation. But, lost for other ways to express my sympathy and outrage, I ploughed on. "It's the same with domestic violence. The wives keep quiet rather than telling the whole world about their bastard husbands or fathers or fathers-in-law. And that's half the problem. That's what allows all this abuse to continue unchecked."

Ilona just sat back and sighed. "It's complicated. I did love my uncle dearly then. By the time I was old enough to know what had really happened and that it was completely wrong, I didn't feel like speaking about it. I was afraid that no one would believe me, since everyone loves this man to death. He really is a charming and kind person...otherwise. And even if they did believe me, what then? It would have torn the family apart. Papa may well have taken a gun to him, and Mama's relationship with her brother would fall apart. Maybe you're right, maybe too many women do stay quiet about this. But it's complicated, all the same. And it's really, really hard to make yourself talk about it; you feel so ashamed, so dirty, so violated, that you just want to cover it up and forget about it. And our patriarchal society often accuses the woman of having provoked or encouraged it in some way. So I've never mentioned it to anyone before."

I stayed quiet, correctly interpreting Laks' glare to shut up. "Anyway...it's better left in the past now", said Ilona.

**

Unless you fly, Khajuraho is not an easy place to get to. The little temple town is one of the few major tourist attractions in India that makes you feel truly in the middle of nowhere. Getting there from Delhi required a half-day train ride south to the city of Jhansi on a long and windy track and then a bus or taxi west for another four hours on a poor road until we reached the temple town. And unlike other remote corners like Ladakh or Lakshadweep, there is no remarkable natural beauty to make you feel like you are, in fact, far away from the rest of the world and alone with the wonder of the nature you have come so far to see. In fact, this is quite the opposite; the Madhya Pradesh plain surrounding Khajuraho – flat as a pancake, topped with featureless, dusty brown fields – seems at first utterly normal, the quintessential Indian countryside. But once your eyes grow fatigued from the sheer unending flatness of the plain, you start to feel, paradoxically, more alone and isolated than if you were probing a remote part of Arunachal Pradesh or the Andaman Islands. The sense of being lost in space while moving through the geographic center of a country of a billion people is a disorienting one. Some historians claim that it's the isolation of Khajuraho that saved it from being destroyed by the Mughal armies (even if they did hack off a few chunks of erotic carvings every time they passed through), and driving through this wilderness made me see the merit in that theory.

Since neither the Delhi-Jhansi nor the Jhansi-Khajuraho trip offered much in the way of scenery, there was little option to break the monotony of the view other than to talk. Intuitively, Laks sensed – far quicker than I did – that Ilona's silence and self-absorption on our return taxi ride from Khajuraho to Jhansi stemmed from feeling raw and exposed after the previous night.

83

He kept up a steady stream of commentary and conversation to help us pass the time and also give Ilona some breathing space. She mostly stared out of the window, turning only to respond to direct questions with uncharacteristically monosyllabic answers.

Then Laks asked me what I felt about all the changes in nomenclature happening to cities around India: Bombay-Mumbai, Madras-Chennai, Calcutta-Kolkata, Bangalore-Bengaluru, Trivandrum-Tiruvananathapuram, and so on.

"I think it's terrible", I said. "Cynical vote-bank politics, narrow-minded chauvinism, treating identity like it's static, in a box. It's also a convenient way to distract people from the government's failure to solve actual problems in these cities like water shortages, power supply, traffic, poverty, etc. etc."

Ilona made a sound that was half-groan and half-chuckle but ended up painting her face into a smirk. We looked at her. "What?" Laks asked.

"Nothing... Well... It's you guys. Do you think anyone who matters gives a shit about these name changes? Look at Avraan pontificating about identity and vote-bank politics. For most people, it's just a return to the natural order of things. These cities were never their Westernized names in most people's eyes. Calcutta was always Kolkata for Bengalis, and Bangalore always Bengaluru for Kannadigas. It's only the urban, English-speaking elite who can even afford to get annoyed by this."

"That's not fair, Ilona." I said. "We grew up in these cities. They're just as much a part of us as anyone else. Just because I speak English doesn't mean I shouldn't care. Actually, it's *because* I care about these cities, and the real problems they face, that I hate these cosmetic name-changes."

"But do these cities care about *you*? I mean, you keep talking about changing India, saving the world and all that, which is fine. You have good intentions and the country needs more people like you. But still, coming from you, it's just...I don't know...a little strange."

"What are you talking about, Ilona? What's wrong with people like us wanting to make a difference?" Laks asked.

"There's nothing wrong with it. And I fall into this category too, don't get me wrong. But how much can we talk about solving India's problems when we're hardly Indian to begin with?"

"What!" This time Laks and I spoke in unison.

"It's true, isn't it? We're not representative of India; that's why people like us don't matter in national politics. Look at us. We're young in a land where only people with grey hair are taken seriously. We're urban brats in a rural country. We come from upper middle-class families in a nation with pathetic incomes per capita by global standards. We're highly educated. All three of us speak English better than we do any regional language. We believe in gender equality. We're liberal and not religious. We have sex with people we don't plan to marry, and our parents don't feel it's their life's duty to marry us off as soon as possible. We've all travelled outside India. We disagree when a historic building is torn down so that a shopping mall can go up. We read literature, not pop fiction – ok, maybe not you, Laks, but Avraan and I do – and can talk about Martin Scorcese films as much as Satyajit Ray's. Laks, you are American at the end of the day. Avraan, you come from a part of India where everyone in your family learns to play the piano – *the piano*, for God's sake! – not an Indian instrument. I'm from backward-looking Communist Calcutta and I don't even fit in *over there* because my Bengali has gotten so bad..."

She trailed off. Laks and I were staring at her.

"Don't you get it? Look around you, at these villages and huts and people carrying their day's labor on their heads. This, as much as I hate the phrase, is the real India. We are statistically insignificant. We are the elite, we are unrepresentative, we are irrelevant."

**

Two days after our return from Khajuraho, Reena and I were conducting a session on environmentalism when we heard a commotion coming from the other end of the field to which we'd taken the class. We paid no attention at first; we were trying to figure out how to kick-start the lesson again, give it some more oomph. Our students had been distracted that morning, the early summer heat made them listless. The warm-up exercise – in which we asked them to figure out where paper comes from, working back from their notebook to the book binder to the pulp factory and so on, until they arrived at the tree – had floundered. We found ourselves supplying too many of the answers. Our objective was to help them see the interconnections between objects they used daily and the natural environment these objects came from, and thus reflect on resource scarcity and the importance of conservation.

We tried again, asking them to work backwards to where their *rotis* came from. We had better luck this time, thanks mostly to Bips, who joked that although *rotis* may come from the hard work of farmers tilling the wheat fields, the farmers wouldn't lift a finger in the fields if their stomachs weren't already full of the *rotis* their wives had cooked for them. This got the class giggling, and me wondering if she'd heard chicken-and-egg jokes before. We paired them up and sent them hunting for waste materials in the mud field we were at. We hoped they would bring back a nice assortment of junk that we could then work with to show how recycling is valuable. Since recycling is a way of life for these children, it would be an easy and fun way to wrap up the session.

Reena and I sprawled under a spindly tree, trying to find patches of shade, still ignoring the excited yelling from the other end of the field. We were feeling the heat as well. Dark splashes of sweat emerged under the armpits of Reena's turquoise *salwar kameez* as she raised her hand to wipe a line of sweat off her brow. I knew my own armpits and back and sides were sodden as well. Reena said, "*Yaar*, I could do with a chilled glass of *nimbu paani* right now."

"Mmm... Or an iced milkshake", I said, sitting up slightly because I'd noticed a few kids running to one corner off the field. "What's happening there?"

"Probably someone found a ball or something to play with", Reena shrugged. "We should call them back soon. Let's finish early and give everyone a break from the sun. I can't wait to get back indoors."

Now a couple of the elder boys were racing towards us. As they got closer, we realized they were shouting. "Reena *didi*, Avraan *bhai*, come fast, come fast, Piyush fell down. He needs help."

"Fell down? Where?"

We stood and began to move in the direction everyone was heading in.

"Into the well. He's screaming. He can't swim. Bips went down to help him but she is not strong enough. Come *fast*, Avraan *bhai*."

"Oh shit!" I began sprinting towards the other end of the field. Piyush was a quiet, withdrawn child. Like most of the kids, his mother held a number of part-time jobs as a maid, going daily from house to house, and his father worked a construction site. He would show up unfailingly to every session but remain almost mute throughout. We'd tried to get him to open up but with little success so far. Pairing him up with Bips for the recycling exercise had been a conscious choice; we were hoping her energy and vivacity would rub off. A little bit of peer pressure can sometimes work miracles.

It was a typical mud field except for a few scattered trees and a clump of weeds and grass on one end. The weeds were longer than they had appeared from a distance. Wading through the fifty meters of their clutching tendrils slowed us down a little. We emerged on the other side to find the rest of the class crouched around a well made of petrified stone.

I reached the well, panting, and looked down. It was a fairly standard well, a series of steps winding down it like a spiral staircase without a hand rail. Bips was clinging to the bottom step with one arm while she supported a limp Piyush with the other. His kicking and screaming had ceased. He now lay inert against Bips' own tiny body, her other hand propping his head and shoulders above the waterline. She didn't have the strength to drag him any higher. "Help me!" she screeched, when she saw me looking down.

I threw off my shoulder bag and started to climb down, careful not to fall in myself because the steps were damp and covered with moss. I felt my feet slip now and then and clutched the side of the well for support. Slowly I descended, yelling to Bips to hang on, cursing the madness that prompted them to come down into this well. When I reached the bottom, I saw that Bips herself had grown exhausted from hanging on. The arm that clung to the step was trembling with the strain of keeping its hold and was covered with several scratches and cuts. Her face was pale, her eyes swinging around. Her body shook every few seconds – it clearly took everything she had not to let go.

Piyush's eyes, on the other hand, were closed. He didn't seem to be breathing, in marked contrast to Bips' rapid and sharp intakes of breath. Fortunately, he was the younger of the two by a couple of years, at an age where each year adds a disproportionate amount of strength and weight to the body. If they were both a handful of years older, she'd never have had the strength to keep him above the water, an ominous black surface broken by splashes of reflected daylight from above. It was slimy and covered with algae, floating weeds and a menagerie of insects, frogs, and discarded plastic bottles.

Slinging my arms under Bips armpits, I asked her to hold on to Piyush, and crouching to my knees, dragged them both higher to the next few steps. I knew that I was being a little rough on them but Piyush looked like he needed medical aid at once and Bips was ready to collapse. As soon as I could, I asked Bips to pass Piyush to me. As she moved aside to push his body through, I heaved and he came up into my arms. When I began the tricky ascent, the waiting faces above broke into cheers. Reena, looking worried, started to come down but I called out to her to stay up because she wouldn't be able to turn around on those slippery steps while holding onto a body. Somehow, clutching a motionless Piyush, I crawled up and handed him into Reena's outstretched hands.

"I've called an ambulance", she said, lowering him to the ground as his classmates moved back into a cordon around them. "I'll need to give him CPR. Hold him down for me."

I had started to climb over the mouth of the well to help Reena when I looked back over my shoulder. Bips lay slumped on the step I had left her, back against the wall and slender legs dangling into the water. I called out to Anuj, one of the two elder boys who had run to fetch us, to help Reena and said, "Reena, if you can handle this, I'm going back down."

"Go", she said, without looking up, placing her hands on Piyush's chest in preparation for CPR. I climbed back down and sat beside Bips. She raised her eyes to me, weeping in fear and exhaustion. "Is he ok?"

"Yes, he's fine", I lied. "But we need to get you out of here as well." Like all wells, especially unused ones, the air at the bottom was a noxious cocktail of gasses. I was afraid the fumes were causing Bips' lethargy, choking the oxygen in her blood.

"I'm so tired. I can't move", she said. "I'll fall in if I stand up."

"No, you won't. I'm here now. I've got you. Come." I took her hand, and raising her gently, led her slowly back up the steps into the sunlight and fresh air.

Back at the top, Reena had succeeded in reviving Piyush a little. She was kneeling behind his body, with his head in her lap. Some of the girls were crying softly, and the boys stood around in a watchful silence we'd never obtain during a class. "He's breathing again", she said, efficient and capable as ever, "But I think he hit his head when he fell in. He may have a concussion...and trauma...and who knows what else. I hope he didn't swallow too much of that water."

The ambulance arrived, bumping over the field to where we stood. We carried Piyush over the weeds and bundled him into it. Reena accompanied them to the hospital while I escorted the kids back to the slum. Bips set off energetically enough but, as she walked along, was unusually quiet. "What happened?" I asked her. She said nothing.

It was Anuj who spoke. "Avraan *bhai*, Piyush saw a multi-colored bottle floating in the water near the last step of the well. He wanted to bring that back for the class. We laughed at him and told him he would never be able to get it. So he decided to go down and prove us wrong."

Ah, Piyush. Who knew under that quiet façade lay a competitive instinct? Or was it just a normal susceptibility to peer pressure?

"So he went down, and picked up the bottle", Anuj continued, "but then he slipped and began sliding off into the water. We heard him hit his head on the stone, it was a horrible sound, and he started to sink. He doesn't know how to swim. After hitting his head, he had no chance. He was screaming and thrashing but he couldn't get back to the step."

I looked at Bips. She was staring straight ahead, expressionless.

"We became really scared", Anuj went on. "Then Bips climbed into the well. She was the only one who went in. After she had reached about halfway, she just jumped in to the water. We lost sight of her too and then we got even more scared. Then she came up, under Piyush, and began to swim with him towards the steps. That's when we started running to get you."

I could scarcely believe my years. Had this ten-year-old girl really dived into the pitch black, fungus-covered, insect-infested water of an abandoned well to rescue a drowning classmate? From where had she summoned up the courage and presence of mind to do that, whilst all her classmates stood rooted in fear?

Anuj and Bips had always had some needle between them, a competitive tension that sometimes got out of hand. Now all of that seemed to have melted away. "Avraan *bhai*, if not for Bips, Piyush would surely have died", he was emphatic.

Bips stumbled a little when she heard this, but otherwise did not change her gait or demeanor. If anything, she started to walk faster. I stepped ahead of her and turned around, crouching so that I was eye-level with her. This forced her to stop.

"Bips", I said, "What you did was wonderful, and it was not an easy thing to do. Most grown-ups wouldn't have been able to do it. Don't worry about Piyush. They have just taken him to the hospital to be sure. The ambulance doctor said he will be fine. And you are an angel. Piyush's angel."

In the days to come, Bips would bask in the glory of the superstar who saved Piyush's life and become even more irrepressible than usual. But now she said nothing. As I finished speaking, holding her shoulders and looking her in the eye, the skin on her chin furrowed. She looked away from me, her lower lip starting to quiver. I pulled her into my arms as she began to cry.

Chapter 5
Revelations in Varanasi

"How did I let you talk me into this?" I groaned as we squashed ourselves into a side berth of the Shiv-Ganga express to begin an overnight journey from Delhi to Varanasi. It was a Friday night. We had decided, at the last minute, to spend the weekend exploring the sacred city. Unsurprisingly, we'd had trouble getting tickets. We were travelling RAC – Reserved Against Confirmation – the Indian Railways' polite shrug as if to say that you can come if you like but we're overbooked, so just be glad you're not on the roof. Laks and I were together sharing one narrow side berth all the way to Varanasi.

I looked out of the window as we slowly rumbled through Delhi's twilight-zone outskirts, finding it hard to believe that it was just this morning that Laks had walked out to join me on the terrace as I drank my morning *chai* and read the sports news, which for those not invested in the stock market is really the only worthwhile section of any newspaper. (Well, all right, the half-naked film stars on Page 4 are also worth a look, and in Delhi, you always want to know how hot or cold it's predicted to get that day, but otherwise newspapers are increasingly just a waste of good forest.)

"Dude, forget the cricket", Laks began, "let's go to Varanasi this weekend."

Ok, Laks", I said, not really listening. Sachin Tendulkar had scored a brilliant double century the previous day and I was gulping down the glowing reviews.

But Laks persisted. "Come on! Let's go. Do something spontaneous for once. You guys are always so lazy."

So he had already asked Ilona and she had refused. "Yeah, she's got a work event to attend on Sunday so she can't make it.

It'll just be us. C'mon! ... Look, I'll book tickets and accommodation and find out everything there is to see. You just have to pack your bag. We'll leave tonight and return Sunday night, back in time for work on Monday."

I wavered. Laks played his trump card. "Please? It's my first full weekend off in months and I don't know when the next one will be. We *have* to go somewhere, and I know you've never been to Varanasi either."

"Ok, but why Varanasi? It's an odd place for an atheist like you to be keen to visit."

"Well, yeah. But I'm also Hindu, and Hinduism accepts atheists too, remember?"

I remembered an Amartya Sen essay Laks had shown me in which he argued that the *Lokyatta* tradition of Hinduism allowed for disbelief in God. Hinduism really was a very large tent.

"But there's another reason too", Laks admitted. "Do you have time now, or do you want to hear the story later?"

"Give me the highlights now", I said. I could afford to be a little late since I don't teach on Thursdays, usually spending the day catching up on paperwork in the office. Laks sat down on the ground opposite me, resting his back against the wall of our house. He was still in his nightclothes, a loose cotton T-shirt and boxer shorts, and his stubble was striding confidently out into its third day. He held a half-full glass of chilled orange juice in his hand. As the sunlight reflected off the glass, droplets of condensation gleamed against their yellow background, exuding a coolness that only made me feel more intensely the heat of the tea I was drinking. Orange juice makes much more sense than *chai* on a hot Delhi morning. But old habits die hard and of all the routines we get into, the morning pre-work routine can really stick.

"When you were in America, did you ever meet Jimmy Statham, the Religion professor?" Laks began.

"No. Why?"

"He was one of my favorite professors in college. A great guy, really approachable and friendly. His first name was Jameson but he insisted that we all called him Jimmy. Not Dr. Statham or Professor Statham, but Jimmy. He specialized in Eastern Religions and his classes were always so popular I wasn't able to take one till my senior year. But as soon as he began speaking that first day of our Hinduism class, I knew I was in the right place. He had this aura about him, a really strong spiritual essence or something. Don't laugh..." Laks broke off, seeing me smile at his self-help book type of description.

"It's really true. The guy had this way about him. He spoke really softly and slowly, and sometimes it was so soothing that you'd go to sleep, especially when he made us practice meditation. Many people actually did fall asleep right there in class, sometimes even when he was lecturing, but he didn't mind at all. He would say that sleep is one of the most profound forms of meditation and since meditation is the core practice of most Eastern religions, it was all right to drift off sometimes, as long as we drifted off with mindfulness."

"Wow", I said. "I wish some of my Economics professors had been so understanding. I swear, as soon as they would begin talking about the Gini co-efficient, I'd be out like a light. I should have said I was 'profoundly meditating' on the Gini."

"I'll bet you were meditating but her name wasn't Gini", Laks retorted.

"Anyway, Jimmy was really something", he continued. "One day in class he told us this story of how he'd had a revelation in

Benaras – he always called Varanasi by its ancient name – one morning at dawn. He was in his mid-twenties at the time, about our age I suppose, and was spending a year in Benaras to do research for his PhD. He said he had stayed up all night, meditating deeply, almost in a trance, and that he had a feeling that some ancient wisdom was trying to reveal itself to him. (Boy, you should have seen the eyes rolling in class when he said that.)"

Laks paused to take a long sip of his orange juice, a faraway look in his eyes as he dug up long-ago memories.

"As dawn approached, he stopped meditating and walked out of his room and up the stairs to the high terrace of the building he was living in. From the terrace, you could see the old city of Varanasi leading down to the Ganges and, at sunrise, as the birds began to call and the city roused itself to life, the river would glow orange, reflecting the sunlight onto the temples and buildings that stood on the banks of the river. On that particular morning, as Jimmy watched the sunrise, he had a revelation, like the universe allowed him to look deep inside it. At that point, he said, everything clicked for him and he knew what he believed in and why. He also realized exactly what he needed to do with his life."

"Impressive", I said. "You think you can manage over a weekend, Laks?"

He ignored that. "You know, one of the most interesting things about Jimmy was that he would never tell his students which religion he actually ascribed to. He knew all the major religions so well (and even more about some of the minor ones), and spoke about each religion with the respect and reverence of a believer, but although every batch of students would ask him what he truly believed in, he refused to tell. It was all part of his aura, which I always felt he carefully cultivated; refusing to divulge his religion added nicely to the legends and myths surrounding him.

After this story though, many of us began to believe he was, in his heart, a Hindu."

"He sounds like quite a guy. I wish I had met him when I was there", I said as I began to rise. I was getting more than a little late now but Laks' story had served its purpose. I was now just as intrigued about Varanasi as he was.

I reached out a hand to help Laks get to his feet. He grasped it, and as he stood, he said, "The thing is. As Jimmy was speaking that day, a sort of glow emanated from him. The process of telling us that story and the memories it made him access had put him back into that trance he was talking about. That's when it really hit home to me – the moment Jimmy had had that morning was the Real Thing, or as close to it as one can get. And believe it or not, when I left class that afternoon, my hands were tingling with some weird-ass energy. It made me feel totally alive."

**

So there we were, trying to fit ourselves into one side berth in a body-heated compartment where we'd have to sleep as best we could while sitting up against the wall. I cursed myself for not agreeing to go until Laks had got confirmed tickets. I've always been a reluctant traveller – happy to visit new places and have new experiences but rarely finding the energy and enthusiasm to do the planning and organization that any trip demands. Laks on the other hand was an insatiable traveller. One of his goals on coming to India was to see as much of his ancestral nation as possible. Whenever possible, he would take off for the weekend to explore a new place. He'd been in India for just under a year, working long weeks, and yet had already weekend-ed his way through most of Uttaranchal and Rajasthan. Although Ilona and I rarely accompanied him, he never tired of twisting our arms to go along. After a full week of work in the slums, I couldn't imagine spending the weekend in touristic traipsing. I was so grumpy indeed at the prospect of such an uncomfortable Friday night. As soon as the train set off, I pulled out my headphones and proceeded to tune out Laks and the world for the rest of the night.

**

By sunset on my first day in Varanasi I was wishing that Jimmy Statham was there to explain just how such a place could lead anyone towards the divine. The old city of Benaras is somewhat like Delhi's Lajpat Nagar market during Diwali – bourgeoisie consumerism on steroids. The narrow winding streets are filled with shops and stalls selling all manner of cheap merchandise, from clothes to utensils to a hundred varieties of *paan*. Crowds throng everywhere and ruminating cows sit right across the narrow lanes, forcing you to jump over them (risking being impaled on a skittish horn) to proceed.

As we walked past the shops and descended towards Dasashwamedh Ghat, the central river temple, the madness moved from annoying to unbearable. Touts and con artists sprouted out of the stone steps leading down to the *ghat*, like weeds from the cracks in the ancient city's streets. A major pilgrimage destination, Varanasi is filled with tourists the whole year round. Fleecing these spiritual mendicants is a thriving cottage industry, attracting a diverse spectrum of traders ranging from cycle-rickshaw *wallahs* to beggar kids, who work on you with a ruthlessness that takes your breath away: "Hello sir, you want cigarette" chimed a girl not more than six years old and "Sir, you come with me, I show you nice college girls" whispered an urchin boy not yet old enough to have one himself. They all speak a utilitarian English designed to find creative ways to part you from your money. We did our best to escape them by walking towards the less crowded *ghats* but without much success. If they were not offering deals on boat trips or a massage, they would come close and whisper sibilantly, "*Chillum*? *Charas*? Hash? Come with me, sir. Round the corner, sir."

Is it paradoxical that one of the holiest places in Hinduism is such a den of thieves? How nice if a Hindu Jesus strode through and upturned everything a la Jerusalem. Not that it would make sense in India anyway – the notion of the spotlessly clean house of worship isn't borne out by the data. So, inspired by the Gospel of Jimmy Statham, I strove to find peace and spirituality in what I did experience in Varanasi. It didn't help that the *ghats* are unkempt. We walked around, invoking to each other the Zen ideal of finding the sacred in the mundane. Laks looked dismayed by what he was seeing; my heart went out to him as he shouldered the crashing of his expectations with as much cheer as he could.

In spite of this rude awakening, both Laks and I experienced a sudden surge of emotion when we reached the top of the flight of stone stairs that led down to Dasashwamedh Ghat and saw the Ganges for the first time in the fading sun. The river was grey, opaque, flecked with the reflected orange of the sun, and calm as it flowed past the *ghats*. I wondered about the awe bubbling through me. It was a pretty sight but not a spectacular one. That strange sensation of wonder must come from a cultural conditioning, growing up in a nation that reveres this river like a mother.

Walking down to the riverfront, we succumbed to head massages that turned into full body massages. As far as massages go, it wasn't great. I was tense with the need to be careful of my belongings even in this sacred space. But it was a nice little experience nevertheless. We lay down on coir mats on the stone floor of the *ghat* as twilight brought some relief from the chaos of the afternoon. A breeze blew over the water, gentle enough to be pleasant but strong enough to cool the *ghat*. The scent of nearby cows settling down for the evening wafted over. Fifty meters to my left, a grand *puja* was being performed in front of the massive Dasashwamedh Ghat. A large crowd stood there watching, absorbing the devotional music and prayers that travelled deep into the twilight air and, through the vigorous kneading of my masseuse, penetrated into and journeyed all through my body, forcing it into a reluctant relaxation. I started to think that Jimmy may not have been flying so high after all.

After our turbulent introduction to Varanasi on day one, we felt that the city could only grow on us. We woke up to take the traditional sunrise boat trip to see the *ghats* from the river, certainly the best place from which to view them since the distance obscures the filth in which they abide. After an hour of gently cruising back and forth past the row of temples, we returned to the dock. Pulling back in, amidst the multitude of boats and early morning bathers and splashing children, I saw a man, waist deep in water, praying. He wasn't a a priest or monk of any kind; he seemed an ordinary man who had come down to the river to pray. His style of moustache indicated he was from the south of the country. He stood in the murky water, broad shouldered and bare-chested, chest hair matted with drops of the holy river, hands folded together in a *namaste*. Eyes closed, he seemed oblivious to the boats and people bustling around him. He was facing the rising sun and his lips were moving soundlessly. And he had the very same glow that I had imagined emanating from Jimmy when Laks told me that story, the glow of an inner assurance of spiritual belonging. It was the purest moment of our trip; I realized that my lack of resonance with Varanasi was, to a large extent, *my* failure. And that perhaps the most lasting moments of spiritual connection are attained only after sifting through layers of grime. Or, as Laks said, "We gotta earn our spiritual stripes, baby".

**

We got out of our boat and headed back to our hotel for breakfast. Laks ordered pancakes with banana and honey, and I asked for cheese and eggs with mine. As we sat back with rumbling stomachs, we became aware of a conversation at the next table. Wally, the hotel owner, was keeping a young British couple company as they worked their way through a large pile of French toast. They were discussing the highly polluted state of the Ganges in Varanasi, and the British man reeled off some miserable statistics about the levels of pollution in the river and dangers it presented to the people of the city.

"Sadly, those numbers are, if anything, understated", responded Wally ponderously. "Every day more than thirty sewers discharge into the river here. Add to that the corpses of people and cows that float down the river daily, and "polluted" becomes a compliment."

"I read that some citizen groups have mobilized to clean it up", piped in the British woman.

"Yes, that's true, but they won't succeed", said Wally, stroking his belly. "It's impossible."

"Why do you say that?"

"Because the problem is not environmental. It's spiritual. They're killing the river. They've already killed it. Look, if the river is so holy, why then do they clog it with carcasses and corpses? Because scripture says so. That's why they will never stop doing this. The only hope is for the scripture to be changed."

Laks raised his eyebrows when he heard this. "For the scripture to be changed?", he mouthed silently in my direction, rolling his eyes.

Our pancakes arrived and we dove in. Later in the conversation, as we were scraping the last dregs of butter off our plates, we heard Wally say, "In India you have to buy your wife. And then you own her."

The subject had changed. But not so Wally's sentiments towards his countrymen. Laks paused with mouth open, his last forkful of honeyed banana pancake quivering in mid-air. Slowly, he allowed his fork to complete its journey and then shut his mouth decisively. He chewed slowly and deliberately, willing himself not to rise to the bait. He loves few things more than a good argument on a topic just like this.

"But what about marrying for love?", the girl asked.

Without so much as pausing for breath, as if he had anticipated the question all along, Wally broke into a Tina Turner impersonation. *"What's love got to do, got to do with it?"* The couple laughed and the rest of the restaurant, pretending like the two of us not to be eavesdropping on Wally's bearish philosophizing, tried to hide its smiles. But Wally sobered quickly. "Love? Love means compassion. These are things that don't exist here. It is all business deals between families. There is no compassion in India."

Wally was Christian, which can't be easy in Varanasi. His family had lived in the city for more than a century, witnessing all its changing moods. His cynicism was, I suppose, understandable, though unfortunate. The previous day, while checking into the hotel, I had endured a rather lengthy interrogation from Wally's wife. "You have a funny last name", she commented. "Where are you from?"

"From the South. I'm Mangalorean. Rebello is not a rare name for us."

She looked up from the register with a look like everything had just clicked. "You're a Christian?"

"Yes."

"Oh, how lovely! We don' get many Indian Christians here. Are you a born-again?"

"No. Born and brought up", I replied, wanting now to end the conversation before I had to confess just how weak my connection with Christianity had become and, more importantly in a budget hotel, lose all the brownie points I had just scored by virtue of a decision my parents had made for me. But she wasn't done yet. "What is the name of your church?" This, I knew, was a veiled attempt to figure out whether I'm Catholic or Protestant.

"I'm Catholic", I said abruptly.

"I see." She looked disappointed but finally handed over the keys to our room. I fled.

**

We finished our pancakes and sat back, content. I asked Laks what he wanted to do for the rest of the day. "Sarnath", he replied.

"Sarnath? Where's that? Why?"

"Dude, that's where Buddha gave his first sermon after he attained enlightenment. It's, like, in the top three most sacred places in Buddhism. Ashoka - the Emperor - apparently built a huge *stupa* there to commemorate it. Let's check it out."

"Is it far from here?" I was dreading more adventures in the cauldron of Varanasi.

"Nope, it's about 15 kilometers, according to the guidebook. It will get us out of Varanasi for a bit. We can take an auto."

Sarnath's tranquility turned out to be worth every bone-jarring bump and pothole it took to get there. Although it had its share of 'guides' and other touts, it was mostly quiet and serene; its green lawns and deer park and quietly bustling Buddhist monks a stark contrast to Varanasi's enthusiastic anarchy.

Despite its religious importance and heritage, Sarnath faded away in very much the same manner as Buddhism did in India. It became a forgotten and derelict town until a Sri Lankan Buddhist pilgrim called Dharmapala visited early in the twentieth century. Horrified by the neglect he saw, Dharmapala galvanized into action. Raising funds from wealthy Americans and Indians, he single-handedly revived the town. Today, though still largely somnolent, Sarnath has been given a face-lift. In the famous deer-park that lies adjacent to Ashoka's massive *stupa*, there is a collection of little shrines representing all the major Buddhist nations – Korea, China, Myanmar, Sri Lanka, Japan, Thailand – on which are carved the Buddha's first sermon in each respective nation's script. These shrines enclose a smaller garden that contains a fenced-off bodhi tree whose leafy branches overhang a collection of statues representing Buddha and the five disciples he first preached to. Each of these nations has also sponsored rest houses, schools and temples for their own citizens to use when they come to pay homage.

After dutifully examining the temples and the *stupa*, we shook off our guide for half an hour, saying we just wanted to sit on the lawns for a while. He said he would wait for us back at the entrance but only retreated to a safe distance from where he could keep a watchful eye on us. Not that we cared. We bought a tender-coconut each and, sipping the cool milk, walked towards a large tree where we could sit in the shade.

We weren't alone under the tree. A German backpacker was already there, sitting with his back to the tree and reading *The Romantics*, a Pankaj Mishra novel set in Varanasi. His name was

Helmut and he was curious to see Indian tourists at a less well-known attraction such as Sarnath, which are generally visited only by the foreign traveller seeking to get off the beaten path. We discussed the complexities and contradictions of Varanasi. He believed the core of the issue was the clash between the deep Indian conservatism of the traditional holy city and the enlightenment-seeking foreigners with very different social and cultural norms.

"Maybe that has something to do with the strangeness of Varanasi", Helmut opined. "The clash of cultures causing some kind of...how you say it in English ... schizo ... schizophrenia. Everyone is seeing an easy market and in the hurry to go shopping, they are losing their hold on the spiritual side. Maybe that is true, maybe not. But that is what I think."

We weren't in the mood to analyze this place any more; we'd been doing it with each other ever since we arrived. Laks tried to change the subject by saying simply that it was nice to be in a more peaceful setting. "It's just a pity that the river is not here as well", he finished.

"Oh, you want to sit by the river where it is quiet? I know a place."

"Yeah, that'd be nice", said Laks, "where is it?"

Helmut put on a sly, conspiratorial face. "Ok, but you have to keep it a secret. One of the *sadhus* in Varanasi showed it to me. He took me there to smoke hash. But he made me promise not to tell anyone since only a few people know about it, and they want to keep it a secret from all the tourists."

"Yeah, yeah, we won't tell anybody." Laks was interested now. As someone who fancied himself a true traveller, he could never resist the words 'we want to keep it a secret from the tourists'.

Helmut considered for a while and then nodded, almost more to himself than to us. "It is a little distance from here, near a bend in the river. You can take a cycle-rickshaw there." We wrote down the directions and decided to set off immediately, hoping to get there in time for sunset.

**

I am getting more and more annoyed with Samar, the main character in The Romantics, *when two Indian guys walk up and join me under the tree, all of us taking refuge from this horrible sun. Every time I start enjoying this book, Samar messes it up for me. Why do so many Indian writers create protagonists that are so vacillating and impotent? No wonder then, as Mishra writes in this book, that foreigners in India have a condescension towards the Indians they meet. Most Indians are either too shy or try too hard to impress. But not these two; they are self-assured; they hold their own in any world gathering. Here they are now, totally at ease with talking to a foreigner, but also smart enough to avoid a debate. They have nothing to prove to foreigners about their India. Perhaps these are the children of the "New India" I see featured in all the magazines and TV channels but noticeably absent from current Indian literature, as rare as a tiger in the wild. I observed them back in the hostel in Benaras where, strangely enough since we're in India, they are the conspicuous ones. Not many traveling Indians stay in budget hostels. I was doing my daily yoga when they arrived, absorbed in the Surya Namaskar (India's greatest contribution to physical fitness – Start with a namaste, stretch up to the sky, bend like a swimmer about to dive, drop to one knee like a runner on his mark, extend the other knee back and arch the back like a cat waking up...it's the greatest exercise of all.) But their arrival disturbed my concentration and, curious to know more about them, I began eavesdropping on their conversations. So it must be karma that, as Humphrey Bogart might say, of all the trees, in all the parks, in all the world, they walk under mine. It's ok I break my promise about the secret place.*

**

It was on the ride to Helmut's secret spot that I first paid attention to the technique of the Indian cycle-rickshaw *wallah*. Cycle-rickshaws are rare in South India, so my time in North India was the first I had seen of these indefatigable transporters. In Delhi, the cycle-rickshaws are used for very short distances, but in Varanasi they can take you several kilometers.

Unlike ordinary cycling, the fact that one is pulling a large – sometimes very large – weight calls for a slightly different style. So as the rickshaw *wallah* moves each pedal downwards, his entire body shifts to that side of the cycle, until he is almost hanging off that end. But just as he looks set to overbalance, he lets go and moves back to the center, before shifting his weight to the other pedal, while leaving the former one to come back up on its own, without the driver's leg on it. When the free pedal reaches its highest point, the weight shifts back and the process is repeated. It is an exact technique, perfected likely out of necessity and years of experience until it is now second nature to the rickshaw *wallah*.

Ours was a dapper man, small-built but wiry, trimmed beard, sunglasses and a baseball cap. Unsurprisingly, he had powerful legs and as he strained to pull us uphill, the veins in his calf bulged out furiously against his leathery skin. He was cheerful and conversational, and I enjoyed the banter as we cleared the crest of the slope and he began accelerating downhill towards the river. "Why", I asked him in my broken Hindi when he stopped at our destination and promptly asked me for more money than we had initially agreed, "is everyone in Benaras a thief?"

He nodded sagely and said, "What happens is God's will. Yes, everyone is a thief here but one day they will get judged by God and punished." A Muslim in Varanasi, he seemed to feel free to lambaste the infidels. "But *I* have quoted the correct fare, have I not, *bhai-saab*?"

"Yes", I replied. He had. Although he was asking for more now, he had initially suggested a very fair price.

"See, I am an honest man. *Inshallah*, I will not be punished by God."

"Yes, indeed. *Inshallah*", I replied, and started to walk away.

"So give me 10 rupees more."

** **

Helmut's secret spot bettered our expectations. It was an ancient houseboat, tethered between the bank of the Ganges on one side and gently lapping waves on the other. It wasn't exactly a deserted spot since a small slum lay on one side of it, but the houseboat itself was unoccupied and there were an assortment of chairs and tables sitting up on the deck. We strolled in, woke up the napping proprietor, and ordered fresh lime sodas before walking up a flight of stairs to the deck.

The view from the deck was magnificent. The blazing heat of Varanasi had turned into a balmy Sunday afternoon away from the city. A brisk breeze picked up off the water. On the other shore, perhaps a couple of kilometers away, blue-green hills shimmered below scattered wisps of cloud. The odd boat drifted by en route to Varanasi, a few rafts ferried devotees to and from a temple on a small island halfway to the other shore. Along the embankment, women bathed and washed their clothes, taking fastidious care over both their laundry and their modesty. A boy in a red dhoti and orange shirt sat on his haunches to relieve himself by the shore.

Overhead, the crows had evolved a unique way of scavenging trash from the flowing river, darting down in quick bursts and getting their beaks under their target before pulling back up again with their bounty of twigs or scraps of rubbish balanced partly in but mostly on top of their beak. An egret, bright white with a yellow neck, hovered across from shore to shore, plunging occasionally to the surface but always coming up empty. It was not a good fishing day. Or maybe it was, for Laks suddenly exclaimed that he saw a dolphin surfacing. I was skeptical that there are any Gangetic dolphins in this polluted section of the river but Laks was adamant.

"Dude, I swear I saw it."

We scanned the surface of the water for several minutes but the phantom dolphin didn't oblige. "Maybe it's one of those mythical creatures that only the worthy can see", I said, and Laks puffed his chest out in mock-pride.

We had the deck to ourselves for a while but then a young couple entered and sat down at another table, sitting not face-to-face across the table but side-by-side as couples do when they're feeling affectionate. I got the impression that they were local, and had sought out this place to spend some private time together. His arm encircled her chair, allowing him to lean in close. She looked down as she talked, which was often and animatedly, but occasionally stole quick coquettish glances at him. He idly touched her hair and she pretended to lean away from the caress. The diffidence of their shadow boxing pointed to early, young love.

Laks and I sipped our fresh lime sodas, not talking much, the peace of the afternoon lulling us into a contemplative silence. Every now and then, the wind would pick up a bit and then die abruptly, leaving the water deceptively still. All around, it was a lazy Sunday afternoon on the magnificent Ganges. For us, away from the heat, dust, noise, and urbanity of both Delhi and Varanasi, it was soul food.

"I'm thinking of quitting", Laks said suddenly. He was gazing out into the expanse of water, sitting very still.

"Quitting what? Smoking?"

"No. Quitting NDTV. I've had enough. It's been ok. I've learnt a lot. But it hasn't been very exciting either. A 24-hour news channel is so much white noise. The few things that matter get swamped by the sheer volume of trash. I'm bored. I want to do something else."

I closed my book – a dog-eared second-hand copy of *The Last of the Mohicans* – and placed it on the table. "You're going back home?" I asked.

"Oh no… No. I'm enjoying it here. It's such a great time to be in India right now; there's so much happening, everything is so vibrant.

"So what next…return to investment banking?"

"No! I am done with that shit, man."

"Great, you can join the social sector, then. Like me."

"Ha. Can you picture me in an NGO? No way. Actually, I'm thinking of starting my own business. Someone's got to make some money while you run around saving the world. Or else who will fund all your grand ideas?

"Hmmm...what business, then? A massage service for bored housewives?"

Laks smiled faintly, as if on autopilot. His thoughts were far away. "I'm going to start a smoothie shop."

"What!!"

He looked at me. "Yeah, a smoothie shop. Delhi weather is perfect for it. And Indian smoothies are crap! All the cafes and trendy restaurants serve them but they have no idea what a real smoothie is. They dish out these glorified milkshakes or fruit concentrates over crushed ice. And there are hardly any options; it's usually the same flavors as in regular milkshakes. Didn't you have any smoothies while you were in America?"

I shook my head. Laks whistled. "You missed out, dude. A real smoothie is at least 25% pure fruit, 25% milk or juice, and the rest a thickener like yogurt or crushed ice. So it all comes out even, and you enjoy the fruit as much as the ice and milk. Over here in India, they usually overdo the ice or the milk, and almost always skimp on the fruit. Overdoing the ice is a common way to cut costs and rip off the customer; but a crappy smoothie is one with too much ice in it. The other problem here is that there are too few flavors on offer – just the standard ones like banana or strawberry or chocolate. A good smoothie shop has dozens of options. You can combine different types of fruits or add chocolate in some or peanut butter in others. Or lime to make it less sweet."

I stared at Laks. It had been a long time since I'd heard him talk so passionately about something that wasn't related to traveling. "How do you know so much about smoothies?"

He grinned embarrassedly. "I've been reading up about them."

"It sounds great, Laks. I'd love to have a smoothie right now, actually. But can you make it work? I mean... How much do you know about how to run a business in India?"

"I think I can do it, man. See, firstly, I'm sure there's a market for this in Delhi. You either have those basic fruit juice stalls all over the place, which are great, but not the cleanest. Or you have the regular café chains, which are so sterile. There's absolutely nothing cool about them. So I think if I can open a smoothie shop with a huge range of smoothies at affordable prices in an atmosphere that's cool, that would be a viable business opportunity. Smoothies are also very healthy and can be a meal in themselves, which should bring the diet-watching girls, which in turn will bring in the boys. I'll probably have to have a small selection of teas and coffees; nothing special. I guess I'll also need a selection of muffins and pies and donuts if people get the munchies, but I won't have much variety with these other drinks and the food. They will just be available so that there's something for everyone – the focus will be the smoothies."

He paused for a moment, and looked back out at the water. A few laborers drifted by, transporting bamboo downriver by sitting on it – they'd even erected a shelter to ward off the sun. On the river, at least, it was business as usual.

"I need to do more research, of course, on the nitty-gritty of starting a business but I don't imagine that will be a problem. I need seed capital but I have some ideas on where I can find it; maybe those years in investment banking weren't wasted after all. Apart from the equipment – which is a fixed start-up cost and shouldn't be very expensive since all we're really talking about is a handful of blenders and a couple of large freezers – the main cost will be the raw materials, which again isn't very much much since fruits and milk are quite cheap here."

"And rental costs, and staff costs", I added.

"We'll see about staff. I can probably manage by myself at first. If it starts to do well, then we'll see about hiring staff. But you're right about rent being a factor. The location is going to be really important. It has to be a place where lots of young people come, since that's the main customer population. But I also want it to be near the expatriate areas because I think foreigners would appreciate good smoothies in India, and in a cool place to hang out for a while and beat the heat. So that rules out places like Greater Kailash and Lajpat Nagar. It will have to be either near Connaught Place or Khan Market, or maybe Vasant Vihar, since these are the areas where I'll get both youth and expats. Actually, Connaught Place would be ideal because then I'll get the tourists too." He stopped speaking at looked straight at me. "Well, what do you think?"

"I think it's a super idea, Laks. Really. Go for it."

"I was hoping you'd say that. How about joining me then?"

I opened my mouth to speak but he cut me off quickly. "Yeah, I know one should never go into business with close friends but I don't think that's necessarily true. I think we'd make a great team."

I let the idea sit with me for a moment. "Laks, I'm sorry but I'm going to stick with teaching and the NGO world. For a while at least. I am not cut out to be an entrepreneur. But I tell you what. If you actually get this shop up and running, then I'll come and help you out – with making the smoothies and serving them and whatever office help you need. I'll come as much as I can after work, and on weekends. And I'll be a volunteer, at least until you start making money. Then you can bloody well pay me!"

"Thanks, Avraan." It was rare that he called me Avraan. It was usually 'dude' or 'bro' or 'man'.

"Thanks for what?"

"For the moral support. Not telling me I'm an idiot for thinking about doing this. You know I'm going to take you up on that offer to volunteer, right?" Laks gulped down the rest of his fresh lime soda and scraped his chair back. "Anyway, we should probably start heading back to town or we'll miss our train."

On our way out, I realized that I had left my sunglasses behind on the table, and we went back up to get it. As I was picking it up, Laks gripped my arm and whispered, "Look...over there...do you see it?"

I followed the direction of his pointing arm and sure enough, there it was: a sleek, grey fin slicing through the surface, parallel to the houseboat. As we watched, the fin slowly turned in our direction and the dolphin's snout broke the surface, upturned, gazing directly at us. We stood transfixed as it paused for a moment and then, perhaps taking a deep breath, dived again and disappeared.

Chapter 6
Such a Lot of World

Laks kept his promise. One afternoon, three weeks after we returned from Varanasi, whilst engaged in heated debate with an auto rickshaw driver attempting to charge me three times the actual fare (in other words, business as usual in the national capital), my cell phone vibrated in the pocket of my jeans. An SMS from Laks: *Have quit ndtv. Smoothie shop here i come! Stay tuned, good souls of delhi.*

Satisfactorily finishing my shouting match, I wrote back: *Awesome, Laks…let's celebrate. My treat. 7:30 Def Col usual place?*

His reply surprised me: *Thanx bro but can't. Busy planning 4 cafe.*

By midnight, Laks still hadn't returned home. I paced around the terrace waiting for him, eagerly looking forward to hearing all the details. Giving up, I sent him another SMS: *You doing ok? What's going on?*

There was no response. An hour or so later, just as I was falling asleep, my phone beeped: *Yeah, doing fine. Just saw ur msg. Smoothie schmoozing. See ya tmrw.*

But when I woke up the next day, Laks had already left. Ilona sat cross-legged on one of our mattress-sofas in the front room, reading the paper. When she saw me knocking softly on Laks' door, she said, "He left already. A few minutes ago."

"Wow…that's seriously early for Laks", I said, looking at my watch to confirm that it was indeed only just after 8a.m. "I've never seen him get up before 9:30 before."

"Yeah, he didn't even have breakfast. He just came out all dressed up – nice shirt, tie, freshly polished shoes – and gulped down a glass of orange juice and left. He said he had a breakfast meeting in Connaught Place and that he would see us later. But, Avraan, he was so lost in thought; like he was already at the meeting. I don't think he even looked at me. Do you know what's going on?"

I told Ilona about yesterday's SMS conversation and how Laks had suddenly become very hard to pin down. "You mean he was serious about the smoothie shop?" she inquired, sounding as surprised as I felt. "I thought you guys were just...I don't know...making stuff up because you didn't have any girl stuff to talk about.

"I didn't think he'd actually go through it either", I confessed.

We didn't see Laks that night. Nor the next. The following morning, he stumbled out of his room in a bleary-eyed haze and made himself coffee, an unusual departure from his usual orange juice routine. (Laks drank two or three glasses of orange juice a day; Ilona and I often declared that he single-handedly kept in business a couple of orchards in the Kumaon hills.) I tried to get a few words out of him but he answered in evasive monosyllables. That evening, when Ilona and I met for an after-work drink at Gola's, she began with Laks. "What's going on? He seems to be deliberately avoiding us."

"Or at least avoiding talking about what he's up to", I said. "I'm sure we'll see him over the weekend. He can't avoid us forever."

But I was wrong. On Friday evening, returning home late from an exhausting lesson-planning workshop, my phone vibrated. *Hoped to see you at home but looks like you got delayed. Am off to Bombay to meet some VCs – venture capitalists – over the weekend. Then will catch up with some of my relatives for a couple of days. Back Tuesday morning.*

By modern standards of electronic speak, where how we write exposes our personality or frame of mind at the time, this was a revealing message. As Laks had gone to the trouble of properly hyphenating his message as well as his complete spelling of Tuesday and Bombay instead of the more typical 'tues' or 'bbay', I could tell that he had been waiting for a while, probably pacing the terrace, before he decided to send his farewell text. He'd been killing time as he waited for his train.

On Tuesday afternoon, Ilona, now getting a little worried about Laks, sent him a message asking if he was ok and to call when he returned to Delhi. She forwarded his response to me: *Doing great...bbay trip went very well. Got back couple hrs ago. Need 2 put in another week running around but its looking good. Will try n call but v busy today.*

Back in Delhi, Laks continued his long days. One evening, as I returned home from work and began to climb the stairs to the *barsati*, Priyanka, our landlady, stopped me. "Avraan, a package came for Laks today. From America. Will you take it up and give it to him? I haven't seen him in a while."

"Neither have I, actually", I said to Priyanka as I took the package from her. It was a large cardboard box, but not a heavy one, from Laks' mother. When I shook it, all I heard was the rustling of papers inside. Wondering why Laks had gotten his parents to send him a box of papers, I placed the box outside his door and went to bed.

The next morning, the box was gone. As was Laks. By now, we had become resigned to just waiting until he was ready to talk. That weekend, he went to Mumbai again. The following Wednesday, by which time it had been almost three weeks since I had last seen my friend, he called me as I was finishing work. "Hey dude, got any evening plans?"

119

"Maybe", I lied, a tad frostily.

Laks heard the chill in my voice. "Don't worry, bro, I'll explain it all tonight. I'll do better than that in fact...I'll show you." He rattled off an address on one of the roads leading off from Connaught Place, and hung up. I called Ilona and confirmed that she had received the summons too. We agreed to meet back at home after work and head out there together.

**

Finding Laks wasn't difficult. He stood outside on the main road, speaking into his cell-phone and scanning the passing auto rickshaws. As we disembarked, he ended his phone conversation and gave us each a big hug, out of sheer excitement and apparently a newly developed inability to stand still.

"Ok, Laks, spill. What's going on?" Ilona demanded.

He laughed, and pointing behind him to a short flight of stairs that led to a closed shutter, said "This way." When we reached the bottom of the stairs, he asked us to close our eyes and open it only when he said so. I heard him sprinting up the stairs and then the crashing, grinding sound of an asbestos shutter being raised.

"Ok, you can open your eyes now", Laks called out. He was standing in front of a glass door that led to a room, which held a number of tables, each surrounded by a few chairs. The door bore the name of the establishment, inscribed in dark red, almost maroon, calligraphic lettering. Slung across the entire glass front of the shop was a white cloth banner with bold multi-colored words painted in large sweeping brush strokes: "A Lot of World Café: Coming Soon".

"Come in", Laks said, and held the glass door open for us. I walked in to face a huge mural of a wooden boat standing on a grassy lawn. The mural covered one entire wall, and was designed to be the first thing someone entering through the glass doors would see. Laks interrupted my scan of the room by pressing a large chilled glass into my hands. "Here's your first proper smoothie, dude. It's made with banana, peanut butter and chocolate. Ilona, yours is strawberry, banana and *chikoo*. Sit down, and tell me what you think."

I took a sip. My taste buds exclaimed as the perfect blend of flavors flowed over them. "Delicious!" I said at the same time that Ilona went "Mmm...Yummy!"

Laks looked thrilled. "You're too kind, *amigos*. Actually, I haven't got the hang of it fully yet, but I've been making progress. There's still room for improvement."

I sat back, took another sip, and looked around. The room was scattered with a half dozen tables and twice as many chairs. More chairs and tables stood folded against the walls of the room. To the right of the mural, and facing me where I sat, stood the service counter, bare for the moment but for a large blender sitting on top of its varnished surface. Behind the counter stood a couple of large freezers and next to them, a doorway leading to what I surmised was the storage room. The rest of that wall was filled with elegantly framed large-sized photographs of exotic (but not unfamiliar) people and locations: a palm tree-lined beach with a swaying hammock, a smiling wizened Buddhist monk creating a mandala, a camel walking across a sand dune at sunset, Nelson Mandela raising his right hand in the air while giving a speech, a South American Indian wearing a poncho and a sombrero flanked by a pair of llamas, a bald eagle soaring over a forested cliff, Boris Becker diving for a forehand volley at Wimbledon, a racing sailboat tilting against the tide and wind, the dark eyes and green irises of a leopard gazing straight at the camera, an aerial view of the Christ the Redeemer statue that overlooks Rio de Janeiro, a palette of seven oil paints containing the colors of the rainbow, a school of tropical fish parting (still in formation) as a pair of dolphins swam through them, Lance Armstrong straining up a steep hill during the Tour de France, and a sunrise over a snow-capped mountain peak.

My eyes continued to sweep the room, panning from the glass front entrance to the wall behind me, covered in a collage of postcards from all kinds of locations. Postcards of temples and churches and mosques, of mountains and beaches and deserts, of crowded cities and seafront markets and ancient monuments, of glamorous female and male models, of movie posters, and even a series of postcards with inspirational quotes. They were jumbled together on the wall in no particular order or formation, some slapped on crookedly and some even upside down, giving the sense of a jigsaw puzzle needing to be assembled before you could see the whole picture.

"Laks, these pictures and postcards...", I began.

"You've seen them before", he nodded. "Some of them at least are from my room in college. The others I collected over the years. I had mom mail them to me."

I rounded the postcard wall, my eyes returning to rest on the mural with the boat. It covered the whole wall, arresting your gaze, demanding your attention. "Take a look at the mural", Laks said. "Just look at it for a minute."

I slurped more of my smoothie, trying to persuade a recalcitrant piece of fudged-together banana and peanut butter to come up through the straw, and looked again at the mural.

The wooden boat stood dead center in the picture, its coat of orange and black paint fresh and still wet. A pair of red oars dangled off each of the port and starboard sides, resting on the grassy shore of a large water body, perhaps a wide Scandinavian fjord. Behind the boat, the green shore led down to turquoise water, its rolling surface interrupted now and then with the white foam of tiny waves that suggested the presence of tides. With no opposing shore, the sea looked beguiling as it stretched across to the horizon. The lagoon or bay, whatever it was, was flanked on both sides by a series of hills, leading higher and higher as the ground rose in a succession of grassy knolls and dark-green forests and eventually gleaming snow-white peaks. Above the boat, the sea, and the hills, the sky was bright blue, without a cloud in sight. Inscribed across this pristine sky, in the same dark red font that graced the glass front of the café, lettering that spanned the breadth of the mural, ran the words:

There is such a lot of world to see...

It was a fabulous scene, a snapshot in time, the kind that makes you think 'picture perfect'. It was also, in an indefinable way, deeply compelling. Despite its size, it possessed a certain quality; one that invited you to gaze upon and contemplate the world through the eyes of this rustic (and, though recently painted, also irrevocably rusted) boat.

"It's breath-taking", Ilona sighed.

"Laks. This picture...have I seen it before?"

"Good memory, Avi", Laks replied. "You may have seen something similar in the States. I got the idea from a scholarship poster in college, although I've made a few changes to make it suit the café better. I brought some professionals in to paint it. I figure the scholarship company won't mind too much, even if they find out about it."

"So, what's the deal, Laks? You still haven't told us anything." Ilona drained her smoothie with one final satisfying slurp and laid the glass down on the table with a little thump, turning to face Laks expectantly.

"Well, ever since Varanasi, I knew I had to give this a shot", he began. "So I began to research it, and once I knew I had a shot at making it happen, I quit my TV job and went to work. I checked with other cafes about who the best suppliers were, for both the raw materials and the freezers. To my surprise, they were happy to give me the information. I then contacted these suppliers and worked out a deal. I found this location through a broker, who made me pay through my nose but it was worth it since this is the perfect location: it's near CP so hopefully once word spreads I'll attract both tourists and *Dilliwallahs*. The big question was financing, especially since the lease on this place runs to a small fortune. I looked around, tapped some old contacts from my banking days and some friends of my parents, and then just followed the trail until I met a venture capitalist in Bombay called Ajay Sanghvi. I put together a business plan for him. He wanted to see the whole thing – marketing strategy, break-even projections, USP, profit projections, long-term market size, plans for scale – and I had to make a lot of it up as I went along. But in the end, I was able to convince him it was a viable venture."

Laks grinned at us. "You are both mentioned in the business plan, by the way, as my initial partners, by which I mean of course the unpaid help."

I laughed at Laks' presumptuousness but I had after all volunteered, even though at the time I had just thought that he was, frankly, talking out of his ass. Knowing Laks, he would hold me to my word, so I would have to make the best of it. Ilona protested a little but gave in soon enough – it was a little thrilling, and that big boat on the wall drew you in and made you want to be part of this place, its journey. Like the little boat facing the rolling waves of open water, Laks' quixotic smoothie shop faced an uncertain future. But the paint was fresh and intoxicating and there was no chance we were going to miss the ride. Everyone loves an underdog, and now that Laks had come through we had to get on board. Our surprise at his rapid progress must have been evident. Laks looked a little miffed.

"And you call yourself my friends!" he snorted in mock-disgust. "Anyway, once I got the funding, it was just a matter of putting the pieces of the jigsaw together. A lot of legwork, but nothing difficult. There are still a few things I need to work on, like a good marketing strategy, but I have a few ideas on that too."

He leaned across the table and put an arm around each of our shoulders. "We're opening in ten days. So get ready to start serving smoothies."

**

Venture Capitalist, Ajay Sanghvi

In my office, he sits there across the desk reminding me of me, with his slides and projections and puffed-out cockiness telling me he wants my advice more than my money. Only it's not me at his age I see but me today, two decades older. Kids these days grow up fast. This one has already attained that meaning-of-life awareness that I, at 45, have only just arrived at. With such a head start, I wonder just how much this boy will accomplish. But how will he react when Life throws him a few punches? We'll find out in time but the raw material is there. So of course I'll give him his seed capital, of course I'll mentor him through his entrepreneurial baby steps. My wife Nikki has always called me a sucker for a Grand Idea and, since she's right I don't protest too strongly. I suspect that's why she had that Salvador Dalí painting, The Temptation of Saint Anthony, *hung in my office, on a part of the wall that, to see properly, I have to lean back in my leather chair and look up. Which she knows is how I always sit when I'm contemplating a new venture. Looking up at the painting from that position – the naked saint dwarfed by the celestial elephants and nymphs bearing down on him – never fails to get me thinking twice about trying something new. But Saint Anthony himself would have struggled to hold up his cross against a younger version of himself. Even the most austere monks groom their successors so it's no surprise that I, more Epicurean in nature, cannot resist the temptation of a protégé. To create a younger mirror image, play the puppet-master, be God. Whoever said 'it's lonely at the top' knew what he was talking about. I've nowhere else to climb so I'm looking back down to see who I can bring up here beside me. Wouldn't that be a fine legacy?*

**

"Say more about the theme, Laks." I was curious. The café's décor was clearly built around some concept.

"It's an international theme, or a traveller's theme", Ilona guessed. "It's meant to cater to *firangs*."

"Sort of", said Laks. "I do think travellers will love this place and they'll provide a big part of my revenue. So I may offer some movie nights and a leave-one-take-one type of bookstore – the kind of value-add stuff that travellers love, especially in Delhi where it's hard to enjoy the nightlife unless you're loaded. But there's much more to it than that. My real target audience is Indians, especially Indians in their twenties – college students and recent graduates."

"Explain", Ilona said, looking skeptical.

"Ok", Laks leaned forward with his elbows on the table. "So, would you agree that both of you are fairly unusual Indians?" He paused, seeing us frowning. "I mean that you are doing 'different' things with your lives. You've both worked in the development sector in your twenties, whereas most people of your background think about social work only after retiring from their actual career. How many of your childhood friends are doing social work? Hardly any, right? That's what I mean by unusual."

We nodded. Fair enough.

"Good. Now, Avi, when you were growing up what sort of career were you thinking about? I bet you never expected to be teaching in a slum.

"Of course not. I wasn't into Engineering or Medicine or Law, so the only option was Economics, since the general assumption is that men who do subjects like History or English Literature are too stupid to get in anywhere else. Then I got an MBA; I thought it was the most useful degree and it would keep my options open."

"Right. You walked down a fairly typical path, the road more travelled. It took the Gujarat riots in 2002 to force you to re-think your life, to look outside the beaten path and see what else is out there. And you discovered this whole set of options. Not just the social sector; so many new industries are booming: fashion, hotels, TV, airlines, mobile phones, and of course outsourcing. The mainstream has broadened massively in the last decade. All of a sudden, there are many more options to get rich than ever before. This is all great for India, but it's only the first step."

Laks paused, waiting. Ilona obliged. "Ok, what's the next step?"

"Exploration. Without a culture of exploration and risk-taking, this progress won't last. There are all these new careers, but most people are still unhappy, aren't they? Everywhere, I only hear people complaining about their jobs. 'Stop whining about how your life sucks', I think, 'Do something to change it'. But no – they simply keep complaining. And this is in their twenties; imagine how unhappy they will be in their forties and fifties."

He looked at me. "I've noticed that your friends in the NGO sector are different. They don't complain about what they're doing. Sure, you guys bitch about your salaries and donor pressure and whether there is any impact from your work. But I never hear any angst about whether it's worth doing in the first place. That belief – in the importance of the work – is what makes the low salaries and all the stress worthwhile. I find it so inspiring! Essentially, this café is meant to be a space where young Indians can dream about doing something worthwhile, something that has meaning to them. It could be social change, sure, but I would love it even more if they also dreamed about starting a business or becoming a painter, or a poet, or a pilot. Whatever it is, they should try and do it."

Laks stopped to take a breath. Outside, the evening traffic was thinning as office lights went out around the city. My stomach began to grumble. I considered asking for another smoothie.

"I still don't get it", Ilona said. "What's the connection between your smoothie café and this little sociology dissertation? How will it help people think outside the box?

Laks heaved a sigh. "Ok, first look around. Just on the surface, is this a cool place? Will it attract young people because of the design?"

We nodded. "And your deadly smoothies", Ilona added. "They'll come for that too."

"Right. So when people come, what will they see? They'll see all these international images and visions, with the postcards and the pictures, but that's just gravy. The main course is the mural and the slogan. *There is such a lot of world to see.* I don't mean just

128

seeing through travel. I mean exploring professional worlds, personal worlds, worlds of ideas and relationships and art. It's supposed to get people thinking about all the different worlds they inhabit, and how many other worlds are waiting to be explored."

He rose and walked over to the door, where the café's name was painted. "I'm sure you noticed that the name of the café comes from the phrase on the mural. Well, 'A Lot of World' is a mouthful, isn't it? People aren't going to say, "Let's go to the A Lot of World Café" or "I'll meet you at the A Lot of World Café". That's too hard to say. Instead, what they will say is..."

"*ALOW*", Ilona's voice came out like a breath. "It's going to become the ALOW Café. Nice!"

Laks beamed, clearly pleased with himself. "And that's what it's all about. It's about *allowing* yourself to follow your dreams, at least give it a good shot. I remember a talk I attended in Chicago, a few weeks before I moved out here. The speaker asked this question: *Have you given yourself permission to do great things in your life?* I had never heard a better understanding of the dissatisfaction people generally have with their lives. They're not unhappy because life sucks; they're unhappy because they don't let themselves believe they have the power to change it. They restrain themselves from fear of failure or what their families will say. The hardest part is to believe it's *okay* to try. That is what the ALOW Café is supposed to convey: have you allowed yourself to do great things, or in other words, to be who you really are? Once you've given yourself this permission, everything else falls into place; you make your own luck. It's like with travelling, the hardest part is leaving your front door."

I was looking back at the mural. I realized slowly that Laks was right. "And the boat adds to it too. You've got this freshly painted old boat, and a beautiful landscape stretching to the horizon, like anything is possible. It tells me that whatever I want to do is worth a try, no matter how good or bad I think I am, because at least it's a beautiful view along the way."

"Now you're talking!" he almost shouted. I had never seen Laks this charged up, like an American basketball coach on the sideline pumping his fists to spur the team on. "The horizon is the goal. We're expanding horizons to show new possibilities. The fresh paint on the boat is intentional – a new coat of paint is a change in perspective. And then... Boom! Suddenly you see it: there's a lot more world out there than you thought. So, guys, what do you think? Are you with me?"

"Well...", Ilona began.

"What!" Laks put his hands on his hips, impatiently.

"One more smoothie and I'm in!"

Chapter 7
Tides and Tidings

"Your girlfriend's a smart cookie", I said to Laks as he finished sharing another Mitali-is-so-clever story. We were relaxing at home after work, trying to decide whether to call for Punjabi or Chinese food for dinner.

"I don't need no smart cookie", Laks mimed the Los Angeles street, "What I need is some hot fudge, you know what I'm say…" He broke off, eyes widening over my shoulder as the front door clattered open behind me.

Ilona stood just outside the door, wiping her shoes on the doormat with an intensity that suggested she wanted to send each microscopic crumb of dirt individually into oblivion. Destruction completed, she stomped through, her face the color of overdone toast. She flung her keys on a cushion, muttering under her breath, and disappeared into her room, slamming the door behind her.

Laks and I exchanged looks but did nothing at first, knowing that Ilona always needed to cool off in solitude. Fifteen minutes later, I went into the kitchen to fix her a drink. Carrying the drinks, we knocked on Ilona's door.

"Go away", came the muffled voice. I turned the knob and we went into her room. Ilona was lying face-down on her bed, still wearing her shoes, apparently either practicing her *pranayama* or counting ten deep breaths so that she wouldn't have to break something. She turned her head and opened one eye as she sensed us looking down at her. I held out the glass of pick-me-up and, with a long sigh, she raised herself into a cross-legged position and took the glass from me.

"To slamming doors", Laks proposed, raising his glass. We sipped our drinks, not saying a word.

"Work or play?" Laks asked finally.

"Both", Ilona said. "Vicky Taj is a complete bastard."

"What did he do now?"

"He's actually started to believe it. The image we created. The hype. He doesn't get that it's all smoke and mirrors, a stupid papier-mâché façade. And now that it's in danger of collapsing around his lazy ass, he's taking it out on the company. Which means me of course."

Work had been bumpy for Ilona of late. A little over a year ago, she'd joined The Talent Management Corporation – TalManC – but with a good deal of skepticism over whether she'd fit into an event and celebrity management company, given her more public sector-oriented professional background as a political reporter with *The Indian Express* and as a project manager with the World Health Organization. Both jobs had left her frustrated and disillusioned – at the newspaper she realized that politicians were too deft at manipulating the media to their advantage, and at the UN she felt like too small a cog in a bureaucratic machine, endlessly creating reports and files that either grew cobwebs on a high shelf or were banished into the abyss of a D-drive folder that may as well have been titled "Files Never to Open Again".

TalManC was created in the late 1980s by one of the country's few successful independent musicians, in a bid to encourage and develop young musicians in India while simultaneously creating a market for non-film music. Despite this narrowly focused infancy, TalManC had unknowingly tapped into a rich vein of latent demand in the country for exactly this kind of service. It had rapidly grown into a mega corporation that managed not just musicians but also actors, models, fashion designers, cricketers, tennis players and even the odd politician. It staged concerts featuring contemporary Western pop icons and organized fashion shows for salivating Western designers to target India's growing *haute couture* market. Yet, despite the rapid growth and expansion into new business lines, the promotion of rising Indian musicians remained a major focus area since it was close to TalManC's founder's heart and still the company's official *raison d'etre*. So when tall, light and handsome Vikram Thejashwin burst on the Hinglish pop scene with the biggest selling single in nearly two decades, it was predictable that TalManC would swoop down and carry him tenderly into their nest.

Secure under a mountain of money exceeding his wildest fantasies, Vikram Thejashwin settled back to enjoy the flight, shrugging as the makeover hawks morphed him into Vicky Taj, endorsing products from detergents to microchips, posing for cameras along with a string of newly-minted models (but only those also managed by TalManC) on his arm at page-three parties across the country. Most of these photo opportunities were arranged by Ilona who, a firm believer in the cause of developing a vibrant national music industry, had been assigned to manage Vicky. Or, rather, Vicky Taj, as the young singer now insisted on being called by everyone at all times – or else he wouldn't answer. No more Vikram or Vicky, only Vicky Taj.

A few months later, aided by that most underestimated aphrodisiac of long evenings in each other's company while on the road, Vicky Taj and Ilona became lovers, one night in a hotel room in Mumbai where they were making a cell phone commercial. It was a no-strings-attached affair; they asked no questions and made no demands of exclusivity on each other. Every now and then, when their romping revealed itself in a telltale bruise, Ilona took care to stay away from Nikhil, who still travelled a great deal on work. But life was normal otherwise. (No 'otherwise', I can imagine Ilona correcting me; life was simply normal).

But the public relations merry-go-round is after all just superstructure. Soon after signing on with TalManC, Vicky Taj released a second album, comprised largely of covers. Unsurprisingly, it bombed. Months went by where he didn't seem to be working on anything new despite several hints, at first subtle and then more direct, from TalManC that he wasn't fulfilling his end of the deal. Eventually, Vicky Taj's sloth began to grate even on Ilona. Soon the gossip-hungry hacks would get bored, for images have a short shelf life and need to be constantly re-invented. Pasted on her desk, the font of the Bob Dylan line which Ilona had made her branding motto grew larger every day, boring into her head like a parental lecture you know better than to disregard: *he not busy being born is busy dying*. The lack of new music meant that in order to keep Vicky Taj in the country's eye, new tricks had to be performed. The TalManC team began to tweak Vicky Taj's public image, recycling photographs and re-stating intentions, a subtle manipulation of the media monster now grown obese on morsels of celebrity gossip. And whenever a genuine question was asked, TalManC would allude to the Next Big Thing, either a third album in the final stages of production or a contract to sing the entire soundtrack for the next Bollywood blockbuster or an all-but-signed deal with a Western label to take the music to the American market *a la* Ricky Martin. Vicky Taj lapped it all up, growing fat on his own hot air.

Ilona's patience dimmed further. She was being harangued at TalManC staff meetings by senior executives, fielding accusations of not being proactive enough in nudging her client towards productivity. Every now and then in TalManC's Kashmiri-carpeted halls she'd make a cynical comment about Vicky Taj being a one-hit wonder and would be quickly shushed by her colleagues. With each day, Ilona grew more amazed how not just Vicky Taj but also her own seasoned colleagues had bought into the cult of the persona they had created.

The situation finally came to a head. Today, at the monthly senior staff meeting, TalManC's still popular founder had wondered aloud why Vicky Taj wasn't releasing anything. Much to her immediate boss's annoyance, Ilona spoke out saying that nothing new was in the pipeline.

"And we've let him know he needs to come up with something?"

"Yes. I've done everything except hit him with a cricket bat."

The founder thought for a moment and then said simply, "Well, then pull out the cricket bat. We can't go on like this. Give him three months and then if he doesn't come up with anything, he loses his minimum guarantee. Make that clear to him." Young pop stars may be close to the old man's heart but he new better than to allow them too much rope.

"The minimum guarantee, or MG, is the binding contract between the agency and the celebrity", Ilona explained, downing her drink and holding her glass out for another. "On signing the contract, the celebrity is assured a minimum sum through endorsements and other promotions. But there are clauses in the contract to the effect that if they don't fulfill their commitments, they lose the MG and the contract is void. In Vicky Taj's case, he has to produce at least one original song every six months."

"So we called Vicky Taj in and told him the deal", Ilona finished. "He said nothing at first and then just walked out. A few hours later, he called and asked me to go over to his farmhouse. When I got there he was in a rage, stamping about, throwing something with each wave of his arm. I managed to catch one porcelain vase that he swept off the table but two others shattered. He said that if I didn't make sure he kept his MG, it was over between us. I ignored that and replied that if he didn't release a new song pretty damn soon then it would be out of my hands. Then he totally lost it. 'Get the fuck out of my house', he screamed. I tried to calm him down, saying that we wanted to help but needed him to fulfill his part of the deal. But he just kept yelling at me so I left."

"What a dickhead", Laks said. "To go ape-shit on you like that when it's all *his* fault. You're better off without him."

"I don't care, really. I could have calmed him down if I truly wanted to. Stroked his ego, said all the right things. But all I could think was 'Time's up, pal. You need to face reality'."

She took another *pranayamic* breath. "I'm sick of it. Sick of the manipulation, sick of the illusion-making business, sick of Vicky bloody Taj. Maybe it's time to quit."

I chuckled, ostentatiously looking at the date on my watch. "Hey look, it's about a year since you joined TalManC. That's about your expiry date, right? You must be itching for a change."

"Oh shut up, Avraan." Then she paused. "Maybe my life is a lesson for everyone else. Ilona, walking metaphor. Maybe I do have a one-year shelf life at my job. I just can't seem to stay anywhere longer than that."

**

"Avraan *bhaiyya*, what are tits?"

I looked down at Bips, somewhat bemused. She had turned from staring out the window of our second class train compartment and was looking up at me; the frank honesty of her gaze told me that this was not a prank or a joke but – even worse – an honest question.

"Where did you hear that word, Bips?"

137

"Oh. One of the *firang* women in Paharganj said it the other day. She was saying that one of the bangle sellers couldn't stop staring at her 'tits'. It made her upset. Then she looked at me and said 'Poor thing, look, her tits are starting to show...now she'll have to endure a lifetime of men."

Every weekend, Bips stalked the streets of Paharganj, Delhi's backpacker tourist neighborhood, selling bangles or other trinkets. Her mother, a trinket-hawker of some distinction herself, had introduced Bips to the trade and, with her fine instincts and natural intelligence, Bips had taken to it like a high-society lady to a shoe store. I often wondered if this exposure to the anything-goes culture of low-budget tourism was responsible for Bips' overdeveloped maturity, and whether her remarkably quick progress through childhood was in fact a good thing. But now she was looking at me intently as I wondered how to explain what tits are.

"It's this area", I made a vague sweeping gesture over my chest.

"Then why did she say it was 'starting to show'?"

"Well, Bips. You know how your mother and other older woman have this area...um...extending forwards." I had no idea what the Hindi word for breasts was.

Bips grasped what I was saying and, to my horror, lifted her scruffy T-shirt up with an innocence much more in keeping with her age than the question she had asked. She wanted me to see the budding swelling of her tiny chest, still at a stage where it looked more like puppy fat than breasts.

"These are my tits, then?"

I pulled her shirt down as quickly as I could. Other passengers were starting to stare. "Yes, those are your tits", I said, abruptly and a little roughly, wanting to end the conversation.

But Bips hung on with the tenacity of a dog wrestling a bone. "Why are men going to be staring at them, Avraan *bhaiyya*?"

Oh God!

"Um... Because men don't have them, right? That's why men like to look at them..." I trailed off, horrified with myself. What was I putting into this child's mind? But I'd been trained to always answer the questions of the children we worked with; ignoring them or responding evasively or commanding them not to think such thoughts would only force them to look for the answers somewhere else. Worse, they'd stop trusting us, which would be lethal for our work.

"Do you like them too? Do you always stare at a woman's tits?" She said the word with elongated vowel sounds – *teets* – indicating that the tourist I would cheerfully strangle right now was either French or Italian.

"No, Bips, I try not to. It's not nice for a man to stare at a woman's tits."

Finally she relented and turned back to the window. We were on our way to her ancestral village, where a partner organization was running what in the jargon of the social sector is called a 'non-formal education program'. It was partly an exposure trip for me, to get a better sense of the type of family background my students came from, and also partly a research trip. I was tasked with liaising with the manager of the program and bringing back a report of the recent work they had been doing. This understanding would help us prepare better as we widened our range of activity in the slums. When Bips' parents heard that I was going there, they asked if I wouldn't mind taking Bips along. They wanted her to spend more time with the relatives they had left behind when they migrated to the city.

**

As my friendship with Bips grew, I learnt more about her family. Her father Ramesh, who now migrated his laborer's body from construction site to construction site, used to be a farmer until the declining fortunes of small-scale agriculture forced him to look for off-season work in the big cities. After a few years going back and forth, with loans accumulating and prospects looking better in the city than in the village, Ramesh handed over the deeds to the land his family had lovingly cared for and lived off for generations into the grasping claws of the local moneylender. Debt free at last, he moved his family to the capital, and the hope of a more secure future.

Unlike many of his friends, Ramesh wasn't addicted to country liquor or other cheap spirits. His vices tended towards a more glamorous universe – the Hindi film industry, or Bollywood. Where his village mates and, later, his slum-dwelling neighbors drowned their wages in the dregs of tinted glass bottles, Ramesh would rush over to the nearest cinema hall and join the crowds in the Stall Section, hooting and whistling as plain-looking-but-courageous or brawny-but-tender heroes seduced simpering starlets and vanquished vicious villains, all while staying respectfully obedient to the strict ethics of traditional society: father knows best, mother stays in the kitchen, never talk back to elders, daughters grow up to marry boys of their parents' choosing, and sons get spoilt by everyone so that they can uphold family honor when called upon to do so. Yet, when Ramesh stepped out of the movie as the all-conquering master of the universe, the harsh sunlight of reality didn't slide his fantasies off him and send them scuttling back to the murky confines of the cinema hall. Instead, he took his fantasies home and re-lived them over and over in his head for days, rehearsing some scenes, re-writing others, refurbishing plot lines at will. When his children were born, it was only natural that they be groomed to take after the Gods and Goddesses of tinsel town. So his daughters were christened Madhuri, Sridevi, Hema Malini and Juhi, and his one and only son was – who else – Amitabh.

But when little Hema Malini was six, the cine world swooned at the feet of a ravishing doll from Bengal called Bipasha. It was a new world in Bollywood – suddenly French kissing was acceptable, saris were shed for mini skirts, dancing around trees replaced by sinuous sliding around poles, wet saris stripped away for bikinis, and rustling bushes pulled back to reveal miles of bare skin and on-camera moaning. This revolution in permissibility was led by a new generation of female stars, with the incomparable Bipasha at the forefront.

The new Bollywood suited Ramesh very well. But there was also a small scratch of disquiet festering in his active imagination. Something just didn't seem right. He thought for a while, offered *puja* at a temple for guidance, and then made his mind up. Yes, there was no other option. Hema Malini, his third daughter, named after the most vintage of his favorite leading ladies, seemed hopelessly outdated. In the new Bollywood, vintage had become passé.

So little Hema Malini was informed one night that she would henceforth be called Bipasha, much to her own astonishment and her mother's strident wails that the train of Ramesh's thought had become completely derailed.

No wonder then, when Bipasha reached the ripe old age of ten, in keeping with her namesake's ability to carry off the outrageous with panache, she began wondering out aloud, with disarming earnestness, why boys would be staring at her tits for the rest of her life.

**

The train deposited us at an isolated one-platform station and chugged off the instant we disembarked, the only ones to do so. A snoozing porter opened one eye and decided we had too little luggage to interrupt his mid-morning siesta. Stepping past more snoring station attendants, we walked out and crossed the road to the banyan tree that doubled as a bus stop. The landscape was empty, flat, and barren, not a soul in sight. Yet when the bus pulled up, materializing as if from thin air, it was heaving with a riotous mix of people, luggage, vegetable baskets, steel cylinders, and assorted chickens. Herding Bips ahead of me, I stumbled inside and inched forward until a little yelp made me stop. I had stepped on a mongrel's paw. She was sticking her tongue out at me balefully.

There was only standing room. After two hours of swaying on our feet, the conductor tapped my shoulder to indicate I was to get off at the next stop. Disembarking, we found a welcome party had gathered. Bips' family had been popular in their village so when word filtered through that one of Ramesh's children was coming back for a brief visit, there'd been much anticipation. Almost as soon as I hit the ground, my bag was lifted off my shoulders, protests waved aside, and we were guided through a thicket of shrubs to a dirt path that led to the village, and marched straight into the *panchayat* chief's house for lunch.

I walked in to find my host engaged in conversation with a slender man dressed fully in *khadi* except for a pair of horn-rimmed spectacles. He looked to be in his mid-30s and introduced himself as Anup Singh, the manager of the local education program, and the person I had come all this way to meet. He was also my colleague Reena's fiancé. They had been engaged for three years but were yet to set a wedding date, as they couldn't agree on how to be together, both of them whole-heartedly committed to the locations in which they worked. I handed over the gift that Reena had sent him. Anup shook the little package against his ear, trying to figure out what was inside, but then instead of opening it, tucked it into his pocket with a little shrug.

As we sat down to lunch, it became clear that Anup was well loved in the village. Due to an air of scholarly detachment that made him seem a couple of decades older than he was, the villagers he worked with affectionately called him '*Kakaji*'. More than any of the reports or numbers he would later show me, this respectful affection was proof that Anup was doing good work here.

Lunch was typical: *roti*, *dal*, a few kinds of *sabzi*, and rice. "Eat as much as you can", Anup whispered. "This is a real feast." So it wasn't typical after all. I tucked in heartily, pausing periodically to announce that this was the best meal I'd had in years. Everyone knew I was lying but also looked pleased. The show must go on.

**

After lunch, Bips went away to play with her cousins and Anup took me for a walk. "I know a good place where we can talk", he said, and plunged into a wheat field that had seen more fertile times. He walked with a slight limp, one leg shorter than the other, often sniffing or blowing his nose into a khaki handkerchief. As I walked behind him, I could see through the scraggly tufts of wheat that the earth below was cracked, the slowly widening lines of breaking soil resembling dry parchment more than actual earth, as if this land, this way of life, was now more historic relic than a current source of livelihood.

Anup kicked up a clump of soil. He picked it up, made his hand into a fist, gently squeezing the clump of earth. It decomposed into a powdery dust and trickled through his fingers back into the ground. "We've had a couple of farmer suicides in the last month", he said worriedly. "And there may be more soon. The fields are dying and even when they *can* grow something, good prices for the crop are hard to come by. Before, most farmers would go into the cities for supplemental work – mostly laying phone lines. But with cell phones spreading faster than gossip these days, the demand for phone lines has come down and these farmers can't find other work. Ramesh was smart –there will always be a demand for construction labor. It was almost visionary of him to sell his land and move when he did. Unless some of these guys follow his example, there'll be more suicides."

He rose and continued walking. "Did you ever think there'd be a link between cell phones and farmer suicides? It's not true that they only make our lives easier."

We reached a small hill and started to climb. It was a foothill for a nearby range and as we climbed the view got prettier; the distance from the ground shielding the cracks like mascara. For some reason, I thought of college, the morning after parties when girls would use makeup to cover the hickeys they'd left on the boys they had spent the night with. In this heartland, though, all the makeup in the world couldn't hide the disintegration of the farmland.

We kept climbing. The slopes were too steep and rocky for crops but a few trees and wild grass bordered our path. Around a cluster of boulders, a small deer darted into the underbrush as we passed. The hill flattened out into a small plateau at the top, on which sat the ruins of an ancient temple. The temple was made of long flat white stone pillars, now greyed with age, standing upright to support stone roofs. Most of the roofs had caved in, but a few remained, creating small square rooms with open walls that looked upon the nearby fields and hills.

"This temple dates back to the tenth century", Anup said. "It's mostly abandoned now but every so often, when times get desperate, we remember the old traditions and come up here to do *puja*. The story goes that during his travels, Lord Ram once stopped here looking for water. He and his companions were very thirsty. They'd been wandering for days in search of fresh water. In frustration, Ram flung his spear down into the ground. It plunged halfway in and shook vigorously. Just as he went to retrieve it, water started flowing out of the ground around the spear. In the tenth century, the village built this temple on the spot where the water came out from, and for hundreds of years this was a sacred place. Today I think the village would prefer to have the water instead of the temple!"

We sat down and talked shop for a while. Anup had achieved an impressive amount with the non-formal education program: facilities had improved, more kids were coming to school than ever before, and the government had started to show interest in this village as the potential site for a new school. The sun began to set and, as I stowed my notebook back into my bag, I felt the air had grown still, as if rain was imminent. Nondescript fields lay ahead of us for miles around, broken up only by clusters of huts. Behind stood a mostly-logged hill forest, also nondescript but providing relief from the flat monotony of the plains. Except for the ruins of the ancient temple, it was an unremarkable place. But for me, far away from everything I'd grown up around, it was one of the most serene views I'd ever seen.

"How did you land up here?" I asked Anup.

"Oh, I was always going to be doing this. Or something like it. I was practically born into it. My parents were closely involved with both Vinobha Bhave and J. P. Narayanan. They accompanied Vinobha on his long walks across India after Independence, helping with his surveys and then the land distribution schemes. Later, when J. P. Narayanan started campaigning, they worked on his team as well, part of his inner circle. I spent my first few years crisscrossing India on my parents' backs."

"Wow! What a way to grow up." It was the first time I'd met anyone with an actively political background, especially one in rural politics.

"It wasn't all good. After all that work, the failure of J. P.'s movement broke my father's heart. The day Indira Gandhi was re-elected, he had a heart attack and passed away. I was just about thirteen years old. But his death also broke my mother's heart. She sent me to boarding school in Nainital and then moved to the village in Madhya Pradesh, near Bhimbetka, where they had planned to live on retirement. She began aging very quickly. I think she just lost the will to live. In 1984, I was visiting her when Indira Gandhi was assassinated. When the news came, she smiled, laughed a little even. It was such a pleasure to see that smile that no one commented on whether it was appropriate to do so. I'm sure she would never have condoned the killing – but once it happened... Well, it's like in the movies, when one thug kills another, you don't think justice was done but you don't feel sorry about it either. Two days later, she died in her sleep. With Indira Gandhi's death, there was nothing left to witness. She felt a strange satisfaction that she outlived the woman she despised more than anything in the world."

He paused for a few moments. "I found all this out only after she died. Going through her things, I came across a suitcase filled with notebooks and letters. Both my parents kept diaries right through their working lives, recording and cataloguing their work, its impact, and then the decline of the J. P. Narayanan movement and the way Indira Gandhi set out to destroy all they had worked for. When they were apart on different assignments, they wrote each other long letters, all of which my mother had preserved. Reading the contents of that suitcase was the best education I ever received. I did my B.A. in Political Science from Delhi University but nothing I learnt in class came anywhere close to my parents' writings. I was an orphan at seventeen, but with a heritage to be proud of. Now I'm just following in their footsteps."

"How about you?", he continued. "Why do you do this?"

I told him my story in brief sketches. "That's interesting", Anup said. He got up and began to pace, limping around the temple, his footsteps resounding dully off the stone floor. He tapped his fingernails against the wall in a staccato drumbeat. "I'm starting to notice more and more people of your age entering the development sector. I interact a lot with NGOs in Delhi and also with the big donor agencies, and I've seen the profile of their staff is getting younger. And they're from of my background, the village-oriented activist, but they're from the cities, they have good college educations, many are lawyers or MBAs, often they have worked a few years in their family business or the corporate sector before deciding they want to do development work. People like you, basically. I'm starting to develop a theory that those of us who willingly choose this line of work have parents that were different-thinking themselves. I think it's in our DNA from the beginning. What do you think?"

"I think there's a bigger change happening. My best friend in Delhi, who's from the U.S.A., says that although everyone in India thinks of America as a highly materialistic society, in fact it has the highest percentage of citizens doing volunteer work of any country. It is also the most philanthropic society in the world – the more you donate to charity, the less taxes you pay. So I wonder if wealth and social work are somehow related. That there's a strong connection between them whereas intuitively we might think they are opposite forces."

"I don't know much about other countries", Anup said, "But there's been a huge change in India in the last few years. There's so much wealth now in the cities; is it any surprise that villagers are rushing there and filling up the slums?"

Anup's pacing and fidgeting had made me restless as well. I too stood up in order to walk around. The evening's first mosquitoes had begun buzzing around my ears. The sun had vanished, and the sky was lined with streaks of dull orange and fading blue. Flocks of birds wheeled overhead. Everything was getting ready for the night.

"It's bigger even than that, Anup. For many people of my generation, our parents have made enough money for their old age. They don't need their kids to support them later in life. So they don't push the traditional middle-class philosophy: study hard, work hard, get married young, have two or three children, educate them, marry them off to the right people, retire, play with your grandkids, and die feeling you have done your duty... Actually, you know what, that's where the shift is taking place. Conceptions of duty are changing. Many of us don't feel that duty lies only in the family. We also want to be fulfilled outside of our families. We want professional fulfillment, spiritual fulfillment, political fulfillment. Our expectations have gone up. People want more out of life than they did before."

"What you're saying is almost a spiritual thing. People are looking for a bigger meaning to their lives?"

I nodded. "Yes. Of course, it is still a small minority. But yes."

Anup interjected, "And with the growth of the development sector, these new activists can see how they fit in, how they can use their education to make a difference without wearing *khadi* and living in a remote village."

"Sadly, that's true too", I smiled at his self-mocking.

"There's nothing sad about it! This life is not for everyone. Many people can contribute better by sitting in an office than working in the field. *I'd* never be able to live with the crowds and pollution and materialism of the cities. But that work is vital also."

I was struck by the contrast between Anup's confidence that more youth were following their dreams and Laks' passionate belief that the very opposite was true.

"Listen, we better move back", Anup was saying. "People will be wondering where I've kidnapped you off to. I'm not the only one here with designs on your time."

I took one final look around the temple, this ancient tribute to a God's great thirst. Following Anup downhill, I struggled to keep up. Despite his congenital limp and more than a decade of years on me, he skipped down the path like a mountain goat while I trundled after like an aged buffalo.

**

The next afternoon, when I went to say goodbye to Anup before beginning our return journey to Delhi, he was teaching in the cattle shed he had converted into a rudimentary classroom. The nearest government school was twelve kilometers away, an impossible distance for the children of the village to travel daily. So Anup had rolled up his sleeves and gotten to work. I stood in the back of the classroom for a while, waiting for a spare moment of his time. It took a while; he was besieged by calls of 'Kakaji', 'Kakaji' from all sides as the children proceeded through the lesson. Since primary school children of all ages study together in the same classroom in rural India, Anup had improvised a system in which each child could learn according to their own pace and interest. As a result, he had ten-year-olds in first standard and six-year-olds in third standard in the same class, all of them learning together. His system had worked so well that many other organizations around the country had copied it. Several State and District governments wanted him to train their own teachers in the method. These days, Anup spent as much time speaking to audiences around India and preparing training modules for others to use as he did teaching. He worried his students were suffering from his desire to spread his method as far as he could. He also didn't like the balance of his time shifting away from teaching and towards more and more paperwork. Although he wanted all children in rural India to have access to education, it was here in this isolated village in central India that he truly felt he belonged, and from these children that he derived his energy and enthusiasm for his work.

Watching him interact with his students and the rapt, eager-eyed way in which they lapped up his instructions, it was easy to see how he needed these students just as much as they needed him; how they were an infusion of purpose every time he became jaded from too many conference tables, hotel rooms, and computer screens.

As I stood waiting, I became aware of a musty pungent odor, one that grew stronger every time a child ran past me. I realized with a jolt that it was the smell of sweat, of unwashed bodies cramped together for long periods in an enclosed space. But of course, I thought. Given the water scarcity here, there was no chance of these children having regular baths or paying much attention to personal hygiene. My mind flashed back to the air-conditioned, escalator-strewn super malls in Gurgaon and Noida, Delhi's satellite cities where the IT brat pack reign. I thought of the young professionals there in designer jeans and elegant shoes, strolling around those malls emitting the aroma of five-thousand-rupee perfumes and colognes. For many observers of India, especially foreign reporters, the defining image of the country's paradoxes, its consistent fidelity to Newton's Third Law, is the high-tech high-rise building standing beside the grimy slum; or the child in rags holding her hand out to the tinted window of a

Mercedes at a traffic signal. After my visit to Anup's village, what always brings the contrast home to me most strongly is the smell of sweat in that classroom against the smell of Calvin Klein in a five-storied mall; or the absence of basic education in India's villages compared with wealthy four-year olds having grueling interviews to join outrageously-priced primary schools in the metropolises.

Anup finally got an opportunity to come over. He thanked me for waiting. I had already grown fond of him. I could see what Reena saw in him, why she was content waiting for their lives to eventually come together rather than pressuring him into a married life he wasn't ready for yet. Walking out of the shed, we shook hands and promised to meet the next time he came through Delhi. He went back into the classroom and I turned to head towards the bus. I felt a touch on my hand. Bips stood beside me, having said her own goodbyes. She slipped her hand in mine and together we began to walk down the dirt path that led to the highway with its banyan-tree bus stops.

Chapter 8
Amritsar's Ambrosia and Delhi's Underbelly

We reached Delhi the next afternoon but it was late evening by the time I had escorted Bips home and extricated myself from her parents' insatiable appetite for village updates and gossip, washed down by many cups of sweet milky tea. Burping *chai*, I made my way over to the *A Lot of World Café* for my evening stint behind the counter.

The *ALOW Café* had had a modest opening a few months earlier. Ajay Sanghvi, Laks' primary investor, flew in from Mumbai and a few of Laks' former NDTV colleagues joined us for the customary ceremonial blessing, followed by a collective clinking of our smoothie glasses together in a loud cheer.

Laks embarked on a marketing drive, flooding the guesthouses and bars of Paharganj and Connaught Place with flyers advertising the Café and promotional deals available in the first month. He pinned flyers to the bulletin boards of several major Delhi universities. He announced karaoke nights on Sundays and a free space for musicians to jam together on Friday and Saturday mornings. He scoured the street booksellers of Daryaganj and scored an impressive collection of books that matched the theme of the Café. And most of all, he devoted countless hours to practicing his smoothie making, until he had the recipes down to a fine art form. Less artful, though, were his friends' progress in picking up the skill.

After a sluggish first couple of weeks, traffic began to pick up. It was nearly the peak of summer in Delhi, and everyone was looking for new ways to stay cool. Initially most of Laks' clientele were tourists, passing through Delhi en route to the hill stations of Himachal Pradesh and Uttaranchal or stopping in Delhi for a few days after months of travelling across the country. Being creatures of habit more than they'd like to admit, tourists often returned to the café for the interior design that made them feel like the globetrotters they imagined themselves as. Many spent long hours in the café, slowly sipping smoothies and reading or journal-writing as they waited for their more adventurous friends to return from sightseeing and shopping. Repeat customers also came for the conversation, which Laks was happy to provide, slipping easily from persona to persona like he was born to it, be it the nudge-nudge-wink-wink banterer or armchair philosopher or the shoulder to cry on or charmer to flirt with.

News of the café slowly started to trickle through Delhi's college and working youth. The rich, fresh smoothies were a genuinely new product in the world of café beverages, a vast improvement over the milkshakes masquerading as smoothies at other cafés. Somehow Laks made *ALOW* appeal to both the disaffected Marxist student – an over-represented crowd on Delhi's campuses – and the modern, ambitious one with an eye on riding the gulfstream of the globalized world one day. Both types of students came in for the décor and the conversation and the opportunity to meet like minds. *ALOW* also appealed greatly to the Outsider, the young rebel alone in the world, for it encouraged drifting into the realm of fantasy and daydream. This type of person typically came alone and occupied a whole table, which initially made Laks fret. "What should I do when the Café gets more full and there are all these loners taking up space others could use?" But eventually the mainstream youth population started to take over from the outcasts and dreamers. This segment was Laks' primary target – not just financially, it was *their* minds he wanted to infect, not the Marxists and the already-globalized. He went out of his way to woo them, offering early-bird deals and after-dinner discounts.

A couple of months after its opening, *ALOW* was doing respectably well, providing enough revenue for Laks to hire a couple of hotel management students to staff the place and let him step away every now and then. But even after hiring these staff, he refused to let Ilona and I off our volunteering duty.

"You're part of the café", he would argue. "Walking examples of the type of Indian I'm trying to promote. You can spend fewer hours here but you have to keep coming."

Just five months from opening day – when business was already so good that it was sometimes hard to get a table in the late afternoon or early evening – ALOW broke even. The speed at which his idea had taken off emboldened Laks to think about opening another ALOW Café elsewhere in the city. He began talks with Sanghvi, his investor, who showed interest. Yet, despite ALOW's financial success, Laks gained the most gratification when he noticed customers staring at the mural, contemplating it, and talking softly to their friends about the beauty of the image or, even better, what it was saying to their souls. In these moments, Laks would swell up with inner bliss and sometimes his staff had to restrain him from announcing a round of smoothies on the house. ALOW was well and truly on its way.

But all bright lights attract insects; approaching full-tilt towards the glow, swooping and diving unabashedly. ALOW was to be no different. When I walked through the glass doors of the café that evening, there were only a handful of lingering customers and Laks was, unusually, not behind the counter. He sat at one of the tables near the back, slumped in a chair with his hands holding his face. Ilona sat beside him, one hand resting on Laks' shoulder in a gentle rub of reassurance. They barely cracked a smile when I walked up. I slung my bag over a chair and, turning it around, sat with my arms over the back. "What's up?" I asked.

"Something happened this evening", Ilona replied. Then she said, "You want a smoothie?" and without waiting for an answer stood and moved over to the counter. Still burping *chai*, but deciphering her signal, I followed and watched as she mixed me a papaya and musk-melon smoothie, with a touch of lime and vanilla essence. Laks sat listless in his chair.

155

A little after four that evening, two men had walked into the Café and chosen the table farthest from the door, a spot from where they could watch anyone who entered or left. They were unlikely customers for *ALOW*, both in their late thirties with large swarthy faces and bulky frames. One had a thick handlebar moustache and the other a thin beard which failed to disguise a heavily pockmarked face. They wore dark glasses, which they didn't remove even while inside, and carried their cell phones in a plastic pouch slung around their neck. Their shirts were unbuttoned halfway, and they perspired freely through them. Everything about their attire and demeanor suggested men who would be more at home in a cheap bar than a modern café. They ordered tea, not smoothies, and took their time, watching the customers in the café a lot more intently than drinking their fast-cooling teas.

"Laks was puzzled by them", Ilona said. "When I came in around six, he asked what I made of them. I was just as perplexed but figured that they had heard about the café and wanted to see what the fuss was about. They were staring shamelessly at the *firang* girls, so I told Laks that maybe they came to letch at the women."

But Laks hadn't liked that idea. "I hope not", he had said, "Because that would be really bad for business. We can't have women feeling uncomfortable in here because of lecherous men. These guys are idiots. Look at them - they're staring!! I'm going to go talk to them."

I looked over at Laks now. He was sitting still and looking into space, but sensing my gaze he pulled himself out of it and waved me over. When we sat back down, Ilona said, "I was just about to tell Avraan what those guys said to you."

156

"Bastards", Laks hissed through gritted teeth. "Mother fucking sons of bitches with their fathers' dicks stuffed up their God-dammed assholes."

Ilona grinned. "That's the kindest he's been to them all evening."

"What did they say?" I was still in the dark.

"They're extorting me, those mother fuckers", he spat. "I went over to ask if they had liked their tea and if they would like to order another since they'd been sitting around for over two hours. I even suggested they try a smoothie. At first they said nothing. They just looked at each other, and then the guy with the beard, said, "Are you the owner?" I said yes, and could I help them with something. "No, we're going to help you", they said, and asked me to sit down. Then the bearded guy said, "We work for Suzuki Shamu" and looked at me meaningfully. I had no idea what that meant, so I said, ok, who is he? They laughed and the mustached guy said, "Oh ho! He doesn't know Suzuki Shamu. Well, he will find out soon enough." And they both started cracking up! Then they told me that Suzuki Shamu is the 'owner' of this part of Delhi. All commercial enterprises – they even used the English words, which sounded weird coming out of their thug mouths – around here only operate under His approval and protection. "But you never came to ask Him permission to start your restaurant here, did you? He is not happy with you." I was stunned. Here I had worked my ass off getting permits and leases and all the other paperwork done, and they were telling me I had to get a mafia don's permission as well. I told them to get lost before I called the police. Then they got angry. The bearded one removed his sunglasses and glared at me. He leaned forward and said, "I don't care if you call the police. I don't care if your father is the *behenchod* Prime Minister. Nobody can touch Suzuki Shamu, so you better listen to us." Something told me that they were not bluffing so I just kept quiet.

The mustached one said, "You know how Suzuki Shamu got His name? He is an expert in stealing Maruti Suzuki cars. You can put whatever lock or whatever alarm on your car but Shamu-*saab* can break it open in less than one minute. Till now, there has not been one car lock or alarm that He cannot disable. But He only steals Maruti Suzukis, and that's how He got His name when He first started. He became a very big man by stealing the cars and redistributing the parts. Also now, even though he has many-many operations, He loves breaking down a Maruti Suzuki more than anything else, more even than fucking His four wives all at the same time. Actually... yes, actually there is one thing He likes better than breaking down a car into its parts, and that is breaking down a *maderchod angrezi* rich boy like you into your parts and feeding each part one by one to his three Dobermans. Now do you understand who you are dealing with, *behenchod*?"

"Holy shit, Laks!" I said. "What did they want?"

"One-fourth of my profits", Laks whispered. "They expect me to keep detailed accounts, which their own 'accountant' will audit every two months, and I have to give them twenty-five percent of the profits. Think of it as tax, they suggested helpfully. The bastards! And that's not all. Since I hadn't asked this Suzuki dude's permission to start my shop, I have to pay a fine of three *lakh* rupees. Where am I going to get three hundred thousand rupees from just to pay them off? I said I didn't have that kind of money but they only laughed some more. "Nobody says they have the money but everyone always manages to find it. You also will find it." They said they would return in exactly a month to collect their tax and the fine. Then they got up and left, not even paying for the damn tea."

"I was standing behind the counter as they walked past" Ilona said, "and one of them puckered up his lips and made a slurping kissing sound at me. I was stunned. But of course not as stunned as finding out what they had said to Laks."

"Who would have thought this would happen! When Mira Chopra told me about the double taxation system, I was horrified of course, but it didn't seem real somehow. Unbelievable." I couldn't help myself blathering whatever came to mind, as I struggled to process what I'd just heard.

"What am I going to do?" Laks groaned. "I can't pay them. Just on principle, my blood boils at the thought of giving them what I've struggled so hard for. But what other choice do I have?" He put his head down on the table, laying it on top of his folded arms, and began to gently bang his head up and down on his arms.

Ilona and I looked at each other helplessly. There seemed nothing to do except close the shop for the night. It might help to get Laks out of there for a while. The thought crossed our minds simultaneously and, after all this time together, we didn't have to speak. Our eyes met and, wordlessly, Ilona rose and began to close down the café, scooping up empty glasses and plates from tables and piling them in the sink for the cleaning lady who came at 8a.m. I put my hand on Laks' shoulder and gave it a squeeze as I too got up to help shut the place down.

**

It was the prolonged honking that first startled us, for it wasn't the staccato *beep-beep-beep* you normally hear in traffic or when you want children or dogs or cows to move out of the way. This was as if someone had passed out and landed heavily on the horn. It was just after 8 a.m.

Up in the *barsati*, we were reading separate sections of the same newspaper – international, op-ed, and sports, for Laks, Ilona, and me respectively – all three of us still in night wear, sitting cross-legged on our mattress-sofas with mugs of tea or orange juice in those precious few minutes each morning before getting ready for work. Because of its strident tone, I thought at first that a car alarm had accidentally been set off and paid it no attention. Then, as the din gradually filtered through my reluctant early-morning consciousness, I realized that this was no alarm. Somebody was sitting on their horn, and had no inclination to get off. We looked at each other with sluggish uncomprehending questions in our eyes before, finally, walking out of our front door onto the terrace to look down onto the street.

On the street below, a white Honda sedan was facing off against a large grey SUV. From our vantage point on the terrace, we couldn't see who was driving the sedan but could make out that the SUV driver was a woman, wearing a white shirt and brown khaki pants, with a small child strapped in the back seat. The honking came from the sedan but since it was directly below us, all we could see was a hand pressed flat against the horn. The two cars had approached each other in the narrow lane of the colony and, with no place to pass, neither driver was willing to back up to the end of the road or into someone's gate to let the other go by.

The sedan reversed a few meters, stopped, and drove forward slowly until, very deliberately, it bumped into the SUV. Laks' mouth dropped open beside me. Slowly, the sedan reversed and drove forward again into the larger car. "Is he crazy?" Ilona murmured. "She can squash him if she wants." But the woman in the SUV appeared unmoved. The sedan reversed and drove forward again, crashing a little harder now. When even this had no effect, the door opened and the driver stepped out.

She was wearing a *hijab*. She marched over to the SUV and yelled into the window. The SUV's door opened and its driver also stepped out onto the street. The two women began yelling at each other, fingers waving and arms flailing as they argued. The woman

160

in the SUV appeared a little shaken and kept repeating 'Don't be silly. I could have run you over if I wanted to' in a tone loud enough to reach us, three floors above. But the sedan driver kept screaming at her in words we couldn't identify. Suddenly, she reached out and shoved the other woman, who stumbled and fell back against her car. "Are you insane, you stupid maniac?" Laks yelled out from the balcony, no longer able to contain himself. But nobody even looked up.

Unexpectedly, the passenger-side door of the sedan opened, and a middle-aged man with a pencil moustache emerged. He walked hurriedly up to the woman in the *hijab*, grabbed her arms, forcibly yanked her backwards and bundled her into the passenger seat. Then he strode around the car, got into the driver's seat, reversed at top speed, and vanished. As the sedan moved backwards, we saw that it bore the white letters 'CD' on its blue license plate, a sign that it belonged to the city's international diplomatic corps. Several onlookers – including the colony guards, materializing now that the incident was over – now approached the woman in the SUV. But she angrily waved them away and got back into her car. Then she too drove off in the direction of the colony's exit gate.

We were still standing on our terrace in disbelief. "Fucking Delhi", Laks said, and walked back to his room.

**

I crossed my arms and rubbed my shoulders briskly to coax some warmth into them. The night was chilly but I needed to stretch my legs, which were cramped in the bus. We were on an overnight ride to Amritsar for a long weekend that coincided with Independence Day holiday. Ilona and I had agreed that Laks could use a break from Delhi. Since the incident at the café, he'd been grumpier than an elephant with anthrax, totally out-of-keeping with his usually carefree personality. He had begun attributing every stray incident or occurrence to Delhi, blaming the entire city for his troubles.

I looked at my watch: almost 3a.m. The trip had started off with several bumps and jolts and Ilona, who had the window seat, complained that every time she leaned against the window to sleep the bus went over a pothole, giving her a painful bump to the head. She asked Laks to feel the small swelling on her left temple from all the bumps, and he had suggested that she was becoming like a character from *The Satanic Verses*. The swelling was her much-delayed and much-deserved outgrowth of horns. Ilona wasn't amused.

But now they were both sleeping soundly in the bus while I, unable to sleep, welcomed the halt for tea and a bathroom break. After walking around to bring life back into my legs, I went over to the *chai-wallah* and ordered some tea. Standing there, cupping my little glass of chai in both hands for warmth, I looked at the boy who had made the tea.

He was a couple of years older than Bips. He kept rubbing his hands together, sometimes blowing warm breath on them, as he poured scalding tea into small glasses for the busloads passing by his little shack. He shivered in the late-night cold but was hard at work nevertheless, surrounded by grown men who crowded around him both for his tea and the warmth of his flame, which leapt up into the night every time the boy lifted his pot to pour out a fresh glass. Each time, the flame jumped higher, as if on a mission to warm the night as well as the water. I watched the shadows of the flames dancing on the boy's face; they were telling a story I wanted to hear. Who was this boy? Where were his parents? Why was he alone forced to be awake at this cold hour, serving tea on the side of a highway in the middle of nowhere?

He looked up then, sensing my gaze, and smiled. He held out his ladle, offering another glass of cardamom and ginger *chai*. I smiled back and shook my head. In that brief exchange, smiles between strangers, we were two ships in the night; this was our single moment of speaking each other as we crossed paths forever.

**

As I pour my chai for the never-ending line of outstretched hands, I feel someone staring at me. It is a young man. He is not from these parts because unlike the other men in shawls and turbans, he's only wearing a long-sleeved shirt. But his shoes tell me he's from a higher class than most of the passengers who stop here. He holds the hot glass of tea like a heater and I can almost see the heat flowing from the glass through his arms and into the rest of his body. I offer him more tea so he can stay warm for a bit longer but he just shakes his head. Well, it's his body, let him be cold. Above his head in the bus I see a woman lying with her head against the glass. She too is obviously high class. I wonder if she is with the man who smiled at me. She looks silly, head against the bus window with her mouth open. I've been on this bus a few times when I've gone to Dilli. But always a stowaway, bribing the conductor to let me get on and promising him that I will sleep on the floor, which anyway is more comfortable than those seats. Something about the woman in the bus reminds me of Suma-didi, my sister who married a plumber and went away to Dilli. Now that she has gone and Ma no longer has the strength to be up so late at night, the chai duty is all mine. Nights like this, when the wind makes the air so cold, I think of my father, who died crossing this same highway one night when a van without lights came from the darkness and hit him, sending him flying into a ditch on the other side of the road. One of the other chai-wallahs said that the van slowed down and he thought he heard girls screaming inside. But then it picked up speed again and took off as if nothing had happened, as if it had hit only a dog or a stone. Now, with him gone and Ma growing sicker and Didi unreachable in Dilli, what is going to happen to me? But I better not think like this. Anyway there will

always be buses needing chai. And that's a good excuse to keep a
strong fire late into the night.

**

Amritsar, the 'pool of ambrosial nectar', is named after the beautiful blue pool at the heart of the incredible Golden Temple complex. Walking through the white marble entrance into the large rectangular space containing the pool which holds in its center the famous golden-domed Harmandir Sahib, we stood transfixed for a few moments, like so many have done at this spot down the years, even before the temple was built.

Ilona informed us that, centuries before Sikhism, the Buddha also once stopped to meditate by this pool. We passed up the chance to dine on rich *dal* and *phulkas* at the Langar hall, where all visitors irrespective of race or religion or gender are welcome to eat, but stopped to watch volunteers washing what seemed like hundreds of plates and bowls for the ceaseless throngs of pilgrims that pass through the temple every day.

Along the blinding white marble walls of the Golden Temple are shrines and memorials to Sikh martyrs and warriors who have defended the Golden Temple from the Mughals and other invaders through the ages. Several of these shrines were decorated with garlands or wreaths by pilgrims paying homage to those who came before them. One such shrine told the story of a legendary warrior who led an army of Sikh soldiers to regain the temple from the Mughal king who had captured and begun to desecrate it. During the battle, the best fighter of the opposing army beheaded the warrior. Just as he was about to die, one of his aides reminded him that he had once vowed to take his last breath beside the pool of nectar and not anywhere else. The warrior gathered his severed head in one hand and marched on towards the temple, killing great numbers of the enemy with a double-edged sword wielded by the other hand. Only after victory was complete did he allow himself to die, beside the sacred pool.

After washing our feet again and putting our shoes back on, we left the Golden Temple and made our way to Amritsar's famed Lawrence Street for a huge lunch of butter chicken, garlic *naan*, *paneer do pyaza*, and *dal makhni*, washed down with a couple of glasses each of frothy white *lassi*, which tasted even better now that we'd been baked by the mid-day heat.

Although the Golden Temple is the highlight of a visit to Amritsar, we had come during the Independence Day weekend in order to take in the scene at the Wagah border separating India from Pakistan. This 'scene' is essentially a changing of the guard, accompanied by great fanfare and camaraderie. Every evening at sunset, crowds gather on both sides of the border to shout patriotic slogans and cheer on their guards while jeering the other nation's guards. The soldiers play to the crowds, dramatizing and exaggerating the smallest movements. Both sides have erected stands for their audiences. The stands on the Indian side are much bigger, almost stadium-like, since greater numbers of Indians show up. But the event itself is not as intriguing as the audience watching it. We were there on August 14th, Pakistan's Independence Day. Over 10,000 people showed up on the Indian side (and at least half that on the Pakistan side). The owner of our hotel told us that there would be 20,000 people the following day, Independence Day.

If the day's heat had abated at all, we couldn't feel it. Last night's chill during the bus ride was a distant memory. Dripping with sweat, our entire section of the audience crowded in to get a better view, unbowed by repeated threats from the guards to throw us out if we didn't behave. Though dominated by Sikhs and other Punjabis, Indians of all regions and religions were present in the crowd, all of us gathering to scream out our patriotism – *Hindustan Zindabad! Vande Mataram! Bharatmataji Jai!*

Later that night, sitting on the third floor veranda of our hotel after Laks had gone to bed, I wrote in my journal:

Claustrophobics would lose it in this crowd. If you get jostled off your perch, you curse and scramble back on, sometimes wondering why you bother because you can't see much in any case. But it's the crowd that's sweeping you along, not the show, and you're part of the crowd so you do as the crowd does. A stampede would have been fatal. And all the while you are jostling for space and clinging to whatever's handy, your sweat mingling with innumerable others' sweat, the guards are doing their thing – bristling their flourishing moustaches, marching up and down with huge goose-steps and great sweeping strokes of their arms, solemnly lowering the flag and folding it with great reverence, pretending to glare at the Pakistani guards the whole time while probably whispering to each other across the border what time they will break open the rum after the show is over and the patriotism-tourists have left.

At the end of the ceremony, the gates close and the Punjabis break out the bhangra. You watch, wishing you were any good because it looks so much fun, but too embarrassed by your two left feet to join in, even though you know you will regret this later. Then, as the crowds disperse and the adrenalin dissipates, you wonder if the same merriment is happening on the other side of the gate as well. It is complete madness.

And yet. And yet... As a Dutch traveller we met said, "It is heart-warming that the people of both sides choose this way to channel their tension. Better this than bombs. The rest of the world can learn a lot from such a ritual." Ok, so maybe that's just eager-beaver tourist hyperbole, maybe this daily evening circus is actually an expression of the

166

hostility rather than an outlet for it. But thinking back to the ceremony, there was something jolly and frivolous about it all, visible most clearly in the grins on the guards' faces as the crowd cheered them on. It was patriotism as spectacle, but a damn fine show all the same.

**

The day we return from Amritsar, I go to one of the upscale cafes in Khan Market after work to meet an old high school friend who's passing through town. When we're done, he walks me to the bus stop and we shake hands as the M-13 rumbles up in a cacophony of squeaking brakes, sparking transmission and lusty yelling from the conductor-cum-salesman. The bus will take me from Khan Market to the bus stop just outside my colony's gate. As is typical with Delhi buses, barely has my hand gripped the side of the door when the bus starts to move again, leaving me to slide and stumble my way up the stairs and into the coach. The only seat available is a makeshift steel box placed just behind the driver's cabin. I have to share the box with two others and sitting there means I'm facing the other passengers, with my back to the direction of movement.

I notice them immediately. Mostly because they are dressed so alike in their tight grey bell-bottom pants and their almost identical shirts: one shirt is blue and the other green but both have two vertical front pockets and are worn tucked in with the top three buttons undone. But I also notice at once the open beer bottles in their hands.

Blue Shirt is sitting in a left aisle seat about midway up the bus and Green Shirt is sitting in a right aisle seat a few rows from the back. They appear to be in their early twenties, slim and wiry, about medium-height. Both have straight wavy hair that falls over their foreheads, drawing attention to the sullen insolence on their faces. Subtle differences in facial structure and skin apart, they could be twins. Brothers, certainly. Their demeanor and attire screams 'Look at me, I'm hot stuff' but they lack the experience to know that you can't be cool if you have to work so hard at it. Still, if it is Bollywood gangster-hip they're after, they're well on their way. Every now and then, they take swigs of beer and look around defiantly, begging someone to be foolish enough to object.

Blue Shirt gets up and walks forward past me to talk to the bus driver. I can smell the beer, along with sweat and cigarette smoke. He begins a pointless conversation with the driver, just passing the time. We come to a bus stop and more people get in. One of them, a dark-skinned patently South Indian man in his mid-thirties, with the thick moustache and conservative shirt-and-trousers uniform of the low-ranking office clerk, walks up and takes the seat Blue Shirt has vacated. Having just got on the bus, he naturally assumed it was an open seat. Blue Shirt is still chatting with the driver and hasn't noticed. At the back of the bus, Green Shirt is gazing out of the window, apparently lost in thought. The rest of us are all in our own worlds, the way evening commuters tend to be, recovering from the workday and mentally re-booting for home.

Eventually, Blue Shirt turns back. He stops short with surprise to see his seat has been taken. Then he strides up rapidly to the older man and demands the seat back. But as far as the older man is concerned, the drunk kid is just making it all up and, in any case, if Blue Shirt vacated the seat for so long, surely he didn't still have a claim to it? When he tries to explain this, calmly and logically, Blue Shirt turns crimson with anger. Raising his voice, he demands the man get up. The older man quietly ignores him and stares straight ahead, tuning him out.

Nine-and-a-half times out of ten, that would have been that. The younger man would accept his mistake in being away for so long and cede the seat with a shrug. But not this time. It suddenly becomes clear to everyone on the bus that there's a subtle change in the air. Blue Shirt is spoiling for a fight.

Furious at being denied, Blue Shirt grabs the older man's shoulder and tugs. The man half-rises and cocks his upper body forward in the mock gesture of throwing a punch that is familiar to school kids all over the country. It's an empty threat, merely a warning, with no genuine desire to fight. Blue Shirt responds by raising his beer bottle and threatening to beat it down on the man's head. A few drops of third-rate beer splatter over nearby passengers. Now of course all eyes are on the two men. There is a watchful silence on the bus. The conductor, in his seat by the window at the back of the bus, also watches in silence. Then Green Shirt moves, coming forward to join his brother in facing off against the older man. Together, they grab his shirt and drag him out of the seat.

By this time, surely someone should intervene. None of us move. Everyone's waiting for the conductor to take the lead – it's his job, after all. But the conductor, tired after a long day's work, is slow to move.

The Twin Shirts drag the older man down to the floor and begin punching and kicking him. He tries to get up but another punch or kick sends him back down to the knobbed steel floor of the bus, writhing deeper in agony. A few moments later, he screams out, "My head!"

As I watch, half my mind is pushing me to get up and do something. But the other half, focused on self-preservation, restrains me: it's not my fight. I don't know what I could say to calm things down, even if that were possible. And what if the Twin Shirts turn on me? Their glass bottles are weapons, and perhaps they're also carrying knives, not uncommon in this city. I'm unarmed and no fighter. Intervention can also have a price: not long ago, a twenty-one year old was thrown to his death from a

169

moving train, in front of several unmoving witnesses, for trying to prevent a gang of thugs from molesting a woman he didn't know. Even more recently, an elderly woman was shot and killed when she intervened to help her daughter-in-law who was being harassed on the street. No, get involved and you die. It happens all the time.

Besides, the Dust is back. It comes slowly, at first filtering through in a gentle trickle but then, as I try and talk myself into acting, it storms in and slams the door of my mouth shut before wreaking its customary havoc on my gums, teeth and tongue. It is worse than usual this time, an unmistakable warning against false valor. I have to clamp my lips down tightly in order not to vomit on the floor of the bus.

In the end, like everyone else, I am rooted to my seat as two young thugs viciously beat a helpless man. The conductor eventually waddles over and pulls the Twin Shirts away. Though their bloodlust rages, the conductor is a figure of authority, and they won't take him on. He tells them to get off the bus but they refuse. Blue Shirt plunks himself down on the seat that caused all the trouble and Green Shirt remains standing by his friend's side. Only now do the other passengers begin to act. Some help the beaten man to his feet. A college student rises and offers the older man his seat. But all he wants to do now is get off. He walks to the front door and jumps out at the next bus stop, not looking back at his tormentors.

Later that night, I'm unable to sleep. I try everything to put the incident out of my mind. I re-read the latest Harry Potter. I put on earphones and pace up and down the terrace, pounding music into my ears: loud music, happy music. I masturbate, imagining erotic happenings in exotic locations.

But I can't rid myself of the images of that beating. The sights and sounds of it keep forcing themselves back into my mind, each time in greater clarity. I'm racked with guilt: despite knowing that I was also protecting myself, I can't get over the fact that it wasn't really an active choice. I didn't consciously hold myself back; my initial, instinctive reaction was to stay out of it, regardless of the consequences to someone's life. But what if the person being attacked was someone I knew, or even a friend? What would I have done if it were an unknown woman being raped right in front of me?

Floating in that timeless void that insomnia puts us in, such scenarios are too easily played out, the reel of my imagination circling inexorably – round after round – over the twin wheels of my cowardice and my guilt. Finally, to force my suddenly stern conscience to let me off the hook, I swallow a sleeping pill strong as a tranquilizer. And lie very still.

Chapter 9
When the Dealing's Done

A searing Saturday morning. Ilona, Laks and I go to Paharganj to see what Bips gets up to there. Paharganj is Delhi's tourist haven, much like Bangkok's Khao San Road but less visibly a madhouse. We walk past uncountable silver jewelers and shawl weavers until we spot Bips circling three *firang* men in a pseudo-Italian café. We sit at a nearby table. Bips, engrossed in her trade, ignores us completely.

Her hook is simple. She pretends to be hawking cheap bangles or earrings or even bookmarks, but this is only to get her foot in the door. It allows her to impress the tourists with her command of English and, as the unwitting *firang* follows her lead, she is the spider shutting the parlor door behind them. For Bips has memorized the capital cities of most major countries in the world. (Some days, when she doesn't know a particular capital, she admits defeat and asks what the answer is. And then her steel-trap mind files it away for future use.) On this occasion, she was up against a canny American but, like any champion, she raised her game when she needed to.

She approached the three men confidently as they sat near the doorway of the café finding refuge from the heat (and the street) in a cold beer. "Good afternoon, sirs. *Namaste.* How are you?"

"Fine, thanks, young lady. How are you?"

"I am fine also. You buy my bangles? 2 for Rupees 50 only!"

"25 rupees for a bangle! No way, that's crazy."

"Ok, sir, for you, 2 for 35 rupees. But only for you."

"No. I don't want any more bangles." And then, to his companions, "If I buy my girlfriend any more cheap jewelry from India, she won't have any bare arm left on which to wear it."

Unfazed by the rejection, Bips put on a sing-song cutesy-pie voice "Where you from?"

"I'm from America. And these two guys are from England."

Without missing a beat, Bips chimed, "Capital of America: Washington; capital of England: London."

"Hey, that's impressive, little lady. Good job."

"I tell you more capitals, then you buy bangles?"

"Well…Ok. But only if you surprise me. What's the capital of Germany?

"Berlin."

"India?" What an idiot.

"New Delhi."

"France?"

"Paris."

"Argentina?"

"Bonnes Eyeres." Bips hadn't mastered Spanish phonetics but her ploy to impress was starting to work.

"Wow, that's very good. What about South Africa?"

I thought it would be Johannesburg, so I was surprised to hear Bips chime, "Pretoria."

The American was also clearly impressed. But he wasn't going to give up so easily. He winked at his friends, and then said, "And the capital of Australia is Sydney, correct?"

"No! Canberra", Bips sang out. "Ok, now you buy bangles."

"I guess so." He handed over a fifty-rupee note to Bips who nonchalantly pocketed it. She acted like it was business as usual but she had just scored big and, sensing there might be more where this came from, she pressed on.

"You very kind, sir. Your girlfriend like bangles very much. If I tell you U.S.A state capitals, you give me 50 rupees tip, ok? I tell you capital of California?"

Bemused and, like everyone else, utterly enchanted by this bright-eyed street kid with the command of a geography she could never hope to experience herself, the American agreed.

"Sacramento", said Bips.

He recovered. "Wait, California is too easy. Hmmm... What's the capital of Maryland?"

Quick as lightning. "Annapolis."

His jaw dropped. Almost in shock, he handed over another fifty-rupee note. Bips skipped out, giddy with excitement, calling "Thank you, thank you".

I was a bit hurt that she didn't come over to say hello. The next time I saw her at school, I asked why. She replied, in a measured tone, "Because of the situation. If I had immediately gone to another table to talk to respectable Indians, they might have thought it was a scam. That they had been cheated."

Despite her sudden riches, she remained, as ever, the lady.

**

After lunching at the scene of Bips' triumph, where we tucked into fettuccines and carbonaras that we wouldn't be able to afford at any Italian restaurant in South Delhi, we made our way back to the *ALOW Café*. As we walked in, a couple of French women got up to leave. One of them was stunning and Laks and I, along with most of the men in the café, stared after her until the door closed behind them.

"Ok, you can put your tongues back in your mouths now", Ilona broke in. "Didn't you ever learn that it's rude to stare?"

"Not if you're dressed like *that*, it's not", Laks retorted. "Did you see what she was wearing?"

The women had been dressed in the international backpacker's uniform for warm climates: thin cotton pants and tank tops. But the beautiful one's pants were extremely thin, gauzy white, and left only a little to the imagination. She wore a red thong under the pants, which only accentuated every curve of her very delectable behind. You could even follow the string of the thong as it disappeared into the crack of her ass. It was perfect – for Ibiza. Certainly not for sex-starved gender ratio-imbalanced Delhi.

Ilona was having none of it. "Of course it's rude to stare. She has a right to her privacy. Otherwise it's sexual harassment"

Laks considered that argument. "Yeah, she has a right for me not to touch her. But otherwise, if she's entitled to dress like that, then I'm just as entitled to look, aren't I? She should expect to be stared at; especially here in India. Actually, I bet she *does* expect it. Beautiful people want to be looked at."

"Arghh! You sound like such an MCP."

Laks looked at me. "Male Chauvinist Pig", I debreviated.

Ilona kept going. "How much about women do you actually know? Don't you get that nobody actually believes they are beautiful? So when you're stared at like that, you feel that maybe your zip is undone or your *kajal* is smeared. At best. At worst, you feel horribly uncomfortable. There's a difference between checking a girl out and undressing her with your eyes, which is disgusting and what you two just did with that girl."

Laks grinned back cheekily. "Whatever. She was practically undressed already. I was just finishing the job. Look, she's crazy to be wearing that around Delhi. Somebody should tell her to be more careful."

Ilona threw her hands up, turned her back on us, and walked over to the counter.

**

The following night, I was in the *ALOW Café's* back room inventorying our fruit stock when I was startled by a loud crash, followed by the sound of breaking glass. Pulling my head out of our giant freezer, I ran into the café as Laks came out from behind the counter, where he had instinctively ducked when he registered the sound. It was after hours and we'd been preparing to close, so there weren't any customers around.

The glass front of the café with its dark red calligraphy lay shattered around us. Jagged shards of glass and fine powder sprawled over the tables and chairs nearest the door. On the floor, amidst the debris, lay a yellow manila envelope tied with rubber bands to an encyclopedia-sized serrated granite rock. As Laks bent to pick it up, I saw a plump bearded man with a pockmarked face and sunglasses walk under the streetlight outside and vanish into the night.

Laks opened the envelope and looked inside. He walked over to the counter and shook the envelope so that its contents – some small pieces of junk and an unlined page of white notebook paper – tumbled out. Laks read the note, then passed it to me silently. With a black marker someone had scrawled 'yeh to shuraat hai, agli bar teri hogi'. This is the beginning, next time it's you.

We ran our hands through the assorted pieces of plastic junk: black and brown and yellow scraps. I picked up the two yellow pieces and held them together, like fitting a jigsaw puzzle. They formed a chassis. Now it became easier to assemble and within a minute we had reconstructed a bright yellow toy car.

"Suzuki Shamu?"

Laks nodded. "Fuck."

"What?"

"One of the henchmen – the fat, bearded guy – dropped in a couple of days ago, exactly a month since they first came to demand their cut. I stalled, saying I was still getting the money together and needed more time. But I don't think he bought it. He told me not to screw around with them and walked out."

"Laks!"

"I know, I know. I didn't tell you because I knew you'd worry and I wanted to call their bluff, I guess. So this is their next move. I'm glad they didn't trash the place."

"Well, it wouldn't be in their interest to vandalize, would it? You'd then have to repair everything and that would eat into your profits, and thereby their cut. This is just as effective. And Laks, don't be an idiot! These guys aren't kidding around."

"But Avi, I can't pay them. I won't. There's no way I could live with that."

"Maybe it is simply the price of doing business here."

"Yeah, dude, it's not a price I'm willing to pay." He looked determined, as if bracing himself for whatever was to come.

"At least now we have something to take to the police", I said hopefully.

Our previous trip to the police station, after the first visit by Suzuki Shamu's men, had been fruitless. They looked at us blankly and said that they were too busy to bother with silly threats. We needed to bring hard evidence. But though we now had some evidence, Laks looked uncertain.

"I don't know if it will do any good. You saw how they reacted when we mentioned Suzuki Shamu's name the last time. Anyway, we should at least try."

Laks was right. The cop dutifully registered our First Information Report, methodically filling out every bit of the form, and promised to look into it. But his lack of interest was transparent, as if the task was worthwhile only in that it gave him something to pass the time. Laks pressed him to tell us what action the police would take but he was evasive, finally abruptly standing up and disappearing into the dark corridor behind his desk. We waited for him to return but after twenty minutes our patience gave out.

On our way out, the cop on sentinel duty by the door said to us in a low voice, "Nobody here can touch Suzuki Shamu, even if they wanted to. It is better to pay the tax. You won't get any police help with this."

We walked out, frustrated and despondent. In the autorickshaw on the way home, I remembered that Mira Chopra, the woman who worked against trafficking, had some experience in dealing with Delhi's extortion mafias. I gave her a call.

**

Although Mira Chopra's office was fairly close to Bips' slum, finding it became a minor adventure. The alley leading into this part of the slum twisted and curved through an astonishingly large labyrinth of by-lanes and gullies, at times leading right through people's houses, all the while giving us the feeling of penetrating deep into a maze. Like the winding and disorienting path leading to Nizamuddin Dargah – the shrine to the miraculous Sufi saint that is my favorite spot in Delhi for its haunting music recitals and aura of hope – I felt that the only way to get a spatial grasp of this location would be to see it from the air. After passing, successively, a Shiva temple, a mosque, a dargah, and a tiny gurudwara, we reached a faded orange-pink building with a sign bearing the logo of Mira's organization.

On our way up to the third floor, climbing stairs stained with dried mud and paan spit, we passed through a classroom of children, not much younger than the eight-to-ten-year-olds I taught everyday. Unlike my boisterous bunch, these children sat quietly: some doodled with crayons, others absent-mindedly played with cheap handicraft toys, but many just stared vacantly at the wall. There was no teacher in sight. In the hall outside Mira's office, a group of sari-clad women sat on the floor, also in silence. Most had their *pallus* covering their faces and their gazes fixed to the floor.

Mira ushered us in to her small office, bare except for a steel desk, a trio of steel chairs and a steel cabinet of the sort used for holding files. The only wood in the room was the frames of a handful of citations and award certificates that hung on the peeling walls. She wore a conservative brown sari, her grey hair in a tight bun behind her head. On the way over, I'd been wondering how to initiate this conversation because Laks and Mira came from such diametrically opposite worlds; one an eternal optimist from a world of plenty where persistence and preparation will get you anything you want, and the other a daily foot soldier on the frontlines of a battle that shows mankind at its absolute vilest.

I needn't have worried. Laks was sneezing as we entered and Mira, instinctively maternal, inquired after his health. When he confessed that as a foreigner used to Western climes he suffered terribly from allergies to Delhi's pollution, she empathized.

"I know exactly what you're going through. And don't worry, it's not because your immune system is any worse. Every time the weather changes the whole city gets sick. I've lived in Delhi most of my life but still, a couple of times every year, I get so allergic to the air that I need to inhale a steroid medicine just to breathe."

Laks brightened on hearing this and the two of them launched into a misery-loves-company chat, happily comparing polyps and histamines and mucosa until, to my great relief, tea arrived to break the spell.

Mira sat back with her tea and asked, "So what did you want to talk about, Avraan?"

I explained Laks' predicament and that I remembered her saying she had to deal with the mafia frequently. "And now, we're out of ideas", I finished.

"And paying the tax is not an option?"

Laks spoke up. "No. I've thought and thought about it. But I just can't."

Mira grimaced, and shook her head sadly. "It's going to be tough, then. I know Suzuki Shamu and he's not the kind to listen to reason. But he's a smart guy nevertheless, much better than his West Delhi counterpart, Ambulance Appu, who is rather prone to shooting first and thinking later."

We all smiled at the names. "Crazy, no? Image is most important to these gang leaders", Mira said. "Not that it's much different anywhere else", she added with a wry smile.

"There was a reverse raid last night", she continued. "Somehow the word got out to Ambulance Appu where we were sheltering the girls we rescued from him last month. Even though this territory is off-limits to his gang, they came last night to kidnap the girls. They raided our rehab hostel and the girls resisted." Her face clouded a little. "We lost three; stabbed or beaten to death trying to defend the hostel."

She gesticulated to the crowd outside. "That's why they're all here today. We need to figure out Plan B, as the Americans would say."

"Mira, this is horrifying!" exclaimed Laks. I'd filled him in earlier on Mira's work against trafficking, the delicate balance she was forced to walk between competing mafias, and the physical abuse she herself had suffered during her work. Now that he had met Mira, he appeared even more shocked. "It must be so tough to be involved in this. How do you… How do you keep on doing this work?"

Mira took a long sip of tea, so long it seemed she was reluctant to put the cup down to answer. When she finally did, she spoke with a catch in her voice.

"I do it because I believe my presence here is helpful. I may not be serving everyone and I may be a mute witness to some terrible crimes. And I know that we won't stop trafficking in my lifetime. But for the women that we rescue, and just as importantly for the children of these women, our intervention makes all the difference in their lives. They start to feel like human beings again, not slaves. I make sure their children – especially the girls, but also the boys – receive an education so that they, the next generation, have the chance for a destiny that's not the same as their mothers' destiny. Otherwise the girls will grow up to become sex slaves and the boys to be pimps and drug dealers. For those few lives at least, we are doing some good."

"For a *few* lives?" I found myself exclaiming. "Laks, Mira rescues hundreds of women each year. She's probably saved more than ten thousand women from being trafficked."

"I can't *bear* violence", Laks said. "Deep down, at a primal level, I hate it. And I come from a country where violence is glorified; the wars we fight in, our so-called 'inalienable right' – the right! – to carry a loaded gun around… I've never been able to stand it. Hell, I've never even been in a fistfight my whole life. So I'm at a loss here. I can't – I won't – be extorted but I don't have the stomach to fight these guys."

"And you shouldn't even be thinking of fighting them, young man", Mira exclaimed. "You wouldn't stand a chance!"

"That's right. Mira, I don't have your kind of courage. Albert Camus once wrote that the only honorable course for our species is to stake everything on the gamble that words are more powerful than weapons. Not simply that the pen is mightier than the sword but, more specifically, *words*: speaking, acting, sharing together. But until I met you I never knew what he meant. And now that I do know, I'm also sure that I don't possess the plain physical courage for Camus' gamble."

Mira pushed her bifocals up the bridge of her nose. "Around the same time Camus was writing in France, there was an American woman called Dorothy Day who said that it takes huge courage to be a pacifist, that someone who can endure mobs, jail, violence, even death, cannot be lightly dismissed as a coward; a true pacifist is that person who can resist the mob that believes violence equals bravery. Like Camus, her words were not original: others realized this before her. Gandhi lived it. And she was too religious for me. But sometimes quotes like these come to you at the right time in your life, when everything that went before prepared you to hear those very words at that very moment. Quotes are meaningful only in context – but when the context is right, a sentence can change your life. That's what Dorothy Day's words have meant to me. I first heard them over twenty years ago but they came when I most needed them and that's why, even now, every time I reach that point where I want to give it all up, her words somehow let me go on."

She drained her cup and put it down with a sigh. "You know, we can continue intellectualizing this; that's the most common way out. But this question – how do you respond to violence? – it isn't something that can be analyzed and measured like a kilo of tomatoes. It has to be felt. It has to be lived. So, Laks, maybe you do have the courage. Maybe it's just that the context isn't right."

Laks shook his head, looking terribly sad. "I believe passionately in the *ALOW* Café, but I can't fight Suzuki Shamu and I'm not going to pay him off. I feel like I'm out of options."

"We'll see, Laks", Mira said. "I'm going to visit Suzuki Shamu today. We need to talk about last night's raid – he's the source of my protection from the trafficking gangs, as you may have guessed. I depend upon him. I'll tell him I know you and plead your case as best I can."

She gave another of her wry smiles. "If it's any consolation, you can be sure that once he's heard about Ambulance Appu's latest stunt, he won't be thinking about your café. He'll have bigger things to settle."

**

Don't get me wrong. I'm happily married and he's not even half my age. But still I'm falling in love with this boy sitting opposite me and looking shocked at what life is like. He's everything that is beautiful about the world; his artlessness, idealism, belief that we can shape our lives as we choose – it's their passionate belief that makes youth so wonderful. The capacity to dream... Like those monsoon clouds last week during my return flight to Delhi after another wasted donor-appeasement expedition to Bombay. I was sitting at the window as we hovercraft-skimmed the mammoth clouds. I felt I could reach out the window and touch them, like trailing my hand through the water as a boat skips over a river. The sunset exploded, spraying the white canvas of the mammoths with lusty shades of orange, gold, and purple. Every now and then a brief parting revealed the depths below, depths yearning to be filled by more dreams, the dreams of youth. I felt restless in my seat, longing to be the pilot, longing to follow these dream clouds to eternity. Then I saw the cloud wall ahead of us; it had wispy edges that turned orange, then red, then magenta, saluting the departing sun. And right behind the cloud wall floated the moon, Noyes' ghostly

185

galleon, radiant and oh so close, impatient for its turn to lord over the skies. A galleon so white that its black craters stood out in outrageous contrast, every contour of the old man's curvy body indecently visible as he sat there smoking his pipe. When we sailed past, the cloud wall dissolved, enhancing the lunar brightness against the darkening sky. How brilliant it was, how imminent it seemed; how it energized me then with its dream-like quality, as this boy energizes me now with his. There is beauty in this world worth fighting for. After his visit, I'm less tired than I was this morning.

**

Mira called a couple of evenings later. We were busy at *ALOW*, as we usually are on Wednesday evenings, when people come in to treat themselves for having scaled the peak of the week. In between processing new orders and wiping down tables sprayed with powdered sugar or stained with smoothie-encrusted spoons, Laks would stand behind the counter and survey his domain. I squeezed his shoulder or patted his back occasionally as I walked past, knowing how hard he was wrestling with his options but also knowing that the demons were his to face and there was little I could do to help.

I bent to sweep some crumbs from a table into my clean-up pan when my phone went off. Straightening, I pulled it out and answered. "Hi Mira."

"Avraan, I have good news. Shamu will lower the tax to ten percent of profits."

"Mira, that's great! Thank you!"

"He was quite reasonable, actually. But I'm afraid this is the lowest he would come down to. Laks will have to hand over ten percent at least. I think it's a good deal, since Shamu is not usually this generous. But I hear he's getting married again, which probably has something to do with it. He wants God on his side."

I chuckled. "Good timing, huh? Well, thanks again. I'll pass the news on to Laks."

Ilona was behind the counter with Laks, wearing a red apron as she whipped up another banana chocolate peanut-butter smoothie, our specialty and biggest selling drink. Laks had the cash register open, giving a customer his change, when I whispered the news in his ear. He smiled, clanged the register shut, and went off to call Mira and thank her personally. Ilona whooped on hearing Suzuki Shamu's new offer and for the rest of the evening, we all walked around just a little lighter on our feet.

After the last customer left, we pulled the shutter halfway down and collapsed into chairs, cups of coffee in hand. The giant red boat rested opposite us on the wall, whispering gently as it always did when anyone gave it some attention. Laks claimed that the boat sometimes spoke aloud to him when he was alone in there, and what it said was usually worth listening to.

Every now and then Laks would utter a statement like that, and I'd glance at him quickly to see if he was pulling my leg. These occasional bouts of mysticism stripped off both his Wall Street machismo and lifetime of conditioned American bonhomie, bringing to the surface another, well-hidden, layer of his personality.

"We should celebrate", said Ilona, raising her cup. "To Mira Chopra!"

Laks didn't raise his cup. He just looked into it, stirring slowly long after the sugar had dissolved.

"What's wrong, Laks?"

"I don't know. It still doesn't sit well. All evening I've been trying to persuade myself that this is a lifeline, a lucky bonus, and I'd be an idiot to turn it down. But I don't know if I can do it."

"What are you talking about?" Ilona sounded incredulous. "You're not thinking of refusing this deal?"

"I..."

"Laks, look, the café is a huge success", I reasoned. "You've even been talking about opening another branch. What's ten percent in all that? It'll be fine."

"Avi, it's not the money. It's the principle. I can't stand to be ripped off like this."

"Oh, what bullshit!" snapped Ilona. "Start living in the real world, Laks. This kind of thing is so common everywhere. It's just how things *work*. Don't give me any of this "principle" rubbish. You'll sleep just fine."

"Look around you, Ilona. If I lived in the real world, do you think I would have created a place this place?"

"She's right, Laks", I said. "You've gotten a huge break here. Even if Suzuki Shamu doesn't retaliate, which I'm sure he will, some other thug will come along. And the new guy may not be as flexible. We're unbelievably lucky to have this connection to Shamu. You *have* to take this deal. Don't even think of refusing because we won't allow it. If anything were to happen to you..."

"Oh no, no", Laks said hurriedly. "I'm not thinking of defying the bastard. That's not what I'm talking about."

"Then what?"

Laks said nothing, looking down at his hands, and then back up at the boat. Following his gaze, we all stared at it. In itself, this wasn't an unusual thing for us to be doing. Quite often after closing the café we'd sit down with our nightcaps and contemplate the boat. It had a surreal capacity to bring us into its world of beauty and lay out our own inner worlds in front of us as we sailed to the horizon. The spell it cast was always restful, and often cathartic.

But today was different; today impatience obstructed the spell. "Laks!" Ilona shook his shoulder. "Wake up."

Laks pulled out of his reverie, coming to anchor. He nodded slowly to himself, making a decision somewhere deep inside.

"I'm going to close the café."

"What?!!" Ilona and I exclaimed in unison, hers high-pitched, almost a yell, and mine sotto voce, a whisper of disbelief.

Laks looked at us, much calmer than he probably felt. "It was a good run but time's up, I guess. I can't keep this place open under extortion. The whole point of the café is to spread the idea that you should be yourself, do whatever is most right for you. To pay this tax would be to squash something that's fundamentally important to me. It would be hypocritical to do so in order to stay in business. Especially for *this* café.

"Shut the fuck up", I said, still in shock. "Life doesn't always work that way. Your bloody principles are just dry pieces of theory, not to be clung on to no matter what."

He smiled at me, but it didn't reach his eyes. "You don't believe that, Avraan. You're even more strong on principles that I am. That's partly why we've stayed friends for so long."

"So that's that?" Ilona asked. "It's that simple for you?"

He reached across and put an arm around each of our shoulders, just like he'd done that first time he brought us to the café. "No, Ilona, that definitely isn't just that. There is, after all, such a lot of world out there.

Chapter 10
Dancing

"It's time for *Ally McBeal*", Laks announced, switching on the TV.

I read once that some intellectuals rationalize magazines like *Cosmopolitan* and *Maxim* with the argument that they need to keep up with the (fast-moving consumer) times, re-christening these magazines *Journals of Popular Studies*. Likewise, Laks and I had dubbed *Friends* and *Ally McBeal* as *Documentaries on Popular Culture* and the two of us, secure in our pretension, avidly watched these American sit-coms. Much to the disgust of the one true intellectual in the house, Ilona, who ridiculed our TV addiction by mocking our masculinity.

As the camera zoomed in on lead actress Calista Flockhart's mini skirt, close enough to cover the screen even with those improbably skinny thighs, Ilona's door opened and she emerged from her room with Jim Morrison's baritone trailing her like a whiff of perfume. *Well, I woke up this morning and I got myself a beer.*

Laks: "Are you trying to get into his heart or into his pants?"

Ilona looked at him balefully and then pointedly turned to me. "What do you think?" she asked. She was wearing a maroon skirt with a slit half-way up her thigh, and a very tight white top.

"You look beautiful", I answered, not being an idiot.

"Ok, I need a guy's opinion." ("And not a bulldog's", she added in an aside to Laks who merely grinned and went into a series of yelping barks and growls). "Should I wear this top or a see-through black shirt instead?"

"I don't know. I'll need to see you in the black shirt."

She disappeared into her room and emerged again in a gauzy black shirt, with a black bra visible underneath. The Doors had moved on as well: *The time to hesitate is through...*

"It's nice...", I said tentatively.

"But..."

"Well, you want him to pay attention, right? Sit up and really notice you. It's that kind of night?"

Ilona was meeting Nikhil for dinner and then we were all – Mitali and Jali included – to rendezvous at one of Delhi's more popular nightclubs. This was an important night for Ilona and Nikhil because she had decided, post the Vicky Taj debacle, to commit exclusively to him. Back in Delhi for an extended stint, Nikhil also appeared to have greater space in his life for Ilona, hinting that they get engaged, or at least move in together. Ilona had at first been skittish by these altered circumstances and even contemplated ending the relationship. But their range of shared interests as well as Nikhil's ability to effortlessly ride the waves of her idiosyncrasies caused a change of heart. To all of us who saw them together, they seemed like soul mates. It was only apart that something seemed to break. So Ilona had decided that they needed to take some sort of step forward as a couple. Tonight, she planned to bring him on board.

Now she winked and said with a grin, "It's *definitely* that kind of night." My relative – relative! – reluctance to make everything sexual amused my flat mates greatly. "Do I want him to pay attention?", she repeated, chuckling. "So quaint, Avraan. I'll put it this way: is this a fuck-me outfit?"

"Go for the white top then. Suggestion works better than revelation. Then again, *I* already know how horny you are."

I raised my arms to catch the cushion Ilona sent flying at me with a sideways flick of her wrist like a Frisbee. "Bloody men", she muttered, turning back into her room to apply the finishing touches to her dress to kill. Thankfully, she'd taken Jim Morrison along with her and we could get back to our show.

"Ok, I'm off then", Ilona waved on her way out a few minutes later. She was wearing the tight white top. "You girls have fun watching your soap opera. I'll see you later at the club."

"Keep your eyes on the road and your hands upon the wheel." Laks sang out after her in his best Jim Morrison voice. Ilona responded with an eloquent thrust of her middle finger as she shut the door behind her.

**

The club was located in a five-star hotel, a pretty standard setting for Delhi's nightlife. A squadron of stunning women marched past us as we waited in a queue to fork over the cover charge. My eyes reeled in the parade of backless tops (held up no doubt by gravity-defying force fields) worn above skintight jeans or miniskirts slung low enough to reveal shadows of lacy thongs. Laks pursed his lips and nodded in approval, earning himself a slap on the arm from Mitali. These women – bold, beautiful, young, restless – were strict adherents to the fashion dogma of paying as much as possible to wear as little as possible. For young urban women, going out on the town requires a uniform as specific as any other, and one not easily earned without determined hours in the gym and a fatwa against food.

Once inside, we made our way to the bar and toasted the night with a round of tequila shots before settling down with our respective poisons: rum-cokes for Laks and me, vodka-tonics for Ilona and Mitali, a *mojito* for Jali, and a whiskey-soda for Nikhil. Drinks in hand, we moved to a vantage point by a pillar and surveyed the dance floor, allowing our bodies to find the groove of the music, letting the alcohol relax us, looking for people we may know, and watching other people dance. All the first rites before hitting the dance floor ourselves.

Nikhil excused himself to go to the bathroom. As soon as he was out of earshot, we turned to Ilona. "How was dinner?"

"Lovely", she said. She hadn't been able to stop smiling since they arrived at the club. "He took me to that Thai place by the Qutub Minar. Soft music, candlelight, great food. We sat in a booth overlooking the Qutub Minar under a full moon. I was so impressed I barely ate at all! It's great to be back together, that he's going to be around for a change…"

Ilona turned as a hand appeared from behind and tapped her on the shoulder. I looked up to see the carefully disheveled face of Vicky Taj, one of the models who had walked past us earlier hanging off his arm.

"V-V-Vicky Taj… What are you doing here?"

"Hi, Ilona. And these must be the famous Avraan and Laks?" We all shook hands. He didn't bother introducing his arm candy, who pretended not to care by composing a faraway look of disinterest. "Private party", he said, jerking his wrist towards the members-only section on the floor above, from where the well heeled and well connected could look down upon the minions on the dance floor. "Saw you down here and came to say hello. Wasn't there another guy with you?"

"That's our friend Nikhil", Ilona said hastily. I felt as much as saw Laks give me a quick glance. Ilona's just-friends description of Nikhil hadn't escaped him either. After another minute of awkward small talk, Vicky Taj excused himself and headed back to his party.

"Don't even start", Ilona pre-empted us. "He was fishing, ok? I didn't want to get into it. Leave it there. Let's dance." We shrugged and followed Ilona onto the dance floor but her desire to avoid questions wasn't lost on us.

**

Nikhil rejoined the group, drawing our attention to a pair of young Punjabi women doing a slow *bhangra* to a hip-hop song by Nelly. They were dressed in typical Western nightclub attire – black pants and silk tops with matching jewelry – but there they were, doing *bhangra* moves to hip-hop. The oddest thing of all was that, somehow, it fit. It looked entirely natural, not in the least out of place. The women had broad smiles on their faces, perfectly aware of the incongruity of their dance steps but reveling in their creativity.

"Looks like even hip-hop is getting Punjabified!" Laks yelled into my ear over the din of the music. India has a long history of taking foreign influences into a deep bear hug and releasing them only after they've evolved into an oddly compelling offspring of both parents. Like secular democracy and tandoori-chicken pizzas, dancing *bhangra* to hip-hop could well be globalization's next calling card.

The strobe lights clicked on, smoke swirled upwards from the floor, the DJ stepped up the pace, and the dance floor was hot. One thing I have to give my girlfriend Jali: the lady can dance. As a Mangalorean, I can handle the formal dances – fox-trot, waltz, cha cha – fairly easily. But when it comes to modern hip-hop, I feel like a lamppost. Jali, being a dance therapist, is trained in the strict traditions of Indian classical dance. Yet, in the psychedelic setting of a good nightclub, she sometimes relents and lets her body take over. When she does so, she makes even a lamppost look good. All I needed to do was stand still and let her slide and wrap her sinuous body around me, hips undulating, legs swirling and face saying 'come hither my man'. I fell head over heels one night at Turquoise Cottage when Guns n' Roses' *Sweet Child O' Mine* came on. Since few enjoy dancing to hard rock, most people just stood nodding along with the music. Not Jali; she turned, backed up against me, and slipped into a maddeningly erotic slow dance, her gifted hips and shampoo-commercial long hair moving from side to side against me in deliberately sensual gyrations, every now and then half turning to wrap an arm around my neck for support as she wriggled down the length of my body with a wink and a grin that showed she was aware of her effect on me, and on the crowd. I could sense a few jaws hanging open around us. I'd never seen a more audaciously conceived performance – and I had the best seat in the house.

Now, however, we danced in a loose group, exchanging smiles every now and then when our eyes met in the staccato strobe lighting. Half an hour later, we took a breather and walked over to a vacant booth. Ilona excused herself to go to the ladies room and Laks began propounding a theory that American pop culture was encouraging men and women to look alike.

"Look at Hollywood movies and TV shows: the women are not just skinny but have straight figures, like men. And all the men are hairless and metrosexual. It's just not natural. In India, women are curvy and men are hairy. But these days, in all the ads and magazines, we're seeing Indians with this American androgynous body: shaved and skinny. Why do you have to shave your chest to get a magazine cover?"

We all took up the debate and it was nearly twenty minutes before we noticed that Ilona hadn't returned. "I'll go look for her", Nikhil said and the girls went with him to scout out the ladies room. They all returned to report that Ilona was nowhere to be seen. Her cell phone was with Nikhil.

Just then, my cell phone vibrated. I fished it out of my pocket and saw a text message from an unknown number: *members section vicky not letting me go pls rescue.*

"Who's it from?" asked Laks idly.

I looked up at them. This wasn't ideal but I had no choice. "It's Ilona. She's upstairs with Vicky Taj but something's wrong. We need to get up there."

"Vicky Taj is here?" Nikhil sounded surprised. He may not have known about Ilona's affair but he did know that the pop star was one of her clients. "So what's the problem?"

"I don't know. But she says to come rescue her. And knowing Ilona…"

"She wouldn't say that unless she was very uncomfortable", Nikhil finished. "Let's go."

Nikhil, Laks and I ran up the red-carpeted staircase to the members' section but found our path blocked at the head of the stairs by a pair of bouncers, dressed entirely in black, with the scarred pug-like faces of World Wrestling Federation aspirants. Both were over six feet tall. They stood ramrod-straight flanking the purple velvet rope that cordoned off the members' section from the rest of the club. They refused to let us in.

"Our friend sent us a message to come up", Nikhil tried. They snickered, not even bothering to reply. They'd heard that one before.

"Vicky Taj is there", I said. "He invited us."

They shrugged. "Call him. If he comes out, you can go in." I tried the number Ilona's message had been sent from. Nobody answered.

"Listen", Nikhil said, starting to sound desperate, "you must let us in because our friend needs help. Something is wrong inside."

They exchanged glances this time but refused to budge. Suddenly Laks pulled out his old NDTV press card and waved it at them. "Look at this! I work for NDTV and I'm telling you that my friend is in trouble inside. If you don't let us in, I'm going to call the media. Do you want TV cameras to invade this party?"

They shifted uneasily. Something in Laks' vehemence had them wondering if this wasn't just another ruse by star-struck fans to enter the club's sanctum sanctorum. "I'll tell the media that celebrities are doing drugs in there", he ventured again.

A lucky guess, but that did it. The bouncers relented. "You can enter but one of us is coming with you. Once you find your friend, you have to leave. No phone calls and no pictures allowed inside."

"No problem", Nikhil said at once.

The bouncer on the right unhooked the velvet rope and led us inside. "Good thing you still have that card on you", I whispered to Laks out the corner of my mouth.

"I knew it would come in handy someday", he replied, slipping it back into his wallet.

The bouncer led us across plush red carpeting, past floor-to-ceiling speakers pounding out trance music, to a large circular table surrounded by deep white leather couches. He gestured towards the table, which was littered with tall bottles of Laphroaig single malt whiskey, several shot glasses, and scattered fragments of filter paper with visible remnants of fine white powder. No wonder they are reluctant to have cameras in here, I thought. However, neither Ilona nor Vicky Taj were amongst the bodies sprawled languidly on the couches, several of whom lay half on top of each other despite the acres of open spaces on the couches. I recognized the woman who had been with Vicky Taj earlier and, looking directly at her, asked where he was. She scanned me up and down disdainfully, like a high priestess defiled by the mere presence of an infidel in her temple. She was shaping to ignore me completely when she noticed the bouncer by my side. Then she waved her arm towards a darkened section of the large room, donning that mask of feigned indifference again. "He went that side with some stupid chick."

"Over here", I said, spotting a couple of dark shadows moving on one of the couches towards the end of the room. Coming into the table's light, we saw that Vicky Taj was determinedly forcing himself upon Ilona. His left hand lay flat upon her right breast, pinning her to the couch as he tried kissing her face and neck, all the while holding off her left arm with his right hand. Ilona was panting with the struggle. Her right arm flailed against his body, trying desperately to push him off her.

"What the hell are you doing?" Nikhil pounced on Vicky Taj, dragging him off Ilona, and pushing him aside. Laks and I simultaneously bent towards Ilona, supporting her as she struggled to a sitting position and re-adjusted her shirt. "Nikhil, NO!" she cried.

"Who the *fuck* are you?" Vicky Taj roared at Nikhil.

"I'm her boyfriend. What the hell does it matter to you? You have no right to touch her!"

"Boyfriend! You have a fucking boyfriend? You said he was only a friend." India's leading pop singer, filled to the brim with cocaine and whiskey, now spilled over, screaming at the girl he had assaulted.

"Don't talk to her like that, man. I'm warning you." Nikhil reached out a hand and gripped Vicky Taj's shoulder.

"Get lost, *man*." He mocked Nikhil's voice, slapping the arm away. "You want to fuck with Vicky Taj, then fuck this, *behenchod*."

Vicky Taj reached into his waist with his right hand and swung it at Nikhil's chest. A flash of glinting silver. Instinctively Nikhil moved his body sideways to block the blow but then staggered backwards, clutching his left arm near the shoulder. Vicky Taj's arm came back around and even in the soft light above the table the dark stain on the blade was visible. Ilona screamed and leapt off the couch towards Nikhil, who had fallen against a wall. Vicky Taj moved forward towards them, knife flashing. Laks and I both jumped to our feet but, with astonishing speed for someone so large, the bouncer got there first, pulled Vicky Taj back, and deftly dispossessed him of his weapon.

"He's bleeding badly", Ilona yelled, putting her own palm across the gash in Nikhil's arm. With her other hand, she unwound her scarf and, with Laks' help, tied it across Nikhil's arm. The scarf immediately darkened but it was thick enough to contain the blood flow.

A rustling of air generated by hurried footsteps and a dapper man in a dark Nehru suit appeared. "I'm the manager here. What seems to be the problem?"

"The *problem* is that this asshole just stabbed my friend", said Laks, turning on him. "We need to take him to the hospital."

The manager summed up the situation in a single glance and then, with an assured calmness that could only come from previous experience with celebrity tantrums, said, "I will drive you to the hospital myself. Come."

"You better, or else this is going to be all over the news", Laks continued to milk his press card.

We helped Nikhil to his feet and supported him on either side as the two bouncers cleared a path for us to the hotel lobby, where a valet had already brought the manager's car around. The four of us piled in, with Laks in front. Nikhil's face was pale. Ilona cradled him against her shoulder and tried to smile reassuringly as she said, "It's not too bad. Look, the blood's not flowing much any more."

In the front seat, the manager addressed Laks as he sped towards a private hospital. "So you're the one with the press?"

"Yes."

"I see. Well, it would be most distressing if any of this came out in the news. It would force the club to shut down and the hotel's reputation could be destroyed. Lots of people would lose their jobs and the means to support their families."

"Uh-huh", Laks grunted noncommittally.

"We will of course take care of all expenses related to this unfortunate accident but would be very grateful if you would not reveal it in the media. I'm sure we can also compensate all of you very generously for the trouble and inconvenience you have suffered."

"We. Shall. See." Laks replied, assuming a matching level of pompous gravitas. I wondered how he kept a straight face.

**

"Are *you* ok?" I asked Ilona.

We were sitting against the spotless white wall of the hospital corridor, waiting while the doctor stitched up Nikhil's wound. Laks had returned to the nightclub to pick up Jali and Mitali and drive them home. Ilona sat slumped against the back of her chair, her legs stretched out in front of her, chin sunk into her neck.

"Do you have angels on your shoulder?" she asked, turning to face me.

Angels on my shoulder? "No. Do you have bats in your attic?"

She made a face. "I'm serious. Sometimes I feel like I've been running away my whole life."

"Running from what?"

"I'm not entirely sure. From what happened with my uncle, from pressure from my community to settle down, from owning any sort of responsibility. Perhaps even running from what's happened to the Kolkata of my childhood. Or maybe it's just that everything seems stale after a while."

"What does that have to do with angels?"

"Well, everyone has the two angels, right? I feel like my good angel, you know, the one that's dressed in white with wings and a halo, is sitting on my shoulder and saying 'Don't worry so much. You're not running, you're just searching for what fulfills you as a person.' And on my other shoulder, my bad angel, dark red with horns and a pitchfork – yes, my angels dress very traditionally

203

– keeps nagging away at me, 'You're not searching! You're running away, you little baby. You'll never find peace until you stop running. Scaredy-cat, scaredy-cat!' Until now, I've been listening to the one in white but I've begun to wonder if I've gotten my angels mixed up."

"You think the red angel with the pitchfork is the good one, then?"

"Maybe. Or maybe they're just bored and playing tricks on me. In any case, there they are, whispering into my ear, usually just after I go to bed. They've been whispering more and more of late, annoying little shits. And they reminded me of what this astrologer once told me."

"Astrologer?"

"Yes. Back in Kolkata, around the time I was graduating university, one of my friends heard about this new astrologer in town and suggested we go ask if we would get into good universities for our Master's. The astrologer was quite striking: a beautiful Bengali woman, over six feet tall, she had her hair tied back very severely and wore no makeup at all. My friend went first and asked about her further studies. When it was my turn, the astrologer stared at me and said, 'You didn't come here to ask about passing exams. What is it you really want to know?' Well, I wasn't going to reveal everything that easily. I'd been fighting a lot with Mama those days so I asked 'Will I ever get along with my mother?' She turned some cards over, looked at my palm and said, 'You and your mother will always love each other but you will never be friends. You are too different from each other.' I was shocked to hear that because the previous night I had wondered in my diary if Mama and I would ever be close. Then she smiled at me and said, 'Come Ilona, ask me what you really want to know.' So I said, 'Will I ever find what I was born to do?' She did the same thing with her cards and my palm and then said 'You will be unsettled until you finish half your third decade. Your restlessness will cause many problems for you and for the people around you. Then you will find what you seek and only after that you will be able to rest. And Ilona – you won't find your answers here in Kolkata.'"

"Wow, she sounds amazing!"

"She is. She's become famous all over Bengal now, and she is often in the papers at the page-three parties. Apparently, her schedule is booked two years in advance and people fly from all over the world to see her for an hour. Anyway, all this was a long time ago. I haven't thought about her in ages but she's been coming back to me more and more of late. She said my answers wouldn't be found in Kolkata, but I wonder if she meant that I had to leave to realize that no matter where I go or what I do, I still have to face my roots and dig up the trouble beneath. As Laks keeps saying, being in India has helped him understand America better. Sometimes you can only get perspective with distance, actual physical distance. Now that I've done the distance thing, I've been thinking about returning to Kolkata, going back home.

I leaned forward, elbows on my knees and chin in my palms, letting those words hang in the air around us, hoping they would float away and leave us alone. I didn't want any changes. But the words were still there, still fluttering slowly, when Laks returned and announced that the hotel had paid all the hospital bills, our girlfriends were safely home, and the manager had offered us free entry to the club whenever we wanted it. "Ha! Like it's going to be top of our list from now on."

He sat down beside us. "What happened back there, Ilona?"

Ilona sighed. "When I left the ladies room, Vicky Taj was waiting outside. He asked me to go up with him for a drink. I said no, but he insisted that he had something important to tell me. He's still a client after all and so much business gets done at these parties, so I went. When we got up there and I saw all the booze and cocaine, I began to get a bad feeling in my stomach. We joined his group for a bit but he didn't say anything other than offer me some dope and put his arm around me. After watching him take a few hits, I said I was leaving. Then he confessed that he is heavily in debt to some dangerous people in Mumbai and that I had to make sure his contract went through for another year. I said I would try, and got up to leave. 'There's one more thing, Ilona', he said and got up after me. 'Let's go over there to talk in private.' The girl he was with asked him where he was going. As he was making whatever excuse to her, the poor thing, I saw an abandoned phone lying on the table. Nobody was looking at me so I quickly grabbed the phone and punched out that text to you, Avraan. Then Vicky Taj dragged me over to that couch and came on to me. When I resisted – I told him I was never going to sleep with him ever again – he slapped me and said 'Shut up and do what I tell you'. He started to force himself on me, and that's when you guys showed up. I've never been happier to see your faces."

She took a long breath. "I feel so shitty about getting Nikhil involved like this. I never thought Vicky Taj was capable of going this far. Indebted to gangsters from Mumbai! His world truly must be collapsing."

"Is that your good angel talking?" I hissed. "Don't excuse that creep!"

Nobody spoke for a while. I told Laks that Ilona was considering returning to Kolkata.

"What will you do there?" he asked.

"I haven't decided yet. Maybe go back to journalism, but not the political beat. More like human-interest stuff: magazine articles on interesting issues without the heat of a daily deadline. I think poking around Kolkata on those types of stories will help me settle back in, teach me things about my city and my culture that I need to learn. In any case, what I'll do doesn't matter right now. Going back is the important thing. Maybe if I stop searching so hard, I'll finally find what I'm looking for. I think there's some Zen poem that says that."

"The wisdom of the ages. But what about Nikhil?"

"He'll come with me. We talked about it over dinner – gosh, dinner at the Qutub Minar seems so long ago now! He is open to moving to Kolkata but if we move anywhere, he wants us to move as a real couple. To live together."

She paused. "That is, if he stays with me after what happened tonight. Especially after Vicky Taj's comment about how I said Nikhil is just a friend. I'll have to come clean with him now."

"But are *you* okay with moving in together?" Laks asked, softly.

"I think I am, you know. It's time."

Chapter 11
In Our Blood

A conversation with Bips six months ago.

"I've got a present for you", I say. "Guess what?"

She looks up, eyes sparkling. "Is it jewelry?"

Double take. She is ten. Granted, she's a remarkable ten. In the couple of years I've known her, I've seen her save a friend's life while risking her own, wonder aloud about her unformed breasts, suggest I get a makeover, and frequently charm unsuspecting tourists into expanding their budgets. She's also been known to give her mother some very sound marriage advice, like when she suggested Mom simply ignore Dad rather than nagging away at him about a major financial decision. "After he's thought about it, he'll agree with you. But *only* if he can come to it himself. You just keep quiet now." Just as Bips predicted, Ramesh came around to his wife's point of view in a couple of days.

But still, she's only ten. What the hell does she want jewelry for? "No, it's not jewelry", I reply.

"Is it perfume?"

"No."

"A new dress? Shoes?"

I'm slowly getting alarmed. "No".

"It must be chocolate then."

Is this all kids today? "No"

She sounds exasperated. "Uff! I give up. What is it?"

"It's a book." Somewhat sheepishly, I hand over a collection of Indian folk tales written for children, hoping to get her reading. I had gift-wrapped it myself.

"Oh."

If I were grading her on how to keep a poker face, she'd have failed spectacularly.

So when Bips announced that she was going to tie a *rakhi* for me, I was touched to be considered an elder brother, but also petrified. What on earth would I give her in return? I even seriously considered flowers. Finally, having resigned myself to the traditional (i.e., safe) route of giving her money, I came across a lovely poster of a pair of leaping dolphins and, thinking it would be a nice addition to their little house, I took a chance.

The *Raksha Bhandan* festival was three days before the incident at the nightclub with Vicky Taj. I went over to Bips' house after class, where she tied the *rakhi*, a cheaply made but extravagant gold and purple affair. I presented the poster in return and held my breath.

I was in luck. A shy smile, a whispered thank you, and a yell to Ma to come see. Phew!

**

The evening after our clubbing misadventure, Jali took me to our favorite Thai restaurant for dinner. She wanted to hear, in pointillist detail, about what had happened in the members' section of the club and at the hospital. We shared a pad thai and a Penang curry, and I filled her in.

She slurped up the last of the gravy and sat back. "I feel bad for Ilona", she said. "But I've yet to meet a woman who hasn't been molested here."

"You too?"

"Oh God, yes. About three years ago, I had a horrible experience. I'd gone to Old Delhi Railway Station to see my sister off on the night train to Lucknow. I decided to return home by bus. Out of taxi, auto or bus, I figured there'd be safety in numbers, right?"

"Makes sense. But you shouldn't have been travelling at all after dark."

"Come on Avraan, it was only 8 p.m.! But the train was delayed, so it was around 11pm when I left the station. Returning home, there were no seats available in the bus. I had to stand. All the seats reserved for ladies were taken by men. They avoided my eyes. Nobody wanted to get up."

"Were there any other women on the bus?"

"None. And at first I didn't mind that I was standing, since I was tired and afraid of falling asleep and missing my stop. I also had a lot on my mind and was lost in thought. Gradually, I began to realize that the bus was getting rather crowded. Then a hand pushed against my ass, and that startled me back into the present. I couldn't tell whether it was an accident or not. But I didn't dare look up. A few minutes later, there was nothing accidental about the grab. I half turned but couldn't see anything. There were too many bodies around me and I didn't want to make eye contact. I began to feel sweat in the air. Also running down my back. November nights are not that warm so my body was reacting to something other than the collective body heat, responding to signals my mind was too slow to pick up. As I stood half-turned in the direction of where the hand may have come from, another hand reached across from the other direction and pinched my breast. Quite hard, too. I turned quickly, but again, too many bodies to really tell anything. My attackers had anonymity in their numbers and they knew it. I was barely able to move. I began to panic but forced myself to stay calm. I tried to look out the window to see how close I was to Andrews Ganj, where I was living then, but all I could see were hands raised to the railings, armpits soaked in sweat, hairy chests and unbuttoned shirts, paunches hanging over stained pants. Then somebody pressed his erect penis hard against my rib and stayed there. Finally I looked up. And immediately wished I hadn't. Every eye was on me. Staring openly, greedily. I knew there was no skin showing anywhere but when has that ever mattered? All those eyes: beady eyes, glazed eyes, red-rimmed eyes, sweat-encircled eyes. All eyes with a bad energy pouring through like a flood. With every jolt of the bus, I felt the bodies come closer. Now I was feeling claustrophobic as well, from being so enclosed. I couldn't breathe. And then there was more than one set of hands on my ass."

"Oh no, Jali." One of her hands was on the table and I reached across to take it in mine. But she didn't want the touch right then. She pulled her hand away, using it to tuck a strand of hair behind her ear.

"I was sure I was going to be raped, and I began to cry in heavy panicky breaths. Just as the tears came, I heard that loud whistle a bus gives when it begins to brake. I felt it slow down and heard the conductor yelling out to potential new passengers. Like a cornered animal, I realized that a window of escape had opened up, perhaps my only chance. I began to push and shove my way to the door. The bodies parted, reluctantly and maybe only because they had to since people were getting on and getting off. But, desperately, vengefully, the hands kept grabbing, pinching, pushing. Harder and harder as they sensed their prey slipping out of their grasp. I was crying loudly now but kept shoving my way through. Finally I breathed fresh air and felt gravity as I fell from the bus, just as it started to move again. Thankfully, nobody followed me. And even more thankfully, I wasn't very far from home, close enough to take an autorickshaw safely."

She continued. "Yes, in hindsight, it was the stupidest decision I ever made, going to the station that late at night. Despite that, I can't understand the atmosphere on that bus. The look in their eyes was terrifying. It was more than lust – it was anger. I feel lucky to have escaped so easily in the end. Every time I read about another girl getting molested or raped in the newspaper, the memory of that night comes back, and I wonder who those men really were. What was driving their mad lust? Where does this rage come from?"

**

Reena joined us as we were walking out of the restaurant. Anup Singh was arriving on the late train and she wanted to greet him at the station. But since his train didn't arrive until after 11p.m., she had asked if I would accompany her. So I kissed Jali goodnight and followed Reena into an autorickshaw, feeling especially useful after Jali's recent story.

But I was also happy to go to the station on my own terms because, over the last few months, I had become pretty close to Anup. Through email and phone, and even the occasional hand-written letter, we had continued our conversation from that time I visited the village where he taught, weaving our way through several more topics worth amateur philosophizing, from the importance of ecology in politics to the quality of regional language novels to the rise of the small town cricket superstar. I had grown to treasure Anup's friendship. He had visited Delhi once since we first met, and our late night murmurings during that visit earned me a severe scolding from Reena, who was understandably unhappy not to have her man all to herself. I felt Anup had come to see me as a younger brother of sorts, someone who needed mentoring and guidance but who also held up a mirror that reflected aspects of his own self for further consideration. We often treasure most those who catalyze new insights about ourselves.

We didn't have long to wait at Nizamuddin Railway Station. Anup's train was on time to the minute. He looked fresh as a morning lily when he disembarked, something I'm never able to manage after a lengthy train journey. After he had affectionately greeted his fiancé, we shook hands with broad grins. "Thanks for coming, Avraan. Let's go get some food."

We walked over to the Comesum food court (pronounced variously by *Dilliwallahs* as 'come-sum' or 'co-may-sum' or, with a leer, 'cum-some') where Reena and I ordered *chai* and Anup ravenously gobbled down a chicken roll, a bowl of *kheer*, and a cappuccino.

The conversation bounced and squirted randomly like a crazy ball, as conversations tend to when people meet again after a long while. Eventually, we moved back to a recurring topic between Reena and me, about the efficacy of our work in the slums. Reena, and the organization as a whole, was mostly content with the incremental progress we made: always three steps forward, two steps back as other commitments, illnesses, holidays, absenteeism, and life in general all conspired to block our path. But I'd been restless with this slow pace, increasingly frustrated that all the hard work I put into my lesson plans often came to nothing as a result of whatever *googly* the day decided to spit at me. I struggled to see how we were making a difference on a large enough scale and often wondered whether, in fact, we were making any headway at all. I believed in the general mantra that helping some children is better than helping none at all, and that if we could demonstrate a working model then perhaps the local government would eventually incorporate life skills into the school curriculum.

Yet, when I walked around the slums, I failed to see how our work tangibly helped a community struggling to etch out a living in insanely difficult circumstances, where each day was a battle for their livelihoods, health, and dignity.

"We need to address all these issues at the same time", I argued. "We need to change the entire system which causes these conditions".

"Avraan, don't take everything so seriously", Anup said, clapping me on the shoulder. "*Yeh to tumhare hasne khelne ke din hain.*" This is your time to laugh and play, to enjoy being young.

I looked at him in surprise. Normally, he loved a discussion like this, and would happily feint and parry with me. But he'd just finished a long journey. And hadn't seen his fiancé in several months.

Unfortunately for the reunited lovers, I was on a roll now. "Well, yes... These are the days when I have fewer commitments and so have greater freedom of choice. But that doesn't mean I'm not serious about what I do, even though my life choices may seem indulgent to people used to the more conventional road. And that's not going to change, no matter how old I become!"

"Ok, ok, calm down, man."

I grinned, taking the hint to shut up. "*Meri puri zindagi hasne khelne ke din hain.*" My whole life is my time of laughing and playing.

Reena's phone goes off as I finish my rant. "Who's calling you at this time of night?" Anup wonders aloud.

"Hello". Reena speaks softly into her phone as Anup and I continue talking. But our attention returns to her when she says sharply, "What!"

We pause. Reena's voice becomes progressively shriller. "What? No!!"

Although the yellow ceiling light falling on her is dim, drawing zebra zones of light and night on her face, it's obvious that Reena has gone very pale. "*Nahin*, that's not possible", she says. This is followed by an agonized "You're not serious" and then, softer, softer, "No, no, no…"

Tears roll down her face. Anup puts his arm around her. She puts a hand up to cover her eyes and slumps against Anup, the phone still pressed to her ear. "I'll come now", she says. Then, nodding quickly, "Yes, I'll have company. Anup and Avraan. Ok, we'll be there as soon as we can."

She stares at her phone as she lowers it. When she finally looks up at us, her eyes are a vacuum.

**

They found Bips in the clump of weeds at the end of the field, by the well into which she'd once jumped to save a drowning classmate. Her body: shattered. Who took her away, how many of them, from where, how… none of these questions would ever be answered. All we learnt is that she didn't come home after another day of trading at Paharganj. Her parents, siblings and neighbors searched everywhere they could think of, all through the night and next day. They were beginning to assume she'd been kidnapped when word filtered through that a pair of teenage boys playing football with a crushed cola can had found the body of a girl in the weeds. But this news came only the following evening. For almost twenty-four hours, including the same period when Ilona was fighting off Vicky Taj in a five-star nightclub, Bips had been assaulted savagely in one corner of a bumpy field outside a slum. Finally, when her little body was so ravaged it could no longer serve the purpose for which they had selected it, a piece of twine was tightened around her neck. Given what had been done to her by then, she may not have cared enough to resist when the cord wrapped around her throat. In a vicious flick of fate, so much is undone, snuffed out forever. Just like that, it ends.

**

We spent the night sitting with her family, holding different people's hands at different times, unable to fight back tears. Her body was wrapped in a white shroud and laid on the floor in the center of the hut in which she'd lived all her life. Up on the wall was the dolphin poster I'd given her just a few days ago, taking pride of place over the obligatory pictures of deities and magazine cutouts of Ramesh's favorite actresses.

I sat there with the rest of them but what I wanted to do was tear away that foolish shroud and lift that stilled body up in my arms, to cradle it against my own, to bring it back to life. In all the time I'd known her, Bips was constitutionally unable to stay still for more than a handful of seconds. It just didn't seem possible that under the white sheet lay that same effervescent little girl. Almost of its own accord, my body would begin moving towards the white figure, to carry out the resurrection my incredulous mind was instructing it to perform. Only Reena's hand tightly gripping mine held me back, my fragile anchor to reality.

Dawn arrived, gentle white rays distilled through the city's thick overcoat of smog, waking up the flocks of sparrows and pigeons to fly their ritual rings around the metropolis, alerting all living things to the emergence of another day. Slowly, people rose to blow out the kerosene lamps and candles that had surrounded Bips' body through the night.

We went home to change for the funeral. It must have been hard on Anup after his journey but he stayed all night and then returned with Reena, unflinchingly supportive. We were back in the hut, sitting with Bips' mother and sisters, when the men from the crematorium arrived. The sounds of a heated discussion outside trickled through our ears. Then Ramesh came in and spoke quickly to his wife.

"They want money to do it. Three thousand. I'm going to speak to Mr. Sharma, the moneylender."

"Wait!" Reena and I spoke almost in unison. She stared at Ramesh in disbelief. "They want a bribe for the cremation?"

"Yes, Reena-madam." Ramesh was wringing his hands in distress. "What to do, that is always the case with these fellows."

"Bastards", she said through gritted teeth and stood up. I was right behind her as she strode out the door and marched up to the small group on the street, most of whom were standing on a carpet of vegetable scraps fallen out of a vendor's wicker basket, the leaves of cabbage and spinach now caked with trampled layers of street grime. Reena began arguing with the two cremators and I followed her lead, matching her high-pitch with what I hoped was a softer but more implacable tone. The two men stood there, heads bowed, arms hanging down and crossed in front, not saying a word as we let them have it, venting our own suppressed grief. After the initial round of abuses, we moved on to a mix of shame and threats.

"You have no right to do this", Reena exclaimed.

"What is your office number? I'm going to speak to your manager." They looked up at me in silence but I stared them down.

"Don't you have any shame? They just lost their baby daughter!" Reena's voice raised a few notches.

"Actually, I think I'll call the police instead." I dug out my cell phone.

It was the standard act; not really good cop/bad cop as much as shrieking woman/authoritative man. The cremators folded, reluctantly retracting their ungreased palms. It was a major victory for Ramesh's family finances, but only a temporary one. Our authority there stemmed entirely from the fact that we occupied a higher position in the class hierarchy. Becoming hostile and raising your voice is sometimes the only way to get things done. If you don't shout and threaten, you're either ignored or seen as a target to be ripped off. When I first moved to Delhi, friends drummed this lesson into me repeatedly. Understanding this truth was the secret to surviving this city, they said. Although I initially rejected that line of thinking, out of principle if nothing else, I gradually came to see how effective it was when I put on a stentorian upper-class voice. Hierarchy rules despotically here, and even more so in the lower rungs of the class ladder. Everyone involved – Ramesh, his friends and neighbors, the cremators, Reena and I – knew fully well that only the presence of Bips' English-speaking teachers had prevented Ramesh from sinking into a painful debt.

**

Before Bips' cremation ends, I abruptly leave the small gathering. About fifteen minutes later, not of any conscious choice, I find myself entering the field and walking slowly towards the well. At the left end of the field, a group of boys are playing cricket with a scuffed-up tennis ball, a piece of wood crafted into a make-shift bat, and three slender twig-wickets. The far end of the field, containing the weeds and the well, is empty. When I arrive at the weeds, I look around carefully but can't make out where her body lay. Those weeds may once have submitted to the weight of a human body but now they've bounced back upright, reaching towards the sky as if nothing has changed.

Ob-la-di, ob-la-da... But life does not just go on.

I lie down on the weeds, looking up at the sky as Bips may have been doing when the final sigh left her anguished body. The last few days have been overcast with dust and smog but today the sky is clear, the clouds are white and adolescent birds are competing to soar higher and higher. It has been a very long time since I have lain down on grass to look up at a clear sky. A ladybird crawls across the hill of my stomach. I reach out a finger and let it run up onto the back of my hand. It briefly flutters its wings, unbelievably fast, as if about to take off, but then has second thoughts and decides to play dead. I rotate my hand gently, like the panning of a movie camera, so that the ladybird is facing me. But there's nothing to see; it has arranged its dark face into the impassive stony visage of the dead.

With a sickening plunge, like the sensation of jumping off a very tall cliff, my heart plummets into despair. I don't feel like I lost a friend or a student; I feel like I've lost a daughter. What could motivate a man to desecrate a little girl like that? Catching a glimpse of the abyss of my grief, I seek refuge in reason, trying to come up with a rational explanation, that elusive Answer. But soon all I'm doing is asking myself, over and over again, the same question that came after the bus fight involving the Twin Shirts, the same question Jali posed after her experience on another bus in the same city, the same question Laks asked when we saw a small car repeatedly drive into a larger one: where does this species of rage come from?

A story from a little while ago.

In an unfamiliar part of town, I had no idea how to get home. At the bus stop, I asked a middle-aged man which bus I should take. "I'm waiting for the same bus", he said. "Get on with me."

We began to make small talk. He was neatly dressed, with a well-groomed beard. He traded automobile spare parts well enough to make a comfortable living. When the bus arrived he invited me to sit next to him. Our conversation veered towards current events, the biggest at that time being a couple of high profile gang rapes, both stunning in their audacity. A Swiss diplomat had been kidnapped from a famous auditorium's parking lot and a young woman was taken from a popular park in broad daylight, where she'd been strolling with a male friend. Both women had been gang-raped, the latter by members of the President's bodyguard. "How shocking", I murmured, shaking my head.

"What's so shocking about it?" snorted my new acquaintance, a sound somewhat unbecoming his dapper appearance. "This is nothing new. Delhi itself has been raped continuously over the last thousand years. Each of Delhi's seven conquerors raped and pillaged the city. Delhi is simply accustomed to rape. There is an ethos of rape in her soil, in her water, in her blood. The only thing new is that it is now happening on an individual level, not a political level."

"Let me tell you a story", he continued. "My wife's sister – we are Kashmiris – married a rich man from another community whose family had been here for generations. Her family was against it but she said she was in love and wouldn't agree to anyone else." He raised his eyebrows in a way that demonstrated his contempt for such a silly notion as being 'in love'. "Anyway, a few years after the wedding, the girl realized that her husband was also bedding the maid. She didn't know what to do. Her mother-in-law stayed with them so she approached her for advice, thinking that the older woman might be able to intervene to save the marriage. But her mother-in-law slapped her and said 'Stop talking

221

this rubbish! He's given you a son; be happy with that. What does it matter who he sleeps with? He is the man of the house. Don't come crying to me with this nonsense'."

The Kashmiri trader paused for a moment to tell me I had to get off at the next stop, and then summed things up. "It was her own mother-in-law who slapped her and told her she had no right to complain. That there was *nothing* wrong with her husband's behavior. When women themselves hold such an attitude to each other, why are you shocked by these small rapes? I'm telling you, rape is in our blood. It is a systematic thing."

> *system (noun): complex whole, organized body of things*
> *systematic (adjective): methodical, according to a system,*
> *deliberate*

Right, then. In India's First City, we have a dark force coursing through our veins, our terrain, our drink. After all the psychological and sociological theories propagated by ivory tower experts, here was a street explanation for sexual violence: it is in our blood.

A tsunami of misery washes over me, deep currents of futility and powerlessness, threatening to sweep me away in a rip tide to oblivion. I do not want to fall asleep at this spot, even though I haven't slept in two nights. I sit back up, cross-legged on the weeds, plucking tufts out by the root and mindlessly tossing them aside. Then I stand and walk over to the well – Bipasha Well, it has come to be known in the area. I sit astride the rim and look down into the black water. Dried leaves and assorted junk continue to float in it. The more things change...

The Kashmiri trader's story doesn't stand alone. Like everything in India, it has its mirror image, its Newton's Third Law. When I returned to my paying-guest house that evening, I narrated his story and beliefs to Debu, my former call-center housemate, concluding with, "I had no idea how dangerous this city is for women!"

He pursed his lips and shook his head. "I don't think Delhi is bad for women. I think it is more bad for men."

"Huh?"

"Just walk on the roads and see for yourself. Look in the cars. Most of the cars in Delhi are driven by women." He folded his arms and nodded, resting his case.

"What does driving a car have to do with anything?"

"It shows women are the ones in control. Hardly any men drive in Delhi."

"Are we talking about the same city?"

Then Debu, seeing that he had not made his case, also told me a story. "One of my friends in college in Kolkata met a Delhi woman studying there. He fell in love with her and she promised to marry him if he agreed to live in Delhi. When he came to Delhi, she said that she didn't love him any more and was getting married to another man. But he was so much in love that this betrayal bloody killed him. She should just have cut off his balls. Now he is back in Kolkata, sitting in his father's house, wasting away. He is not even capable of holding a job. Total, good-for-nothing, loser. And all because he fell in love with a Delhi woman. So you see" – he nodded triumphantly – "Delhi is much more dangerous for men. I have noticed that you have a few girlfriends here. Please be careful. Have fun-shun with them but, whatever happens, do not fall in love."

Rape-infected blood in a city of dominatrix drivers. And the green grass grew all around and round, and the green grass grew all around.

**

"Hey, is there room for two over there?" Anup Singh shuffles through the weeds towards me, his limp more pronounced than normal. Lost in my own thoughts, I hadn't noticed him approaching. "Reena thought you might be over here", he said.

"Yeah."

He straddles the rim of the well to sit beside me. "Are you doing okay?"

I look down into the well. "How deep do you think the water is?"

He gently squeezes my arm. "You're right, stupid question."

We sit for a while on the rim of the well, watching the cricket game in the distance. The boys' excited yells are muffled when they reach us, but its the only sound apart from the occasional frog jumping in and out of the water below. Despite being very much in the city, this field beside the slum has always seemed unusually isolated, somehow cordoned off from the urban chaos surrounding it.

"She wasn't just my friend", I say at last. "She was my best student. She could have become anything she wanted, despite where she came from. It's such a fucking waste."

Another long silence. "Do you ever wonder what the hell we're doing?" I ask Anup. "You've been doing this much longer. Do you ever feel it's all a waste of time?"

"Of course! All the time. That's a totally natural reaction to the difficulty of our work. The question every social worker has to confront at some point in their life is this: how do you balance the cynicism that comes from observing the world around us with the optimism that change is possible?"

"Well?"

"It's tough. Everybody's got to make his or her own journey through this question. But the way I see it is that the problems we're trying to solve have taken decades, centuries, sometimes millennia, to become the beasts that they are. That's why they seem so unchangeable. So the solutions to these problems will also take a long time. It's not realistic to think that you or I can solve them in our lifetimes. We just have to keep working with the faith that one day our efforts will bear fruit, like the faith of the workers who built the great temples of ancient India. Most of them knew they'd never live to see the temple completed. But that didn't prevent them from doing the best job they could. You've got to go on, keep putting another brick in the wall. Or even just *be* a brick. And that's your life."

"Life as a Brick. Someone should make a movie on that."

"Yes, with Shah Rukh Khan and Aishwarya Rai running around trees", he smiles.

"It'll be less depressing at least. Your answer sucks, by the way."

He shrugs, but not without sympathy. "Like I said, everyone's got to make their own peace with it. It is *the* fundamental test in our work. I've experienced it, and so has Reena. And I've seen many people fail this test.

"How did you pass it?"

"I can't say I have, to be honest. Because I also still ask myself the same question. But the way I get through the tough moments is by making a big deal out of the incremental change that you were so critical about last night. Really celebrate the small successes. When I was your age, I did similar work in a slum in Lucknow. My organization had a policy of throwing a party every time our kids passed a big exam. Not just a quiet celebration but a huge party, as if we'd won the Nobel Prize. In terms of the overall mission, it was nothing worth celebrating. But for those of us who worked in that slum, it was the only way to keep ourselves sane."

In the distance, Reena enters the field and begins to walk towards the well. I'm touched to see that Laks and Ilona are with her. Anup sees them too and jumps down off the rim. He looks up at me, his eyes telling me that he understands, that things will get better, that I will go on.

"Come", he says.

Chapter 12
Dust to Music

Dust to dust. All these years, and I can still taste the dust.

The final of The Wilson Cup. My high school is up against archrivals, Jairam High School. Any cricket match between our schools was a tense affair, partly because of the rivalry that dated back over a hundred years and partly because people took school cricket very seriously where I grew up. This was particularly true of The Wilson Cup, by far the most prestigious school cricket tournament. On the day of the game, which was always widely covered by the local press (nobody questioned the absurdity of 15-year old schoolboys making headlines), both schools declared holidays so that students could support their respective teams – a prudent decision because only a handful of students would have attended school anyway, and they'd sit in the classroom alone while their teacher was out watching the game. In addition to over two thousand schoolboys, about five hundred other spectators comprising parents, dedicated (read: unemployed) alumni, members of the city's cricket community and miscellaneous other interested individuals would also show up, creating a cauldron-like atmosphere around the small ground.

That particular year was my last in high school. For us seniors it was a chance to graduate with distinction. We'd lost in the semi-finals the previous year, and were determined not to let the school down again. Furthermore, the end of high school usually meant the end of our cricketing lives; most boys would aim at careers less capricious than sport once we got to university. The situation was exactly the same for the seniors of Jairam, also a public boys' school with a tradition of sporting excellence. Possibly our last ever competitive sporting experience, we had to make it count.

Jairam had a glittering team that year. But the jewels in their crown were their opening bowlers, both local legends already. They made a fine pair: Ravi, of medium-height, was a wiry, acne-spotted left-armer who could swing it at pace, and Jason, tall and giant-shouldered, was a hairy right-armer blessed with the priceless ability to generate steep bounce off a good length. They had dismantled batting line-ups over the last three years and right through this competition. There was a buzz around that they'd both make it to the State team in the next couple of years – indeed, a couple of State selectors were rumored to be in the audience. Although we possessed a strong team of our own, only our captain Vinod was a serious contender for further cricket honors. He was a precociously talented, tall, opening batsman who had scored consecutive centuries in the lead-up to the final. We were relying on him for inspiration against the opposing fast bowlers.

The day of the final was overcast. We were playing on a typical Indian school playground: all sand and mud. Schools cricket was yet to graduate to proper turf fields. The stiff wind every now and then raised the sand off the ground and swirled it around like a troupe of whirling dervishes, forcing players and spectators alike to turn their backs and cover their faces.

We lost the toss and were sent in to bat. As our openers walked out to the middle, the coach turned to me and said, "Avraan, pad up. If we lose an early wicket, you're going in at number three."

I was an off-spinning all-rounder with a better defensive technique than attacking stroke-play. My role typically was to provide stability at one end as the stroke players went about scoring runs. In that year's Wilson Cup, I had been in good form with the ball but had struggled with the bat. My highest score in the first three games of the group stage was a labored 36 off 65 balls and I'd been rewarded for that performance by being demoted down the order. With the rest of our batting in fine form, I hadn't been needed since. I was low on confidence as a result of not enough recent match practice. And in sport, confidence is often just about everything.

So when the coach told me to pad up, I gulped. I understood without being told that my role would be to ward off Ravi and Jason's dangerous opening spells, and then do my best to get out so the hitters could come in and do some damage. Like many in the team, I was apprehensive of facing the fast bowlers, both of whom were renowned – at least in our little world – for their aggression and hostility. Jason in particular had a reputation for preferring to hit the batsman rather than the wickets. My hands shook as I buckled on my pads and thigh-guard. I found myself praying that the openers would get a decent partnership going.

Padded up, I sat back down as my captain Vinod, who had bent to take guard, now stood to examine where the fielders had been placed. The bleachers on one side of the field and the outdoor basketball courts on the other were crammed with students from both schools. It was standing room only and they were already raising a ruckus, feet thumping, conch blowing and loud drumming accompanying each side's cheers. Representatives carrying their schools' flags ran up and down either side of the ground, the fluttering flags inspiring greater cheering and shouting as they floated past. A teammate made a crack about wishing we were in co-ed schools so there'd be cheerleaders in short skirts but I was too nervous to join in the laughter. My eyes never left Ravi as he handed his hat to the umpire and measured his run-up.

As Ravi warmed up, tossing a few practice bowls to the mid-on fielder, the crowd grew quiet. Suddenly, like in a group of divers who have just seen a shark approaching, the atmosphere around the ground became deathly still. "Come on, Vinod", someone muttered as, amidst the pin-drop hush, our captain bent elegantly and confidently into his batting stance.

The first ball of the match sent one side of the ground into frenzy. Ravi charged in and bowled a slow swinging full toss. It seemed he was nervous as well because the ball ballooned up from his hand and took an eternity in getting to Vinod. Deceived by Ravi's unintentional slower ball, Vinod brought his bat down too early with an ugly swish most unlike his usual graceful technique. Still a full toss, the ball cannoned into the middle stump and sent it somersaulting into the hearts of the Jairam supporters, who erupted as one from their bleachers.

Packed into the basketball courts, our supporters stood in horrified silence, many with hands over their mouths. As captain of the cricket team, the tall and cocky Vinod was a full-time hero to the whole school. But here, in our hour of need, he had failed spectacularly. A collective gasp went around the team. The coach turned to me and said, "Go, Avraan. Just hang in there and play out some overs. Don't worry about scoring runs."

I jerked to my feet and began to walk towards the matted pitch, adjusting my helmet and playing a few practice drives to get my arms moving. Vinod had stood rooted in shock as the Jairam High School fielders mobbed their opening bowler – the tournament's leading run scorer had been dismissed first ball in the match that mattered most. But now he turned and began the long walk back. The stunned look on his face as we crossed sent shivers down my spine. I stepped onto the pitch and asked for a leg-stump guard, my heart pounding like a band of tribal drums sending a distress signal across the landscape of my nerves and synapses. My right hand shook uncontrollably as I tried to draw the white chalk stripe on the brown matting in line with leg-stump. The chalk slipped out of my hand and I had to pick it up and draw the line again.

"Ravi, he's shit-scared", the observant wicket keeper called out. "He's pissing in his pants! This one's going to be easy." I'd have retorted back but all I could do was agree that I was, in fact, shit-scared. "Don't worry", Jason called out behind me from his position at square-leg, "If Ravi doesn't get him, I'll break his head in the next over."

Doing my best to tune out their heckling, I stood and slowly pulled on my gloves, drawing a mental map of the open spaces in which I could get a run or two. Ravi was rubbing the new ball against his trousers vigorously, like a vicious horse chafing at the bit. My feet seemed unsteady on the crease so I spread them a little wider to lower my center of gravity. On this cool overcast day, sweat was streaming down my sides and soaking into my white uniform. I looked up in my stance, the umpire lowered his hand, and Ravi crouched into his run up.

With no warning, the dust storm came. No one felt a sudden gust of wind; raised from a vacuum, it swirled and twisted, ripping a long blanket of sand from one end of the ground and hurtling it towards the other end, gathering more and more dust in its wake. A brown avalanche. Everyone ducked and buried their heads in their hands. I managed to shield my eyes but the visor of my helmet proved impossible to cover and dust hurtled in, seeping into my mouth and forcing its way down my throat. Crouched down with the gale battering me, I felt like I alone was the target of the vicious storm.

The sandstorm passed. Everyone slowly regained their positions. I stood and removed my helmet. My eyes were clear but my mouth was full of dust. I spat and spat, and spat some more, ejecting as much sand as possible. The umpire gesticulated at me to get on with it. I put my helmet back on and took guard again.

As I bent into my stance, I registered the utter silence on our side of the field, in glaring contrast to the rowdiness coming from the Jairam side, as if the sandstorm had been just an opportunity to rest their throats. Then, from out of nowhere, our Head Boy Sanjay Iyer screamed in a tone that penetrated the heart of the oppressive silence and ripped it wide open, "Come on, Avraaaaaan!" And, like a tidal wave bursting through a dam, the rest of my school took up the cheer.

"Avraan! Avraan! We want Avraan..." The chants rang out suddenly and thunderously, causing Ravi, who was halfway through his run-up, to pull out of it disoriented. Glad of the withdrawal, since the sudden yelling had also broken my own tenuous concentration, I stood back upright and looked towards my schoolmates, screaming out my name like banshees. Conscious of the pride at stake, I gave an involuntary shrug to shake off the expectations. Over ten minutes had passed since the first ball of the match, with five thousand eyes on me the whole time.

And I still had dust in my mouth, dust mixing with my saliva into a muddy paste that caked my tongue, dust lodged between my teeth, dust bruising my lips and gums.

Ravi charged in to the crease and, in a flurry of arms and legs, the ball zoomed towards me. Again it was a full toss, almost a replica of the delivery that flummoxed Vinod. But this one was intentional, controlled, quicker, lower and deadlier. My feet had turned to stone and I was slow in reacting but somehow jammed my bat down just in time. The ball hit the bottom part of my bat and squirted away between cover and mid-off. As I set off to scamper a quick run, I heard a roar from the direction of the basketball courts. It was as if I'd hit a last-ball six to win the match and not, in fact, a nervous out-of-form batsman desperately scurrying a single to get off strike. Rather than encouraging me, the vociferous cheering actually depressed me further.

In the end, it was all a blur. I scored very little, getting worked over by both bowlers and surviving two dropped catches before Jason ended my misery with a ripping leg-cutter than pitched on middle and uprooted the off stump. Three hours later, we'd been bowled out for 94 and thrashed by nine wickets. The winning runs for Jairam High School came off my bowling, an effortlessly swept six by their captain.

In the shame that haunted us for months after this defeat, I relived again and again the moments before that first ball I faced. Especially the taste of the Dust. Every subsequent moment in my life when I've been in the public gaze, when I've felt the pressure to perform in front of an audience, the Dust comes into my mouth from some dank Pavlovian recess. If there isn't much riding on the performance, the dust is slight and can be swallowed, like the fine mist covering a laptop keypad. If the stakes are high, however, the Dust overwhelms my mouth with millions of tiny pieces of sand and gravel, grating my tongue, rolling against my teeth, slicing out small chunks of my lips as it slides out of my mouth and into the pores of my face to form scars. Unable to swallow these dunes of sand, I'm choked into inaction, frozen like a cockroach under a flashlight, like when Bips challenged me on my first day in class or when I watched passively as a pair of thugs beat an innocent man.

It's numbing: pressure, stage fright. *Loaded guns in your face*, Billy Joel sings. A sandstorm in your mouth, I reply. But we agree on one thing, joining our voices together in a mournful chorus: you can't handle pressure until you have the scars on your face. Like a baby moth or an infant crocodile, the active process of breaking out of your protective shell is what gives you the strength to enter the environment where your predators lie in wait.

Jali rolls her eyes when I finish telling the Dust story. We're out at dinner to celebrate a year of being together. She has made us dress up for the occasion. I'm wearing a nice shirt and have even polished my shoes. She is resplendent in a satiny *kurta* over a tight black skirt.

Though we began our relationship with no claims of commitment, things have evolved in a more serious direction. Her acute sense of the possibility inherent in every day is the right foil for my own navel-gazing and perpetual analyzing. Sometimes being with her was like skydiving, as if jumping off a moving plane is the only way I can describe such exhilaration. Jali led me out of myself. I'll always win 'where's the strangest place you've gotten action' games because of a certain burst of passion behind a terracotta sculpture in the National Museum. We got caught that time and turned over to the police. But we laughed for days afterwards over the memory of the curator's lips quivering with indignance. In return for all the excitement, I like to think I keep her grounded – just a little.

I wonder if Jali's recent attempts at being naughty together is part of a purposeful, loving, plan to shake me loose from the swamp of despair I've been thrashing about in since Bips' death. This moves me. But then I conjecture that her impatience with my analytical ways will eventually begin to grate on me. And there I go deconstructing again...

"Dust in your mouth, I believe!", she snorts. "Darling, you're one hell of a weirdo sometimes."

We finish our dinner and walk slowly back to her tiny *barsati* in Defence Colony. Her fuckpad, she calls it. Knowing I'm right behind her as we walk up the steep staircase, my eyes level with her ass, she deliberately sways her hips more than usual. Teasing, for Jali, is an essential ingredient in foreplay.

"You're very quiet", she asks, fishing out her keys to open the door. "What are you thinking about?"

"Nothing", I say.

She closes the door behind me and turns with a skeptical look in her eyes.

"Ok. I'm just wondering if I should change my job. Maybe I'm not cut out for this grassroots work after all. You develop individual relationships with your students and then… Anyway, we're not making fast enough progress. I feel like I'd fit better in an organization that approaches social issues more holistically."

"You may be right. And your grassroots experience would be an asset, no? You'd have firsthand knowledge of the realities."

As she says this, Jali flops down into the one chair in her apartment, a large orange armchair in a corner.

"Exactly", I respond, approaching her. "I think I would enjoy the change. Starting to look at issues in a systemic way…"

I trail off. She is looking up at me with a wicked gleam in her eyes. I look into her face quizzically. She lifts her legs off the floor and places her feet against my hip, the black skirt riding up her thigh. My line of vision follows her legs up from her feet until they disappear inside her skirt – when I suddenly realize that she isn't wearing any underwear. Startled, I look up at her. She cocks her head to the side and raises her eyebrows with a grin as if to say 'What are you waiting for?'

I sink to my knees, putting my hands on the hem of her skirt on either side of her thighs, pushing it up further. Higher and higher it goes, and I lean in.

**

Someone dies and a battalion of memories gushes out to center stage. You realize you didn't think about them very often while they were alive. It's only their absence that inadvertently creates room for all that's avoided and treasured, as if our existence limits our occupancy in each other's minds. We forget the vast majority of people we meet in our lives, but we also carry surprising parts of others for a long time. With some people, even if our interaction was brief or occurred without word or look, but still triggered something in ourselves, with them, we weren't just ships in the night speaking each other in passing. No, one person leaves something profound for the other, to be reeled in and consumed later. We're always, always touching each other, and we have the power to impact deeply. Maybe that's why we have such taboos on public displays of affection – the touch means so much that we load it with heavy meaning.

Touches that are fleeting in time yet leave something behind: a glimpse of the past to a lonely singer, an image of friendship to a café waiter, a vision of progress to a tourist, a mirror of comfort to a lonely executive, a sad memory to a little boy, a renewal of purpose to a tired social worker. Or, more generally, a word of encouragement here, a piece of writing on a random page there, the opening notes of a song, an unexpected gesture of generosity, the sensual thrill of a mutual second glance. They say not to sweat the small stuff, but it's the small stuff you never forget.

We're rarely aware of the meanings we hold for each other.

**

I'm often accused of being harsh on Delhi. This is easy to be. Delhi lends itself to harshness, to extremes, as easily as the Australian outback or the Alaskan wilderness. When you live here, one of the rare places on earth where people die of heat in summer and cold in winter, the phrase 'harsh reality' makes literal sense. Love or hate it, there's rarely middle ground. Writers down the years have tried to explain this harshness. William Dalrymple, in his biography of Delhi, quipped that the reason Delhi has been conquered so frequently and so easily is that the inhabitants were too pre-occupied slitting each other's throats to worry about invaders.

Yet, like the monsoon providing relief from the summer, Delhi is not without its charms. It's just that acknowledging those charms can take a bit of coaxing, like a lover rousing you on a lazy monsoon weekend morning. She may straddle you and work on your ear – kissing softly, gently biting lobes, probing boldly with her tongue – before letting a trail of butterfly kisses lead her to your lips, which of course you turn away from in your sloth, but she follows, running her lips and tongue over yours, and then down your neck to your chest before she reaches down to confirm her endeavor hasn't been in vain, that she has, after all, transformed you into readiness. Take a little time, spend a little love, probe in the right lobes, and sure, I'll admit Delhi ain't all bad.

It comes down to love. I found love in Delhi over three years after I first moved there. As soon as I did, I recognized the truth that we rarely like a place for itself; what we love is the memory of the people we loved while we were there. There are plenty of bright sparks; memories and moments that ensure it isn't 'all doom and gloom', as Laks might put it.

**

Late in the morning after we returned from the hospital where Nikhil was stitched up, and a few hours before we found out about Bips, Ilona knocked on my door. I was lying in bed, trying to still my mind, and failing. She perched on the bed beside me, not saying anything. Then she pushed me over and lay down next to me, facedown, burying her head into the pillow. Her body shook as she sobbed. I put an arm around her, gently rubbing her back.

I thought of how quickly Ilona moved on from things, whether jobs or men or philosophical anchors. Anticipating loss almost compulsively, her strategy to overcome it was by speeding past. Like a racecar at a pit stop, she stopped not to reflect or grieve or regret but only gather more fuel. So she sped through painful relationships, cutting ties without a flicker of the hesitation

238

that makes us pause in matters of love. So she switched jobs on a yearly schedule, seeking novelty served on a platter. So she speed-dated religions without asking why God mattered to her so much. So she stayed away from home because of a trusted person's betrayal. And from the force of her velocity when she moved through loss, she gained a tremendous gift: she never doubted that at any given moment she wasn't doing what she thought was best.

Introspection does not come naturally to people like Ilona. For them, the outside is the place to fill, explore, and sink into, until the inside clicks into place. Ilona is the most passionate person I know who doesn't feel passion for anything. Yet, as passion has the same root as pathos, this might be her loss-replacement talent at work again, only this time acting as shield not bandage, protecting against the potential disappointment of the answer to the oldest question of all: why am I here?

She's starting to answer this question, Ilona writes from Kolkata, where she and Nikhil have found new jobs and a one-bedroom apartment, much to her family's horror. It's an actual handwritten letter, on that jazzed-up paper with petrified bits of hair and twigs floating in it that women use for special occasions. She's still holding her shield, she says, not ready to cast it away yet. But thanks to all her time away, she feels strong enough to begin slaying some old demons, even at the price of a fresh wound or two. She doesn't elaborate further. What she does go on to say is that she accepted Nikhil's proposal to 'never get married as soon as possible', but crossed her fingers behind her back as she did so. Returning to Kolkata has been like the comforting sensation of putting on a pair of old jeans: tight from the recent wash and fraying at the edges, but it just feels right.

**

Laks mourned the closing of the *ALOW Café* for precisely two weeks. The first seven days, he spent the mornings and afternoons in bed, the evenings contemplating various ancient ruins around the city, and the nights getting noisily drunk. On the eighth day, having run out of drinking partners, he picked up his backpack and headed north, trekking through the Valley of Flowers for a week. On the fifteenth morning, he returned to Delhi on an overnight bus from the hills, unpacked his trekking gear, packed his business clothes, and jumped on the next train to Mumbai. There, he met with Ajay Sanghvi, explained what had happened and talked the man into backing him again. Laks was going to re-open *ALOW* in South Delhi.

With the capital he had already saved, and more from Sanghvi, Laks opened two new *ALOW* branches, one each in the popular markets of Greater Kailash One and Vasant Vihar, both places reputedly less complicated to work in. Four months after shutting down the original *ALOW Café* in despair, Laks launched two new cafés on successive days. Sticking to the marketing strategy that worked so successfully the first time around, he soon had his clientele streaming back. The unavoidable decrease in foreign tourists was more than offset by the phalanx of local yuppies inhabiting the two posh neighborhoods, particularly on weekends. Eight months after his first failure, business had never been better.

"In some ways I have to thank Suzuki Shamu", he reflected. "Without his threats, I would have taken way longer to get this far. I guess I, like, *owe* him!" But he also wasn't one to forgive so easily. "Shit, I hope the bastard can see me in his dreams", he said with a glint in his eye. "I'm sticking my tongue right in his face."

I laughed. We were in the Vasant Vihar *ALOW Café* late one evening. The place was packed, many customers sharing tables with complete strangers. Looking at the crowd, I was glad Laks no longer needed me behind the counter.

"You're living the dream", I told him. "The young Indian entrepreneur, spreading his tentacles across the city with a sparkling new idea. And not just America-returned but a red-white-and-blue American in the flesh. Talk about reverse brain drain! I bet you'll soon be on one of those TV shows about India's 'Young Turks' and on the cover of *India Today*. And then on the lecture circuit", I teased.

"I had to, Avi. I couldn't let Suzuki Shamu chase me away. I want to be a part of this period in India. I want to contribute. I believe we won't know the importance of these years – these first 10 years of the 21st century – until at least 2050. I know you should never make predictions about the future but I'll bet that in 2050 we will look back and say that these were the years when India began to change forever."

**

I am sitting alone on another Saturday night in another bar. The music's great – a combination of classic rock for the purists interspersed with Bollywood *bhangra* for your shoulder-flinging pleasure or a sample of the latest one-hit wonder starlet. Such a lot of world – something for everyone. The DJ is good not because he can rip and remix but in fact the opposite: he understands that when people relax on a weekend, they like what's familiar. A jaded Queen anthem usually hits the spot better than an innovative rave beat.

Before heading to the bar, Ilona and I helped Laks shut down *The ALOW Café* for the night. It was the last time Ilona would help shut down; she and Nikhil leave for Kolkata tomorrow. After Nikhil recovered from his wound, they fled to Naukuchiyatal for a long weekend during which they both confessed everything that happened when they were apart and, after several rounds of tears, decided to strike forward together. What doesn't kill you makes you stronger, Ilona declared was their new leitmotif, ducking as

Laks threw a coaster at her for using the word leitmotif in a sentence.

At the bar, we celebrated our years together, raising glass after glass in hastily conceived toasts that ranged from our landlady's Nepali butler to Suzuki Shamu's wives. Although Jali is out of town (gone home to break the news to her parents that we are moving in together), and Mitali and Laks have split up, Nikhil joined us, dragging everyone onto the karaoke stage for a corny best-days-of-our-lives jingle. After we had roared it out, he remained on stage, serenading Ilona. In reply, she downed a tequila shot and jumped up to respond with Alanis Morrissette: *You've already won me over, in spite of me...*

Ilona and Nikhil left after that, going home to finish packing. So they said. Laks and I shared another Cuba Libre. Halfway through It he found a dance partner and shimmied onto the floor. I stayed behind, perched on my barstool, nursing my drink and watching the crowd.

Now, I look down at the Sudoku puzzle on the coaster upon which my Cuba Libre sits. I ask the bartender for a pen and begin to fill it in, doodling circles on the side as I try persuading my drizzled brain to do the puzzle. Soon the loopy spirals of my doodling run out of space on the coaster, trailing away into the rhythmic beats banging out of the speaker a few feet away. The curves I've drawn show that you never really come full circle. Instead, you always end up a little to the left or right of where you started. The question is: are you now at the center of an upward spiral or at the edge of a downward one?

The smoke from the dance floor makes me sneeze: once, twice. I drain my glass and decide to go home. Laks looks like the fun he's having on the dance floor may extend much later into the night so I just wave at him to signal I'm leaving. He waves back with a grin and a thumbs-up. Making a final survey of the crowded bar,

Delhi's nightlife pulsating with the energy of a thousand mini-stories, dramas and dreams, I find myself humming, even above the thudding base coming from the speakers, a line from Bob Dylan: *Ah, but I was so much older then, I'm younger than that now.*

I pay my bill and leave, walking out into the Saturday night traffic. I can't stop humming.

Glossary of Indian Terms

acchar – Indian pickle, cooked in oil with lots of spices.

angrezi – person from England

arrack – a highly distilled, locally brewed alcohol drink made from fermented grain, coconut, or other plants

barsati – a dwelling created on the roof of someone's house, typically used as a servant's quarters or rented out for additional income

behenchod – common Hindi abuse word, literally 'sister-fucker'

beti – an affectionate, diminutive term for a little girl, or daughter

bhai-saab – literally 'brother-sir', a common Hindi term of semi-respect, though also frequently used ironically.

bhaiyya – brother

Bhangra – popular music and/or dance from Punjab in North India, commonly associated with weddings and Bollywood dancing outside India

bhindi – lady's finger, or okra

bidi – a thin roll of tobacco wrapped in a leaf and tied with string at one end. Like a regular cigarette, but with more of all the good (read: bad) stuff.

chai – Indian tea, with nearly as many variations as tea-makers

chaiwallah – person (typically male) who sells tea

chikoo – Indian word for the fruit zapota or sapodilla, a brown fruit with soft interior native to Central America

dal – lentil dish common in India

dargah – an Islamic Sufi shrine built over the grave of a religious figure, often a saint

desi – derived from the Sanskrit word for 'country', it is the term used for people and culture from the Indian subcontinent (including its diaspora)

dhaba – highway restaurant, usually serving a rich, local cuisine.

didi – elder sister

Dilli – local way of pronouncing Delhi

Dilliwallah – person from Delhi

firang – foreigner

ghat – a series of temple steps leading down to a body of water, usually a river

googly – a cricket term wherein a ball goes the opposite way than it is expected to. Used commonly in India to describe when something unexpected happens.

gurudwara – Sikh house of worship

inshallah – Arabic for "god willing", very commonly used by Muslims the world over

kajal – everyday make-up used by Indian women to darken the eyelids and as mascara for eyelashes

khadi – handspun cloth, usually made out of cotton. Historically significant as a movement started by Mahatma Gandhi to promote the idea that Indians could be self-reliant on locally made cotton. Khadi clothes are still worn by many grassroots social workers in India, often to the amusement of more 'modern' Indians.

kheer – rice pudding made by boiling rice and other ingredients with milk

kurta – type of upper-body garment worn by men across South Asia, with many regional variations of fashion and form

lassi – popular yogurt-based drink, sometimes with spices, sugar and/or fruit

maderchod – common Hindi abuse word, literally 'mother-fucker'

naan – leavened, oven-baked flatbread central to North Indian cuisine

namaste – customary Indian greeting made with a slight bow and hands pressed together, palms touching and fingers pointing upwards. It is meant to signify "bowing to the divine within" the recipient

nimbu paani – literally, 'lime water', like regular lemonade but usually with salt and/or sugar

paan – a stimulant made from the betel leaf, usually chewed and then spat out *panchayat* – the oldest local government system in India. Literally means assembly (ayat) of five (panch) respected elders chosen and accepted by the community to manage local governance.

phulka – a flat bread made with wheat flour, also known as roti or chapatti.

pranayama – refers to a range of breathing techniques used in yoga and other Indian traditions

rakhi – common name for Raksha Bandhan, an ancient Hindu festival that celebrates the love and duty between brothers and their sisters with a set of rituals in which 'siblings' (who may or may not biologically related) exchange tokens of love and protection.

raath-ki-rani – literally 'queen of the night', a shrub with flowers that give out a strong aroma at night. Very noticeable in Delhi in the autumn.

roti – a traditional flat bread made with wheat flour

sabzi – vegetables cooked with spices; generic name for all such dishes

sadhu – a religious or holy man whose life is dedicated towards achieving liberation

salwar kameez – traditional outfit in India, mostly worn by women (but traditionally can be worn by men too). Salwar are loose pajama-like trousers, where the legs are wide at the top and held up by drawstring, and narrow at the ankle. The kameez is a long, sometimes embroidered, shirt or tunic.

stupa – a mound-like structure containing Buddhist relics, used as a site of meditation

wallah – a suffix to a name or activity that indicates a person involved in that activity; in this book, rickshaw-wallah (rickshaw driver), chaiwallah (tea seller), etc.

Acknowledgements

Thanks are due first to Harsha Bhogle who, a long time ago, took a gamble on a kid he barely knew and pushed me into a journalism internship. If not for his hunch, I may never have written a word in public, let alone a book.

This manuscript was first drafted in 2006. After that, apart from one revision in 2009 when I was staying in to heal a broken heart, it simply sat there, somnolent on a shelf and hibernating in my hard-drive, for eight years. Then, one evening over sundowners on the roof of the Best Western Hotel in Nairobi, Ciku Kimeria, whom I had just met, explained how she had self-published her first novel despite working as a consultant and how I should do the same. "This is how...", she began. Often in our lives we have to thank someone for a well-placed kick in the butt. This is one such occasion.

Going back to 2006, there are a number of people whose boundless generosity in New Delhi made my life there possible. To Mridu Mahajan, Perveen and Larry Malarkar, Pervin and Kapil Malhotra, and Geeta Nambissan - I hope one day I can repay your hospitality and many acts of kindness.

A large portion of this book was written as a guest of Jose Dominic in his wonderful beach resort SwaSwara in Gokarna, Karnataka. There are few lovelier places to write.

In a world where violence, corruption, and crime surround us (and often don't make the news), there are thousands of people solving major problems every day, sometimes laying their own lives on the line to help others. The social workers depicted in this book were, in part, inspired by the fabulous work being done in 2006 all over India by tremendous social entrepreneurs who are too many to acknowledge here. They are patriots, in the best sense of the term; long may they continue being catalysts for a better India. Yet I would never have known about their work if not for my own employment at Ashoka: Innovators for the Public, the most inspiring organization I have ever known.

Several people provided invaluable feedback on that first manuscript back in 2006. My heartfelt gratitude to Nidhi Paul, Gared Jones, Manmeet Mehta, Javier Rodriguez, Shreyan Singh, Dilip D'Souza, and Suba Sivakumaran. The many faults in the book are of course mine.

Lastly, immense thanks to Kainaz Unvalla of Kai Design Sense for the cover, and Gautam Shah for the photographs that grace it.

Roshan Paul
Bangalore, 2014

About the Author

Roshan first started writing in primary school when his father sat him and his sister down on Sunday morning and made them write an essay on the question, "My Perfect Day". This was in Bangalore, India. He has since lived, worked and travelled in more than fifty countries around the world, writing widely on travel, cricket, social entrepreneurship, and higher education. This is his first novel, and he blames it on his Dad.